THE DEAL

KAREN WOODS

Harper
North

HarperNorth
Windmill Green
Mount Street
Manchester, M2 3NX

A division of
HarperCollins*Publishers*
1 London Bridge Street
London, SE1 9GF

www.harpercollins.co.uk

HarperCollins*Publishers*
Macken House, 39/40 Mayor Street Upper
Dublin 1, D01 C9W8, Ireland

First published by HarperNorth in 2023

3 5 7 9 10 8 6 4 2

A catalogue record for this book
is available from the British Library

ISBN: 978-0-00-852867-6

Printed and bound in the UK using 100% Renewable
Electricity at CPI Group (UK) Ltd

This novel is entirely a work of fiction.
The names, characters and incidents portrayed in it are the work
of the author's imagination. Any resemblance to actual persons,
living or dead, events or localities is entirely coincidental.

This book is produced from independently certified FSC™ paper
to ensure responsible forest management.

For more information visit: www.harpercollins.co.uk/green

For Brenda Birch, the wife of Samuel Birch,
always missed by her family.

As always, our kid, our Daz, our Woody.
Miss you always and forever.

And my son, Dale, goodnight God bless x

Chapter One

Macy Taylor stood on Rochdale Road and waited for her friend, Joanne. The weather was against her, fine rain and dark clouds hanging from the sky. But she was used to it. You had to be, round here. She gazed across the road into the middle distance. There it was in its full glory: Tavistock Square. A chill crept down her spine. The Square never changed, and it was almost as if it stood looking back at her, laughing at her, knowing all the secrets it kept, everything it had witnessed through the years. If the place could have spoken, lives would have been wrecked, feuds fuelled, people flung into the big house for a very long time.

Every parent in Harpurhey warned their children about the area they lived in. The Square was right in the middle of the estate and for years it had been all over the news, the backdrop for reports about the darker side of Manchester, the side that not many liked to admit existed. It wasn't so far from the bustle of Deansgate or the glass towers of Spinningfields. But it could have been another world.

Invisible to most people: until you stood here, watching who passed through the Square, who stopped in the shadows. If you wanted something you couldn't get elsewhere, or needed something sorting, then the Square was the place to be. Drug dealers, armed robbers, shoplifters – anyone you needed was only a whisper away here.

Macy had been raised here and she'd had some good times on the Square too, she supposed, and some she wouldn't want her own kids to know about. Yes, growing up she'd blazed bud and sat there with her friends, drinking and smoking, but she was a teenager then and doing what most kids her age were doing. Macy loved Harpurhey back in the day when she was younger, and she had never had a bad word to say about it then. Even now, she knew most people here were her kind of people: they had her back, always there to help her out if she needed a favour or a sub until she got paid.

Money had always been tight for Macy, even more so since she'd given up shoplifting. The fastest fingers in the North of Manchester, people had said, and they were right: she had the art of nicking things down to a tee. Magic it was. Now you see it, now you don't. She was trying so hard these days to keep her fingers still but sometimes she couldn't help herself.

Macy stared over at the Square again and this time her eyes locked on a small alley leading off one side. The hairs on the back of her neck stood on end. One glance was all it took, and she was back *there*. That night was forever fresh in her mind: the blood, the screaming, the police interviewing her, her mother crying all the time to tell what she knew. But Macy had kept the code of silence, never breathed a word of what she witnessed, not now, not ever. She would have to take it to the grave. She'd never say who killed Nathan Barnes.

Chapter Two

Jayden Foster lay on the tattered brown leather sofa and shoved the last few crisp crumbs into his mouth, licking his fingertips, getting any last bit of the flavour. This was a smart sofa in its day; soft leather, comfortable, cost a right few quid. Jayden launched the empty packet on the floor, screwed up in a ball. The Mrs would pick it up when she was cleaning around, she always did. It was how she earned a crust, so he was leaving it to the expert, he claimed, when she went off on one about it. He looked over at Macy now with his puppy dog eyes, the ones he always used when he wanted something doing or when he was in trouble.

'Macy, do us a brew, love. Strong coffee with three sugars in it. Honest, I don't know what's up with me lately, I can't seem to find the energy to do anything. I'm sure I've got the lurgy or something.' He forced a cough, banging his clenched fist against his chest, eyes making sure she was watching him.

Macy flicked her long chestnut-brown hair over her shoulder and growled at him. Born lazy, he was. She'd seen more get-up-and-go in a sick-note. And, if he thought she was running around after him all day, he had another think coming. She felt like she barely had a moment to herself between cleaning up after folk at work, then cleaning up after her family at home. Things were going to have to change. Hands on her hips, she eyeballed him. She was sick to death of this couch potato doing sod all in the house every day. Fetch me, carry me, feed me, wipe my arse, it would be if things carried on like this.

'You can sling it. I'm going to work soon. You've got a case of lazyitis, nothing more. You've not moved from that spot all day. Oh,' she tilted her head to the side. 'Hold on a minute, my mistake. You *have* shifted – but only to fill your face or go for a piss. There is nothing wrong with you, so you and your so-called man flu can do one. I have to carry on, so man up and move your arse.'

Jayden ran his fingers through his thick black hair and smirked over at her. He loved winding her up. He shifted his weight among the heap of cushions on the sofa and tried to get comfortable. 'Wow, stop bleeding moaning. What's up with you, are you on the rag or something?'

Her cheeks went beetroot, steam practically coming from her ears. How dare he say she was hormonal. If she was or she wasn't, it had nothing to do with the way she felt towards him. He was like this every day, and she was finally sick of fetching and carrying for him. She was on one now, letting rip. 'You can make tea too. Leanne will help you, so don't give me all that 'you can't cook' business because it doesn't wash with me anymore. 'Ping' meals take ten minutes tops. All you have to do is bang them in the microwave and 'ping', they're done. It's not rocket science, is it?'

Jayden sat up and sighed, aware he might have to actually do something. Popping a cigarette into the side of his mouth, he gave her a cocky look. The one he always did when his cage was rattled. 'Nah, sack that, woman. Man's got places to go, people to meet. You know what I mean, nudge, nudge, wink, wink, say no more.'

He was really pushing her buttons today. She let out a laboured breath and her face said it all. 'Oh, change the bleeding record, Jayden. I don't even know why I'm even with you anymore. You bring nothing to the table, and you don't do a tap in this house. Open your eyes and look around you: this place is a shit tip. There has been paint in the cupboard for over a year now and every time I mention giving the walls a lick of paint you come down with some bleeding illness or excuse. It's bullshit, I'm sick of it. I don't even know why I bother. You can do one, jog on.'

He plonked back down on the sofa, shaking his head. 'Oh, for crying out loud, you wonder why I'm never in this gaff when all you do is moan, woman. You would think you was twice your age to hear you talk. I swear, I can't fart these days without it upsetting you. You're turning into your mother.'

Macy reached over to the brown wooden table and pulled a cig out of the packet. She clutched the rest of them tightly in her hand and rammed them into her cardigan pocket. Given the chance, this freeloader would have blazed the lot of them without a care in the world. And, as for her turning into her mother, she needed to remind him of all the times she'd bailed them out. Tenners here, tenners there. Yes, he was forgetting about that, wasn't he?

Grace Taylor hated her daughter's partner with a passion, and yes, she was forever telling her to kick this waste of space to the kerb. Jayden would only ever be the kind of man to take, take, take. Grace Taylor wasn't one to see her daughter suffer so she was always give, give, give. Plenty of times, there wouldn't have been money in the meter or food on the table without her helping out.

Jayden stood up from the sofa and promptly shoved his hands down the front of his trackie bottoms. He was thin as a rail – despite all the crap he ate. He needed a few pans of chicken broth down his neck to fatten him up. He walked over to Macy and stretched his wiry arms around her body, picking her up slightly from the floor, squeezing her. Despite his thick skin, he was aware he'd upset her – properly this time. And he couldn't handle any more grief right now so he decided he'd better pour some oil on troubled waters. Anything for a quiet life. 'Stop pecking my head, Macy. If it's doing your head in that much, I'll paint the bleeding living room. I will do all the house if it puts a smile on your kipper. Just stop being a miserable cow. I'll get Simon to give me a hand too. He'll do anything for a few spliffs. Well, that's if he's alright. His Mrs fucked off a few weeks ago and I've not been to see him yet. I can't be arsed with listening to all the drama when it comes to domestics. I have enough of my own going on.'

He released his grip on her and smacked her bum as he walked back to the sofa, confident his usual banter would win her over.

She was still fuming. 'You can kiss my arse if you think that thieving bastard is coming in here again. I don't even know why you didn't chin him when that money went missing. It was defo him, there was nobody else here. Come on, even you're not that thick?'

Jayden picked up the black remote and pointed it at the television. 'Nah, I'm not having that, Macy. I would know if the guy was a wrong un. I graft with him all the time and he's never had me over. I am a good judge of character. You've got it wrong; he's sorted.'

'Oh, how did I know you would say that?' Macy scoffed. 'You think the sun shines out of his arse. No wonder his wife pissed off. Anyway,' she quickly shot a look at the silver clock on the wall. 'I need to be going. Joanne's meeting me in five minutes and I can't be late. You should have heard the bollocking I got from her the last time I was late. She gave me a right lecture about how many other people would bite her hand off for a job. She's lucky I never told her to shove the job up her arse, talking to me like that. I will scratch her eyes out if she does it again. If it wasn't for that judge saying he would slam me if I got caught nicking again, I would be out there earning some decent cash, not bleeding pennies like I do with her. Honest, every day I'm fighting the fact that I used to be coining it in.'

Jayden sniggered to himself, not really interested in her dilemmas. As long as she was bringing money into the household, he was happy to kick back and reap the rewards. 'So be on time then. This job is money in your hand, and we can't afford to lose it right now. Money's tight. But if you're that fed up, you *could* always go back to Bobby and the gang. Just don't bloody get caught this time.' He raised his eyebrows high as he continued. 'You're right, you earned proper money when you was grafting with him and the team. Top cash. My wardrobe was top too. New jeans, new T-shirts, I looked dapper.'

She let out a laboured breath and scooped her hair back into a ponytail before twisting a band around it. Macy had great features, big saucer blue eyes and a clear complexion. She'd never had a weight problem, but she always said if she won the lottery she would go abroad and get herself a nice set of tits. She had boobs like two fried eggs, or so she said when she looked in the mirror. 'Shut up. I've told you before that I'm not chancing my freedom with Bobby and that lot. Shoplifting is a fine art but it wrecks your nerves. My anxiety was through the roof, and it was just a matter of time before I got slammed,' her voice got higher. 'Did you not hear what the judge said the last time I was in court?' She rolled her eyes and shook her head as she continued. 'He told me that if I ever appeared in front of him again he would throw the book at me. So, end of. Stop even bringing it back to the table because it's not an option anymore just a daydream. I'm only saying that money was never a problem when I was grafting, that's all. Maybe, if you got your head in gear, we would have more money. This is meant to be a partnership, Jayden, not me working all the time and you dossing all day.' She walked about the front room and had one last pop at him before she left. 'And anyway, you were paranoid about me working with Bobby. I know you hate the guy, so fuck knows why you're telling me to go back working with him, because you would shit a brick if I did.

Remember Jayden, the phone calls, the text messages, you threatening to punch his lights out every time I was late home? So do me a favour and pull your finger out of your arse. If you're not out working, the least you can do is not sit about all day. Maybe do a bit of cleaning up. Look,' she pointed to the table behind her. 'You can put that washing away for starters.'

He rolled his eyes and forced a smile. 'Stop stressing out, woman. Let me enjoy the peace and quiet. I'm not a well man. My head is banging, and my nose is blocked up.'

Macy took her dark blue parka from the back of the chair, pulled it on and zipped it up, completely ignoring his attempt at getting some sympathy for his supposed man flu. 'Alex's teacher will probably ring you too. He's been a right little bastard lately in school. Every day she's belling me out about him. It's his last year, and he needs to try his best to get good grades. I don't want him ending up living hand to mouth like we have.' A sadness filled her eyes. 'I wish I had listened more in school. Maybe now I would have had a decent career, a little bit of luxury and not be working a dead end job that nobody else wants.'

He snapped, fuming that his boy was messing about in school and not listening to the teachers. 'So, ground Alex, then. How many times have I told you to take that PlayStation off him? Then he'll soon see the light. You're too soft with him. You should let me deal with him.'

Macy snarled and her nostrils flared. The vision of Jayden pinning Alex up against the wall and his fist slamming his body was never far from her mind. It had just been the once, but she'd told him, if he ever even thought about it again, she would not only leave him in a heartbeat, but shop him for it as well.

'You keep your bleeding hands away from him. Social services were right on our back when the school seen the bruise on him. If I hadn't smoothed it over, you would have been in the big house for assault. The only reason I didn't let it go on your record was so they didn't take my boy from me.'

Jayden's ears pinned back; teeth clenched tightly together. 'He should keep his big mouth shut then – learn how to speak to his parents properly. Cheeky fucker he is, no respect.'

She sighed. Who the hell did he think Alex was going to learn respect from? Certainly not his dad. 'He's a kid, Jayden. He's fifteen years old. Maybe he is more like you than you care to admit. Like father, like son, eh?'

'I won't have no kid of mine talking back to me the way he does. He knows the script now, anyway. I've told him, any back-chat and he's out the door.'

Macy shook her head. She hated the way he spoke, but she knew he was all talk and no action now – he had begged her not to leave him when she threatened to walk. She'd told him then – and he'd believed her – that she would put up with a lot but she wouldn't put with anyone hurting her boy. Still, she was fed up with the constant bickering between father and son. Alex would never back down from his father, even if he was wrong. The two of them were a nightmare when they were together. She was actually glad she was getting out of the house, even if it was only for work. 'Right, see you in a few hours. I'm off to clean shitty toilets and other people's mess up. Not that bloody different from home, eh?'

Chapter Three

Macy leant against the rough brick wall, as she did most days, waiting for Joanna to take them to today's job. Day in, day out – work came around too soon. She thought about what Jayden had said – about going back to lifting. Mind you, she hadn't told him she still kept her hand in. Never anything big, not anything risky that would get her sent down, and certainly not for Bobby and his team. No, this was just a little bit of something now and then – old habits die hard, after all. And it wasn't like they didn't need it. Jayden helped out when something fell into his lap but most of his money got spent on weed and gambling. So, if she wanted something, she had to go out and get it herself. But she'd slowed down loads in the last few months – she wasn't nicking to order anymore, and only from places she reckoned wouldn't miss it. No, these days it was odds and ends from the local supermarket when she was skint: pieces of meat, a few bits of cheese – the kind of stuff she'd always run out of money for. And yes, the occasional bottle of wine when she was feeling down. She tried her best to keep on the straight and narrow, but it was so hard, so bleeding hard not to let her fingers go wild. She hated the desperation that drove her to it. And, after the adrenaline of getting away with it crashed, she hated the fact she'd done it again. But everyone was on the take somehow, weren't they? Everyone had a hustle, she figured. Rich people, poor people: everyone bent the rules. It was just a lot easier to get caught nicking a bottle of gin than some fat-cat not paying their taxes. It wasn't like her family were any different, she thought.

Jayden was as bent as a nine-bob note, always ducking and diving, always promising her that the next graft he did would be the one to set them up for life. It never happened and the family never had a pot to piss in. Always living on the edge.

Sometimes she let herself think about how life could have been different. But she knew she was tied to this place, to this life. After all, she still passed through the Square almost every day. It was a reminder she could never escape what had happened. And maybe that was her penance. She might have stayed silent, but she'd also refused to run away.

Nathan's family never let it lie though. Every time she saw them they would shout abuse at her, spit near her feet. They knew she knew something about the night he died. She gave them a wide berth and whenever they were nearby she would make sure she was gone before they spotted her. But in a place like the estate, you couldn't avoid people for long – and now trouble was closer to home than ever.

Her daughter, Leanne, had started knocking about with some of the Barnes kids – even spending evenings on the

Square with one of them. In fact, it seemed like she was always chilling there, and Macy was sick to death of telling her that she would end up in a bad way if she continued hanging out with the people she did. She wished she could tell her daughter exactly why she should steer clear of the whole Barnes clan, but she knew if Leanne got a whiff that she was hiding something, she'd be on dangerous ground. And Leanne had changed over the last few months. She'd got gobby, always complaining she was tired, giving her back-chat. Macy was sure she was dabbling in drugs. Her daughter was seventeen now, and she'd already heard a few rumours that she was up to no good, but could never prove it. How could any parent prove their child was smoking weed, having sex, when there was no firm evidence? Macy knew alright – her mother's instinct was never wrong – but she also knew she'd push her away if she tackled it the wrong way.

Macy froze as she saw a dark shape move in the small alleyway. Her eyes wide open, her heartbeat doubled. That was the exact place it happened. The gun shot, the scream-ing. She closed her eyes tightly, not wanting to see the vision that looped in her brain like a flashing light in her mind that she couldn't ignore. A scream like an injured animal, Nathan's pleas for help.

A voice at the side of her cut in, bringing her back to the present. Joanne opened the passenger door and spoke again. 'Are you getting in or what?'

Macy took a few seconds to shake the memory, then jumped into her friend's car and started to fasten her seatbelt.

'We need to be quick today, Macy. I'll clean the down-stairs and you can do upstairs.'

Macy frowned as the car pulled out onto the main road. 'What, again? Why am I always the one who has to clean the toilets? You know this family are scruffy bastards. You should have seen the state of the bedroom last week. Dirty dishes by the bed with food all over, clothes flung every-where. They have no respect for the place they live in. They have more money than sense.'

'It is what it is, love. We are there to clean, not judge.'

'I know that, but it still pisses me off that those kids are brats. I mean, as parents why haven't they taught them to respect the stuff they have? Some people have it so easy, it bugs me.'

Joanna agreed and carried on driving. 'Anyway, how's your day been? Is Jayden working yet?'

Macy cringed, knowing Joanne was having a dig at her about her boyfriend. She was always bitching about him and told Macy straight that the man was a wanker and out for what he could get. She replied in a softer voice, trying to hide the fact that Joanne was right about her man. 'No, he's doing bits here and there, but he's not got a permanent job yet. It will come though, he's always looking,' she lied.

'You want to kick his arse to the kerb. The guy drags you down all the time. Look at the other month when he nicked the gas money and you had to come to me for a sub until you got paid.'

Bloody hell. Joanne was going to town today. Macy rolled her eyes. Joanne was right but still, she hated hearing the truth. She could call him out but she didn't like anyone else having a pop at him. 'I've told him time and time again to sort his head out, but it's hard for him, Joanne. You're alright with Paul. He had a good start in life, decent education, helped you set up your own business. Me and Jayden are not what you call qualified in anything. I can only just about read and write and he's no better.'

Joanne gasped. 'You're as sharp as a tack, Mace – you might not have the exams to prove it, but don't you go talking yourself down. Not like Jayden. Don't make excuses for him, Macy. I offered him some cleaning work months ago, cleaning gutters and gardens, and he turned it down. If he wanted to change that much, he would have got off his arse and done it. Beggars can't be choosers.'

Macy hung her head low as they pulled up outside the house they were cleaning. This was a top gaff, five bedrooms, in the Prestwich area of Manchester, a nice respectable place. Macy opened the car door and stood with her hands shoved in her pockets. She sighed and waited for Joanne to lock the car up. The two of them plodded down the garden path and Joanne knocked on the door. Here it came: the different accent for customers, almost a complete change in her, shoulders back and the posh tone Joanne always used when she was dealing with clients, high pitched, minding her Ps and Qs. Macy smiled to herself as a woman opened the door wearing a cream silk housecoat.

'Hi Agatha, how have you been, my lovely?' Joanne smiled.

The woman was in her late fifties, but you could see she had had plenty of careful work done: lips, fillers, the lot. The door opened wide, and they followed her inside. 'I'm not going to lie, Joanne; the house needs a good deep clean. Steph has been studying all week and she's not had time to clean her bedroom.'

Macy stood looking about the hallway. This was how the other half lived. You could see money wasn't in short supply in this household.

Joanne shot a look at Macy. 'You start upstairs, and I'll be up to help you when I have finished downstairs. Agatha, is there ironing to be done today, because I'll get cracking with that?'

The woman nodded. 'Yes, I've got mountains of it. I've not had a minute to myself this week. Tony has been working away and I've had so many lunches and meetings to attend.'

'Lah-de-fucking-dah,' Macy mumbled under her breath, inhaling the sweet floral smell as Agatha walked past her. She loved perfume. If this had been a friend, she would have asked her what the name of her scent was. But no, this woman was not the type to answer, so she kept her mouth shut, head down. Back in the day, Macy had had her own perfume collection, expensive ones. Even if they were shoplifted, they'd been the real deal. She had a lot of things back then, never wanted for anything, always had money in her pockets, designer clothes, bags, the full monty. Now her wardrobe was tatty and tired.

―――――

Upstairs, Macy inched open the bedroom door and was horrified. She hesitated before she opened the door fully.

Bloody hell, again there was food left on plates scattered around the room, dirty underwear on the floor, cups tipped over, empty cans on every ledge. Forget the fact that this was a million-quid house. It was a shit tip. But there was no point standing there looking at it. It wasn't going to clean itself. Macy rolled her sleeves up and entered the bedroom ready to blitz it. Suddenly a girl popped her head from under the bedclothes and nearly scared Macy half to death.

'Fuck off out of my room, will you. Come back later, I've hardly had any sleep.'

Macy was sick to death of these rich bitches and replied to her in a steady tone. 'Sorry, your mam wants a deep clean so, if I was you, I would get up and go somewhere else while I clean this bedroom.'

Steph was around twenty years of age. A pretty girl and with a look of her mother. She flung the duvet from the bed and stormed out of the bedroom, sneering and mumbling obscenities under her breath as she left. Macy rammed two fingers up behind her back and mumbled under her breath again. 'Off you trot, Mrs Attitude.'

Underneath all the crap, this was a beautiful bedroom, Macy knew. She looked at all the nice things inside it – imagined how she'd have taken care of it if it had been hers. Macy didn't have a lot in life but what she had she looked after. She started to clean up and pick the dirty washing up from the floor with two pinched fingers. This girl had no shame. Imagine leaving worn underwear on the floor for anyone to see. A noise shook her from her thoughts: something dropping to the floor as she picked up a balled-up pair of pants. Macy screwed her eyes up, looking more carefully.

Her knees bent slightly, and she reached out and picked up a gold diamond ring. She held it up to the light and admired the way the colours in the diamond changed. This was clearly an expensive piece of jewellery, not something that should have been left lying about. To her mind, it should have had pride of place in a jewellery box, or even in a safe. Macy froze, eyes flicking one way then the other. Her fingers rolled slowly around the ring, and she quickly pushed it deep into her pocket. Old habits. Stephanie would probably never miss it anyway. If she cared about the ring that much, she would have never left it lying about. Ungrateful bint, she was. Finders keepers, losers weepers. Even if the spoilt cow looked for the ring, she'd probably have no idea where she'd left it. Macy continued cleaning; she was smiling now. Jayden would be able to get a good price for the ring, and she'd get some gas and electric and food. Forget all that *Thou Shalt Not Steal* stuff: her needs were greater than this toffee-nosed cow who had left it lying about.

Chapter Four

Leanne walked into the front room and growled over at her step-dad. Jayden was oblivious, sleeping on the sofa.

Her half-brother, Alex, barged past her, went straight over to the armchair and started to set his PlayStation up. *Grand Theft Auto, GTA,* was his life and whenever he got the chance he was always on the game. His mother always said that was where his aggressive behaviour had come from, the bad language, the way he spoke to his parents. He didn't believe it for a minute. He got all his attitude from right here at home. He rustled about, kicked his shoes off and curled up on the chair with his legs tucked underneath him. A double of his dad: a cheeky smile, trouble written all over his face.

Jayden opened his eyes and yawned. 'Leanne, your mam said you are on tea duty tonight.'

She snarled and made sure he could see her. 'Not a chance. Me and Kerry have made plans tonight and I have to wash my hair. You can do it. You're not paralysed, are you? Or ask your son to do it, why don't you?'

Jayden growled over at her. She wasn't his blood daughter and, even from a young age, Leanne had always thrown that fact in his face whenever he challenged her to do anything. And at nearly seventeen years old she was firmly in the stage of life when she was full of attitude.

He raised his eyebrows at her. 'Not my orders, love, they're your mam's, so take it up with her if you have a problem. I'm just passing on the message. As you can see, I'm not feeling too good, and your mam thought it would be a nice gesture for you to help out and cook tea for us all. I mean, I don't want anything, it's just for you and Alex and your mam.'

Alex turned his head from the TV. 'I'm not hungry. I'll grab something later.'

Leanne smiled at her brother and gave him a cheeky wink. He knew the score: when his mother came home she would make him a scran.

Jayden stared over at his son. 'Have you been behaving in school today or what? Because your mam told me you've been a little bastard lately.' He never told him that the school had tried ringing him and he'd ignored the call several times. *Top Boy* had been on and there was no way he was missing a second of it.

Alex never took his eyes from the screen as he replied to his old man. 'It's a load of shit, Dad. Just because I threw a chair across the classroom at Paddy Turner, they flung me out of the classroom. He's lucky I never one-bombed him. The guy has got attitude and he thinks I'm some kind of a prick who won't answer him back. Nah, I don't roll like that. He got told.'

Jayden nodded his head. He'd been a kid who could handle himself and remembered how he was in school. He'd got flung out because of his behaviour and had hated the way the teachers spoke to students. No respect whatsoever, treating them like animals. He nodded in agreement. 'Fair dos. Don't let anyone take the piss out of you, son, otherwise I'll be up at that school telling them straight. What do they expect you to do, just sit there like some little melt? Nah, you done right, and if they ring, I'll be telling them that.'

Alex smirked. His dad was a bit of a headcase, and when he got a bee in his bonnet, he would go off on one and let everyone know what he thought about them. His mam was a lot quieter than Jayden and, to be honest, he would have never put the two of them together. He knew she could hold her own and she was nobody's fool, but these days she'd calmed down a lot. Even if she was always on his case about school.

Leanne plonked down at the end of the sofa and fanned her long bright blue nails out, looking at them. All the girls she knew wore acrylic nails, and she was forever at the salon getting infills or a new set. She examined them more closely: they were dulled and growing out now.

'Jayden, when can I get my nails done? You said if I cleaned the house from top to bottom last week for you, you would sort me out with twenty quid?'

He gulped and chuckled. 'That was our little secret, and when I get some cash, I'll weigh you in. I've been ill and I've not been earning, have I?'

She let out a breath. Same shit, different day. 'No, you just lie on the sofa all day eating us out of house and home.' This girl was a straight talker for sure.

Jayden bolted up from his horizontal position and faced her. 'Oh, have you been listening to your mother again? I put money on the table all the time in this house. Where do you think all my universal credit goes, eh?'

Leanne let out a sarcastic laugh. 'You mean the money that's used to pay your weed bill off every week? I've heard you myself when it comes to coughing up money. So don't try and blend it with me.'

His eyes were wide open, and he swallowed hard. 'Bleeding hell, I have a few spliffs every day and you begrudge me that?'

'Telling you how it is, that's all. My mam is always skint because of you, and you should do something about it instead of sponging from her all the time. Don't think that the guys on the Square don't tell me about serving you up every day, because they do.'

Jayden jumped up from his seat and he was up in arms. 'Are you having a laugh, or what? That's below the belt, Leanne, knocked me sick it has. I do what I can for you all.'

'Just saying what I see.' Leanne carried on picking at her nails.

Jayden marched about the front room ragging his hands through his hair. 'Where's my trainers? I'm not sitting here listening to you insulting me like this. Out of fucking order!'

Alex smirked over at Leanne and kept his mouth shut.

'It's the truth, Jayden. A relationship should be equal and when I see my mam grafting all the time and you're lay on the sofa, of course I am going to say something.'

Jayden sat down, putting his grubby Nike trainers on. 'Cheeky cow, you are. You're forgetting I was the one who brought you up, aren't you? Your real dad wanted fuck all to do with you, and I was the one who stepped up and looked after you. Where is the thanks for that, eh?'

Leanne was used to this. Every time he was feeling sorry for himself, he would bring up her biological father. 'Blah-de-blah. Wow, how did I know you would bring that up? We all know you're not my dad. Change the record, will you?'

'No, I bleeding won't. You need reminding about it, that's why. When you was growing up, I was the one who made sure you never went without. I was the one who bought you nappies, picked you up when you fell, stroked your head when you was ill, no fucker else.'

Leanne folded her arms tightly in front of her and licked her lips slowly as she listened to him waffle on. 'Go on, tell me to go and ask my dad for money, because that's what usually comes next.'

'Nah, the man is a wanker, I wouldn't waste my breath. He's never given you a penny. He wanted nothing to do with you. It was me here, muggins, who looked after you.' Jayden stood up and kicked the bottom of the table, fuming. He gripped his coat from the back of the chair. 'Tell your mam I've gone out because I can't stand your mouth, Leanne.'

She rolled her eyes. 'Face. Bothered? Go and do what you always do, get stoned and get bladdered.'

He stormed out of the living room and slammed the front door shut as he left. The room shook.

Alex turned to face his sister. 'The guy is a muppet. I didn't say anything to him because I would have ended up punching his lights out. You're right in everything you say about him. I know he's my dad, but he's a lazy twat.'

Leanne sat up straight and twiddled her hair. 'And now he thinks he's the victim. He'll be ringing my mam now telling her a load of bullshit, feeling sorry himself.'

'Why does he always bring your dad into it? The man hasn't been in your life from the start so there's no need to keep gassing about him, is there?'

Leanne dropped her head low, sadness filling her face. This was a side she very rarely let anyone see. 'I thought about going to find him, you know? After all he is my dad, isn't he?'

'You should, but don't tell anyone. Imagine my dad if he found out. He would have the house up saying you have disrespected him and all that.'

'I know, I can imagine it. But, he's the one who keeps throwing his name into the mix. If he never mentioned him then I would just crack on with it, but he's always bringing him up, making me curious to what he's really like. It's alright for you. You know your dad – even if he is a pain in the arse.'

Alex dropped the control pad onto his lap, giving his sister his full attention. 'Sometimes I wish Dad would fuck off and leave us alone. The house is calm when he's not at home and he only brings trouble to the door anyway. Have you heard the way he speaks to Mam? No respect. I'm sure he gave her a belt last week, too.'

Leanne was alert, fist curling tightly. She'd heard them fighting in the past and he'd promised her he would never lay a finger on her mother again. Leanne delved deeper. 'So, when exactly was this and what did you hear?'

Alex picked up the controller again, glad for a reason not to meet Leanne's eyes, and carried on playing the game as he spoke. 'I heard shouting and banging, and I'm sure I heard Mam crying.'

'Why didn't you tell me? Better still, why didn't you go and steam into him?'

'Coz, like I said, I wasn't sure.'

'So, from now on we listen out for her. Anything, and I mean *anything*, and we will both go in team-handed and sort him out. There is no way I'm standing by while he batters her. I've got a few lads from the Square onside and they've told me if I ever needed anybody sorting out, that I could speak to them.' Her eyes were wide open, and her voice was quieter. 'And they will, you know. If I tell them what he's been doing, they will do him in good and proper. Nil by mouth.'

Alex's voice changed, concerned. 'And who are these lads? You know hanging out on the Square is nothing but trouble and if my mam finds out she will go ape. She's always telling you to keep away from there.'

'Shut up, you. Don't be telling her, either. The last thing I need is her on my back, pecking my head. I'm a big girl and I can look after myself.'

'But, you know as well as me what goes on there and it will only be a matter of time before you end up getting caught up in it. You'll be arrested or stabbed up.'

26

'Nah, I don't do anything to get me nicked. Me and Kerry just chill with Gino and Kyle. Top lads, they are. You know Kyle Barnes, don't you – Jacko's mate – everyone knows Gino Gallagher. I think Gino has a thing for me. I'm not going to lie, if he wants me on his arm then I would jump at the chance.'

This was too much information for Alex. His sister's relationship was not something he wanted to hear about. 'Be careful, that's all. Some bad-arses knocking about over there. And, I've heard that Gino is a bit of a head-the-ball.'

'Yeah, yeah, whatever. I know him, so don't be listening to people who don't. If he gets wind of it, he will cut them up, trust me. He hates people talking behind his back.'

Leanne stood up and looked around the front room. It was a state and she knew before she went out that she needed to clean up. She had to keep in her mother's good books and if it meant doing a bit of cleaning then she was all up for it. 'Alex, turn that off for a bit. You can help clean up.'

'Nah, man's chilling, sis,' he replied as his fingers pressed rapidly on the control pad. Like father, like son. Allergic to a bit of proper graft.

Chapter Five

Jayden stood looking up at the top window, walking one way then the other. Cream blinds moving about. A face appeared at the window. He waved his hand about and smiled up at the man. 'Yo, Simon, open up. Come on man, I'm freezing my nuts off out here. Are you deaf or what? I've been here for time.'

The face disappeared. A light went on in the hallway. The door opened and a man was stood there wearing only his boxers: tight-fitted, they were, budgie smugglers. 'Yo Jayden, lad, where have you been, pal? I've not seen you for time.'

'Just been chilling, mate. Had to get out of the house though. Them lot are doing my head in. First Macy was on one, you know what it's like, then it was Leanne.'

Simon rolled his eyes. Of course he knew about women. His own Mrs had left him and, if he was being honest, he was enjoying the single life now he'd got used to it. He could come and go when he pleased, sleep when he wanted to. It was heaven, as he was telling everyone.

Jayden followed him inside the house. 'So, what you been up to, have you had any decent gigs, or what? I could do with earning a few quid, mate. I'm on the bones of my arse.'

Simon plonked down on the sofa and shoved his hand down the front of his boxers, scratching his nuts. 'I'm branching out. I've been doing a few grows of my own. I've got two rooms upstairs kitted out, got the full works, you know the dance.'

Jayden's ears pinned back. 'Since when have you been growing? Who sorted that out?' He was intrigued.

'I bought the lights and that, and our Terry's mate set it all up. It's ready for chopping in a few weeks and I'll get a right few quid from it. A few grand, at least. I'll show that slag what she walked out on. I'll be fucking minted, buy what the fuck I want, new clobber, and maybe a holiday. The world's my oyster.'

'Fuck me, mate, why didn't you let me know and I would have been in with you? I always sort work out for you when you have none. Shady, you are.'

Simon pulled a sour expression. 'Are you having a laugh, or what? Sally left me weeks ago and while I was on my tod, depressed as fuck, you have been nowhere to be seen. I swear it's only these last few weeks that I've pulled myself together and sorted my napper out. She's dead to me now. I wouldn't piss on her if she was on fire now, the slapper.'

Jayden stuttered; he knew his pal was right. Yes, he'd heard about the breakup, but what bloke in their right mind wants to sit with someone who is crying all the time and miserable? Jayden's tone changed, softer. 'Mate, I know I should have been here with you, but I've had shit going on myself. The kids are in trouble all the time and to tell you the truth I've not been feeling myself, no energy.'

Simon wasn't letting him off the hook that easy. 'I hear you but, a text or a phone call wouldn't have gone amiss. I was in a bad way, mate, even thought about ending it all.'

There was an eerie silence for a few seconds, both of them just staring into space. Both men thinking about friends they'd lost, guys like them who'd been brought up to think men didn't cry, didn't let on when they were hurt. But the hurt always came out in the end. Even if you couldn't find the words for it.

Jayden looked shifty before he changed the subject. 'If you're growing now, rather than on delivery, has your Tez got any work for me, or what, then? I know he's got his finger in a few pies.'

Simon reached over to the table and picked up his cigarettes. He popped one into the side of his mouth and held the brass Zippo lighter underneath it. 'Yep, Tez was asking me only the other day for a driver. You know, to do drops and that.'

'Dropping what? Are we talking class A or class B?'

'A bit of both. I don't really know all the details, but you know as well as me where the money is.'

Jayden sucked hard on his gums. 'How far would I be driving, where is it going to?'

'The last one I done was in Wales,' Simon said. 'Three ton I got for it, but mate, my arse was twitching all the way there knowing what I was carrying. It's not for me that. I would rather take the chance growing my own weed and selling it. If the dibble come booming the door in, I will say some guys rent the room and I know fuck all about it. You know the score. That's what everyone else does and they get away with it.'

Jayden knew exactly what he was talking about – and he understood why his friend had moved into growing, instead. He'd been along for the ride on a few drops in the past and he knew being a driver was no easy job.

He was apprehensive. 'Macy won't have no part of that life. She fucking moans when I'm carrying even a bit of bud on me. You know what she's like since she nearly got time. Lost her bottle and now she's a goody two-shoes.'

Simon chugged hard on his fag. 'She won't be moaning when the money starts rolling in, though, will she?'

'Correct, Simon. Women are all smiles and that when your hand is in your pocket and you're treating them, but the second you're skint they are on your back, packing your shit and telling you it's over.'

Simon flicked the ash on his fag. 'That's why I'm never getting a girlfriend again. I'm staying single. I can't be arsed with relationships. I'm just gonna shag them and then do one. I'm a free spirit from now on. Riding solo.'

Jayden started laughing. It was so obvious that Simon still had feelings for his wife. Who was he trying to kid here? But it wasn't worth a fight, and so he sat back in his seat. 'Skin up, then.'

Simon shot his eyes to the small wooden table to the left of him. Rizla, a small plastic bag of weed, and a few lighters. 'Help yourself, pal. I've been blazing all day so I'm chilling now for a bit. It's decent weed too, haze it is.'

Jayden reached over and gripped the things he needed to build a joint. Once it was complete, he lit it and sat back and inhaled deeply. 'I'll give your Tez a shout, then. I suppose one or two drops will sort me out for a bit. Get the Mrs off my back at least.'

'Better than nothing, Jay. When that's ready upstairs I'll give you a treat but until then, I'm like you, potless.'

Jayden was stoned, eyes barely open now, words slurring. 'I always thought my life would turn out better, you know. I had big dreams – owning my own garage and that – when I was growing up.'

Simon chuckled. 'You and me both, mate. It's this area, it draws you into the underworld and, once you're in, there is no way back out. Look at us two, how long have we been grafting now? Must be over ten years. And barely a fucking day of that has been on the right side of the law.'

'Yeah, it must be about that. We were practically kids when we started out – simple days, they were, doing a few burglaries, whatever looked easy.'

'We did anything that got us any money, Jay – remember those days? Shoplifting, car theft, credit card fraud. I tell you we are lucky we've not been to the big house for a long stretch.'

'Tell me about it, mate. We've had a few near misses, though – admit it – and got away with it by the skin of our teeth. What about that house we broke into, and that old guy woke up and steamed into us with his walking stick?'

Jayden held his stomach as he burst out laughing. 'That old guy was former SAS or something. He had balls of steel, I'll give him that. My face was bruised for weeks after he landed a cheeky one on the side of my jaw. Still, they were good times. We were fucking wild when we were kids.'

Simon looked serious and tilted his head slightly. 'Talking of kids, you might know, but I've heard a few stories about your Leanne on the Square. She's chilling with some right head-the-balls. Ruthless they are, they don't give a fuck. Tooled up, ready for action.'

Jayden squirmed and fidgeted about in his seat. 'She's a gobby cow at the moment and she's not listening to me or her mother. Every time I say something she throws in the old *you're not my dad* card, so what can I do?'

Simon sighed. 'You brought the kid up, though. What was she, three or something, when you met Macy?'

'Yeah, something like that. I can't remember now, too much weed, done my memory in,' he sniggered as he continued. 'She's going down the wrong road and I'm sick of telling her where it will all end up. She'll be preggers next, mark my words.'

Simon shook his head. 'Well, keep her away from the Square, mate. It's a bad place.'

Jayden stared into space as he replied. 'Do you know what? Sometimes you've got to just look out for number one. It's my time now. Forget everyone else. I'm not arsed anymore, mate. Fuck her, fuck the lot of them.'

Chapter Six

The Square was busy, motorbikes skidding about, kids shouting, music being played. The strong smell of weed hanging in the air. Kids getting high, swigging vodka like it was water, every teenager's dream and every parent's nightmare. Anyone stumbling across the scene might have wondered where the police were. They should have had some presence, making sure all the kids were safe, at least. But even the law wouldn't have stopped this gang. The Square was that kind of place – normal rules didn't apply. The shop was still open, and a lot of youths were stood outside it. Whenever the shopkeeper's back was turned, they were in there like a rat up a drainpipe, filling their pockets. They had no fear, this lot. Fuck the law and fuck anyone who dared to cross them was the standard attitude. A force not to be messed with or so they told everyone. They ranged from kids to teens to young adults and, to be honest, society had ignored them for enough years when they had been in need of support, of structure, of care, it was hardly surprising that now they rejected society and set their own rules.

Across the way from the shop stood five youths, dressed in black, caps pulled fully down, dodgy-looking characters. Leanne Taylor stood next to them with her friend Kerry, chatting. Her black skirt barely covered her bottom and the white belly top she was wearing only just contained her boobs. Her black leather jacket hung from one shoulder like she was an extra from *Grease*. The lad nearest to her draped his hand around her shoulder and pulled her closer and whispered something into her ear. Leanne's eyes were wide open, alert. Gino Gallagher passed something into her hand and she walked quickly away from him towards a man who had just walked onto the Square. No words were spoken as Leanne reached the man. She took some money from him and passed him the small package. And that was how easy it was. Job done.

Leanne walked back to Gino with a big smile spread across her face. She smirked at Kerry as she passed him the money. Kerry squirmed and shook her head slightly. She clearly knew the score, this girl, and she was sick to death of telling her bestie to let this wanker do his own dirty work. Kerry could read him like a book. Gino was using Leanne, having her over. But Leanne never listened. She thought the sun shone out of Gino's arse. He said *jump*, and she said *how high*. A fool in love was Leanne.

Gino pressed his cold lips on the side of her cheek. 'Cheers babes, you're doing well.'

Leanne snuggled into his body and kissed his neck softly with her heart-shaped lips. She looked up into his big blue eyes and spoke in her sexy voice. 'I like to make you happy.'

Kerry was listening and rolled her eyes. She rammed two fingers towards her mouth and imitated being sick. Gino was one of the main heads on the Square and he was well known for being a snapper, a right piece of work. She wanted to keep her friend well away from him, but she was fighting a losing battle. Leanne was mesmerised by him, smitten. The more she told Leanne to keep clear of him, the more she clung to him. Maybe her friend thought she was jealous, but she wasn't, she was looking out for her.

'Are we going to get off soon, or what?' Leanne ventured.

Gino shot a look at the other lads and winked at them. 'Yeah, just got to earn the cash first and, with you helping me out, it shouldn't take us long. Another hour or so and me and you can have some special time.' He reached behind her and squeezed her bum. The other lads sniggered and whispered to each other. Gino was the man on the Square, and he was always with a different girl. The guy had banter, the gift of the gab. His friends said Leanne was all over him like a rash, too needy.

Gino seemed a lot older than Leanne, but you grew up fast around the Square. They hadn't put a label on their relationship yet, but they'd seen each other a couple of times and he'd whispered sweet nothings into her ear, made her feel special, made her feel like she was the only girl he was interested in. Gino moved her out of the way now as a figure rounded the corner, and he squinted at the newest arrivals onto his patch.

'Oi, oi,' he said as he nodded his head at the other gang members. He spoke through clenched teeth. 'Look at this cheeky cunt coming on here when he knows *we* graft here. What, he has a few brothers backing him and he thinks he's untouchable? Watch, just let me see him trying to lick shot here and he's getting his jaw snapped. Fucking liberty-taker.' Gino stepped forward, ears pinned back, chest expanding. He popped a cigarette into his mouth and lit it. Sucking in deeply, he blew out a large cloud of grey smoke from his lips. He walked slowly one way then the other, weighing up his rival: Leon Walsh. Could he take him down? Take on his brothers? It was clear he wasn't sure, but one thing was certain: Leon wasn't welcome on the Square.

Kerry walked over to the shop. She knew exactly what she was doing. Pretty and with a curvaceous body, Kerry looked more developed than her friend (*thank God for the push up bra*, Leanne always said), and whether her swagger was real or faked, she looked the part as she approached Leon.

Leon Walsh clocked the eye candy straight away. He was with two of his boys and licked his lips slowly as she neared him. 'Yo, what you saying, sexy?'

Kerry flicked her hair over her shoulder and licked her cherry-coloured lips. She could feel all eyes on her from both sides of the Square. She eyeballed Leon for a few seconds before she replied. 'What did you say?' Of course, she knew what he'd said but this gave her time to think of her next line, and get a better look at his gorgeous features.

'I said can I have your snap or what?' He chuckled now stepping nearer to her, confident.

Gino looked on from the other side of the Square, his feathers well and truly ruffled. He twisted his head like an owl in a barn and snarled at Leanne. 'You need to have words with her, fucking slapper. Is she right in the head, talking to our ops? She makes a choice right here and now what side of the fence she sits on. I'm not having any slag thinking they can chill with us and then go dropping their knickers for them pricks over there. Word her up before I do, you get me?'

Leanne swallowed hard; her voice was low. 'She's not doing anything, Gino. She's only gone to the shop; it's not her fault that Leon is making a play for her.'

The other lads looked at each other and cringed: they knew what was coming. Gino went nose to nose with Leanne and backed her up against the wall, his hot breath spraying into her face. 'Oi, fucking gobby, don't you start giving me back-chat, otherwise you can fuck off over there with them pricks too. No woman of mine speaks to me like that. Do you understand me?'

Leanne's eyes were wide open, her breathing doubled, mouth dry. She stuttered as she replied, 'Gino, just chill, will you? I'll have a word with Kerry, alright, just get out of my face.'

He backed off, twisted his head around and watched as Kerry went into the shop. He'd spat his dummy out big time. 'Come on, let's do one. My blood is boiling watching him. I swear the day is coming when that Leon wanker will get his comeuppance. Trust me, he's living on borrowed time. The clock is ticking.'

Kyle, Jacko and the others nodded in agreement.

'Catch you later, lads. Stay put for now and make sure everything is running smoothy. Any problems, bell me.'

Kyle stepped forward. It was his show now and he was more than ready to stab some wanker up if they tried any funny business on his watch. In fact, he was looking out for any chance to show his worth, prove his status. If you looked hard enough for trouble around here, it didn't take long to find some.

Leanne hung her head low as she started to walk off, a couple of steps behind Gino. She turned to one of the others. 'Jacko, tell Kerry I'll be back soon. Tell her to wait for me and I'll walk home with her.'

'Yes, sorted,' he replied.

Kyle whispered something to Jacko and they both sniggered. It was their show now and they loved the power they held while Gino was away.

Gino was in a mood. He'd hardly spoken to Leanne all the way to her house.

'Is your mam home tonight or have we got the house to ourselves?'

'Dunno, it is what it is.' Leanne had to squash a smile. All the main men round here, so used to acting the tough guy out on the street, most of them still lived with their mothers, would do anything for a bit of privacy. At least she usually got that from her lot.

'We'll go to my bedroom anyway. Nobody will bother us in there. It's the only place I can get some privacy.'

Usually, she would have put any lad in his place who'd treated her like Gino had. She'd have told him to fuck off for talking to her like that but, over these last few weeks, he'd got into her head, and she was doing anything to please him. Sometimes she hated the power it felt like he had over her. She'd found herself practically begging for his approval. True, her home life hardly helped the situation and, deep down, she knew she was just looking for someone to care about her, to give her some attention. Everybody at home had their own thing going on and it felt like nobody really cared where she was anymore. Jayden was a stoner and he spent most of his time asleep on the sofa – he didn't really care where she was or who she was with. Her mother was always working, and when she was at home she was too tired to talk, let alone ask about her daughter's social life. Meanwhile, Alex was the one who got all the attention at home, and she always felt that Jayden favoured him because he was his blood. He'd always denied it when she brought it up, but she knew blood was thicker than water. He only said nice things to her when he was after something, to run to the shop for him or borrow a cig from the neighbour. He was a right cadging fucker, or that's what the neighbours said about him behind his back. She'd stop defending him.

She sat on the edge of the bed, playing with her hair. Gino was sorting the music out and rolling a spliff. He seemed to have calmed down. He flicked the lighter under the joint and made his way over to the bed.

'Move over, then,' he said.

Leanne slipped her trainers off and got onto the bed and lay down staring at the ceiling, nervously twiddling her thumbs.

He was next to her now. 'Yo, get a few blasts of this down ya neck, helps you relax.'

Leanne had never smoked weed before and she wasn't sure it was something she wanted to do. She'd seen what a hold it had on Jayden. But Gino held the spliff out in front of her and she knew it would be less hassle to smoke it than to refuse him. Two long hard drags she took, and she quickly passed it back. She smiled over at him, wanting to show him that she was game for anything, not a wuss. Gino had a few more drags before he placed the spliff in the ashtray, then sat up and pulled his black T-shirt over his head. Leanne had to give him that, he was ripped and in great shape. His lips met hers and he started to kiss her. Leanne had only kissed a few lads, although she'd spoken to Kerry only last week about taking the next step. Most of her mates had been having sex since their early teens, so she wouldn't be judged, would she?

Gino was horny. He lay on top of her and pressed his crotch onto her. Her head felt woozy, and she could tell she wasn't thinking straight. The kiss became more intense, and Gino tried his luck at getting into her knickers. His hand disappeared under her skirt.

'No Gino, I'm not ready for that yet. Just let's kiss.'

Gino rolled from her and punched his clenched fist into the pillow, snapping. 'You're a fucking prick teaser. Go on, do one. I've put time and effort into you for weeks now and

I'm sick of waiting. It shows me how immature you are. Maybe I need an older girl, someone the same age as me. A girl who's not frigid.'

Leanne panicked. She sat up and reached over and touched his arm. 'Gino, stop being like this. I didn't say I didn't want to, just maybe not right now. I've waited long enough for the right person.'

He sucked hard on his gums. 'So, I'm not the right person, then?' His eyes were wide, and his temper was rising as his nostrils flared. She swallowed hard, brought her knees up to her chest and cupped her hands around them. She never replied.

He repeated himself as he gripped her cheeks, squeezing them together. Looking her straight in the eyes. He was waiting on an answer. She was scared, he could see it in her eyes. 'Yes, you are, but...' She never got chance to finish what she was saying.

He mounted her again and this time he wasn't taking no for an answer. He kissed her with force, small bites to her neck, holding her hands over her head, the skin turning white. His hands were in her knickers, and she was rolling about on the bed trying to get him off her. Every time she tried to shout, he placed his large hand over her mouth and smiled down at her with menacing eyes. 'Keep it shut. Relax and enjoy it. You love it really.'

Leanne lay frozen, eyes wide. He was inside her now, moaning and groaning. Between her legs was burning, pain like she'd never felt before. This was rape. But the minute she even let herself think that, she froze as she thought what people would say. Gino didn't take long; it was over very quickly. He rolled from her and gasped his breath. She was in shock as she rummaged about the bed, trying to find her knickers. She needed to be covered up, not let him see her private parts.

'That was bang on, that. See, I told you you would enjoy it.' His voice sounded a million miles away.

Her eyes clouded over as she stared at the wall facing her. This was not how she had imagined her first time. There were no candles, no soft music, no nothing. He reached over and dragged her onto his chest, stroking her hair back from her face.

'So now it's official, you're my girl,' he chuckled.

Leanne closed her eyes slowly and lay lifeless next to him.

'Why are you so quiet?' he asked, after a few minutes had passed.

She gulped. 'Gino, I said I wasn't ready, and you just did it to me.'

He pulled her head up and looked deep into her eyes. 'Listen, you wanted it, so stop gassing. Ask anyone, you've been all over me for weeks, so what did you expect me to think?'

She stuttered. 'I wanted to wait, that's all.'

'So, you're saying you don't have feelings for me like I have for you? I don't say soppy stuff, but that – just then – that shows you how much I wanted you.'

He had feelings for her. He'd never told her that before. Maybe she'd been naïve asking him to wait. She'd told Kerry how much she fancied him – no one would believe her if she told anyone he'd raped her. She swallowed the bile in her throat. Perhaps she could rewrite history, convince herself Gino was telling her the truth and that she could go back to how she felt about him before this. After all, what was she going to do? Tell the police? Like they'd believe a girl from the Square...

'I do have feelings for you too, Gino.' That was it. The first step was convincing herself.

He chuckled and looked her in the eyes. 'So, no harm done then, is there. We love each other and we've just had sex? That's what couples do.'

Leanne tried to raise a smile and lay back on his chest. No one had said anything about love to her before. Maybe he was right, she'd overreacted. And, if they had feelings for each other, then what he'd done was part of being in a relationship. Her hand played with the small cluster of dark hair on his chest. She replayed the words in her head, running over the words until she almost believed them. He was her man now and they were in love.

Chapter Seven

Macy sat drinking her cup of coffee when Jayden walked into the living room. His hair was stuck up and he had his hand down the front of his boxers. Bloody hell, he could have done with a few weeks in the sun. He was as white as a bottle of milk.

'Brew us a drink, love. It's bleeding freezing in this gaff. Is there no heating on?'

'Nope, it ran out last night. But you won't know that because you was out until God knows what time.' Macy had been freezing, even under the covers.

'I was in before midnight. I come to bed and you was snoring your head off. Don't you remember I kissed you and asked if you wanted some rumpy-pumpy?'

She sipped the hot drink and squirmed. 'Nope, I was out for the count as soon as my head hit the pillow. I'm not even sure what time Leanne come in. I lay on the bed for a bit, trying to get warm, and the next thing I can remember it was morning time.'

'Aw, my little sleeping beauty. Except I was tempted to do more than wake you with a kiss, if I'm being honest.'

Macy started laughing and placed her cup back on the table. 'You would have got a slap if you would have woken me up. You know what I'm like if someone wakes me up.'

Jayden sat down on the sofa next to her. 'Do us a drink then, it's like the North Pole in here.'

Macy stood up and left the room as he dragged a few cushions from the sofa and placed them on his body. He smiled. He hadn't got in until well after midnight and yet he was in the clear for now. Macy wasn't off on one. What a result: no moaning and he was in the good books for a change. Macy was back holding a cup of tea in her hand. 'Here, get it quick before it burns my fingers off,' she shrieked. Jayden reached over and took the mug from her hands.

Macy walked over to the table and rummaged through her coat pocket. She sat down next to him and unfolded her fingers slowly. The ring. 'This should get us a few quid, shouldn't it?'

His eyes lit up and he quickly gripped the jewellery in his grubby fingers. 'Lovely. Is it real? Where's it from?'

Macy smiled and sat back in her seat. 'I found it when I was cleaning. I was going to put it back on the side but, as I see it, that family is loaded and it's not like they would ever miss it anyway. Honest, they have more money than sense.'

Jayden wasn't listening. He held the ring up to the light and tried to look at the hallmark. 'I'll take it to my mate, and he'll give us a right few quid for this. I bet we get about a ton for it.'

'So, stop gawping at it and get it sold. We need gas and the electric meter only has a few quid on it. We can go food shopping and get some freezer stuff too. It should help us out, shouldn't it?'

'Yeah, let me have this drink and I'll scarper with it. I went to see Simon last night and he's got a bit of graft for me too.'

Her expression changed and she folded her arms tightly in front of her, aware that whatever he was going to say, she wasn't going to like. Simon was always getting his collar felt and since his relationship had fallen apart she'd heard lots of stories about him and his antics. 'Nah, Jayden, keep well away from him. Jodie told me he's been going to the brass gaffs since his Mrs left him. Rotten, he is.'

Jayden went bright red and stuttered. 'Stop listening to gossip. How many times have I got to tell you about the big mouths around here? They chat shit all the time. No truth in that comment whatsoever. He's a sorted lad and so what if he is sleeping with brasses? His wife left him, and he probably needs to empty his sack. Who are we to judge him?'

'Dirty thieving bastard, he is. He wants to try paying for his kids instead of paying for fanny. I bet he's riddled with chlamydia.'

Jayden started laughing and changed the subject. 'He's asked me to do some drops for his brother Terry.'

Macy shook her head. 'How many times have I told you that's the worst part? If you get caught and you have that amount of drugs on you, because let's talk straight here, it's boxes and boxes of weed isn't it, well you're the one that goes down for it, despite you only getting a pittance. The last time you did it, you was carrying four boxes, so about forty grand's worth? Course the big boys never risk being near that much stuff. They pay a few quid to someone like you they can afford to lose.'

'Fucking hell, Macy, put the dampeners on it, why don't you. We are skint, and I need to earn a crust to put some food on the table.'

Macy was in a strop now. The mention of Simon's name made her blood boil. No wonder his wife had left him: he was a lazy bastard who never had a day's honest work in him. She hated Jayden chilling with him too, and she couldn't hide that fact. 'Get a normal job, for crying out loud, is it too much of a big ask?'

'Wow,' he shot a look at the clock on the wall. 'It's not even ten o' clock and you're kicking off already.'

'Just saying, that's all. Tell Simon to do one and get someone else for the drops. He must think you are green or something.'

Jayden stood up and stretched his arms over his head as Alex walked into the room. 'I'll get ready and take that ring over.'

Macy opened her eyes wide, letting him know to keep his mouth shut in front of Alex. That was the last thing she wanted, her kids knowing she was a thief when all she ever lectured them about was getting a good job and staying out of trouble. They wouldn't understand how she crossed the line so they didn't have to.

Alex plonked down on the sofa and his lips were purple. 'It's freezing, Mam. I need another duvet on my bed. That bedroom was cold last night.'

'Your dad is going to get some gas, love. It must have run out during the night.'

'Dad, when are we getting the new *Call of Duty* game? It came out last night and all the lads are on it.'

Jayden was on his way out of the room and turned back to answer him. 'When I get some more bleeding money, son. And, if you keep talking and keeping me here, then it will take forever. I'm gone, going to get ready.'

Jayden walked out of the room and Alex reached over for the television remote. He shot a look around the living room.

'Where is our Leanne?' Macy reached over for her fags and sparked one up.

'Probably in her bedroom as per usual. I think Kerry stayed over so she'll be in there all day, if I know her.' Alex smirked, cheeky smile. 'Kerry should have come and got in my bed to keep me warm.'

Macy burst out laughing. He had his dad's sense of humour for sure. He was lucky he hadn't talked his way into trouble, the stuff he came out with. 'Oi, dirty bollocks, you stick to playing on the PlayStation. I don't need the stress of you with girls for now. Not that you'll get one of your own unless you learn to treat them with a bit of respect.'

'Girls are all over me, Mardukes. It's only a matter of time before they are knocking on the door for me.'

Macy chuckled. 'Yeah, whatever, but until they do, go and get that room cleaned. I popped my head in before and it stinks of sweaty feet and cheese.'

'Mother, stay out of my bedroom. I will clean it when I'm ready. Like I keep telling you, it's a work in progress. Go in Leanne's bedroom. That's where the real trouble is, make-up all over, bath towels on the floor and rubbish on her window.'

'Never mind your sister, you just concentrate on you. Grass.'

But he wasn't listening to a word she said. He was watching the television now, back in a world of his own.

Macy stood in the hallway looking at Jayden who was ready now. She had to make sure he was coming straight back with the money once he'd sold the ring. In the past he'd been to cash her benefit money and got on his toes, missing for days, leaving her without a pot to piss in.

'Jayden, do you want me to come with you? Give me ten minutes to get ready and then we can go shopping straight after.'

He gave no eye contact, head dipped low as he fastened his shoelaces. 'Nope, you wait here. My mate Gazzar is funny about people going to his gaff.'

She eyeballed him. 'Straight there and straight back, do you hear me? Because, if you go on the missing list like you have in the past, I'll cut your balls off.'

He stood up and held his hands in the air. 'Macy, fuck me, stop worrying. I'll come straight back, so wind your neck in, woman.'

She watched him from the corner of her eye and followed him out of the room as he headed back down the stairs. He kissed her on the cheek before he left.

Leanne lay on the bed and twisted on her side to speak to Kerry. 'Gino was going sick last night about you speaking to Leon Walsh.'

Kerry raised her eyebrows. 'Like I'm arsed what he says. I'll do what I want. He doesn't run the Square, or me for that fact.'

'So, has Leon messaged you?'

'Yeah, all night he's been on to me. I am meeting him later.'

Leanne was alert. 'Don't be bringing him on the Square. Gino has already said you can't chill with us lot if you're talking to Leon.'

Kerry sat up and folded her pillow behind her head. 'Leanne, that guy is brainwashing you. I've told you before and I'll tell you again. I don't trust him. There is something about him that doesn't sit right with me. He's controlling and thinks he owns you already. Come on, it's not like you two are a thing, is it?'

Leanne took a deep breath. Her voice was low. 'We are now, after last night. He said he has feelings for me.'

Kerry burst out laughing. 'What, and you believe him? He's trying to get into your knickers.'

Leanne was beetroot and anyone could see she was pissed off. 'We had sex last night and it was afterwards that he told me, so put that in your pipe and smoke it.'

Kerry gasped and stared at her best friend. 'You didn't tell me you were going to shag him. I mean, we sat chatting last night until the early hours and you never mentioned it once.'

Leanne stuttered as she twiddled her hair. 'I've told you now so what does it matter? Wow, Kez. Don't make a big thing out of this. It is what it is.'

Kerry stared at her friend for a few seconds and said. 'I'm just saying, that's all. Be careful with Gino. Donna

Moffat from the Shiredale estate was seeing him the other month and I've heard some nasty stories about what he did to her.'

'Stories like what?'

'Like slapping her about and stuff.'

Leanne let out a breath. 'Well, that's her own fault then, isn't it? She probably deserved it. He's not raised his hand to me, so that proves he loves me.'

Kerry let out a sarcastic laugh. 'Yeah, for now. Be careful with him. There is something about Gino I don't like. I've said it before, and I'll say it again, you are too good for him.'

Leanne lay chewing the skin on the side of her thumb as Kerry spoke. 'So, come on then, what was sex like? Did it hurt?'

Leanne blushed and checked the bedroom door again to make sure nobody was listening. Many a time she had found her brother outside her door, snooping about, trying to listen to her conversations. The coast was clear. 'It was over pretty quick. I just feel sore underneath, that's all.'

Kerry covered her mouth with her hand and sniggered. 'So did he have a big-un or what?'

'I don't know. I didn't look at it.'

'So, you had sex and never seen his willy. What, did you close your eyes all the way through?'

Leanne was on the spot and knew she had to come up with the goods. She needed to convince Kerry she'd wanted it, that she'd enjoyed it – as much so she could believe it herself. There was no way she was going to tell Kerry the truth. That her so-called boyfriend should be in a cell right now. She let her mind wander to how she'd always thought it was going to be. 'We were kissing for ages, and he was so gentle with me. It just kind of happened so natural. He kept asking me if I was alright all the way through it.' What a load of bullshit she was saying. It was rape: nothing more, nothing less. She needed this to sound more convincing. How was she going to tell herself she wasn't a victim if she couldn't even convince her best friend?

Kerry looked sour. 'I never had the guy down as the caring type.'

'Well, he doesn't show that side to everyone, does he? I'm special, he said.' Leanne was creating a world that wasn't true; complete fantasy. She should have told her friend the truth, told her how he forced himself on her, and grabbed and bit her body during the ordeal. It hadn't been a special moment at all, it had been an attack. Why couldn't she say it?

Kerry lay in silence for a few seconds, but then, luckily, she filled the quiet that hung in the air between the friends. 'I need to look mint tonight when I meet Leon. I think we're going to go to Maccies for a burger and that.'

'So, it's like a proper date, then?' Leanne tried not to sound envious. It was just a *McDonalds*, she thought.

'Of course it is. I'm not just standing about with a guy on the Square all night and counting it as a date. No, dates are like going to the cinema and all that.'

Leanne knew she was right and when she got the chance she was going to speak to Gino and ask him if this was something they could do with each other. Kerry was right: if you were in a relationship you were meant to go on dates, not stand about on the Square all night long selling drugs.

Jayden walked through the estate with his tracksuit jacket zipped up tightly. Big fat grey clouds hung low in the sky and any second now it was going to start tipping down. The area was quiet for a change, just a few locals pottering about, dog walkers, the postman. Jayden stopped by a shabby house and walked down the path. He stood back slightly. Dogs barking, a male voice shouting from behind the door. A man with a bald head and arms full of dark blue tattoos opened the door.

'Alright, Jay mate, to what do I owe the honour of this visit? I've not seen you in like forever. Have you been in the big house or what?'

Jayden stretched his hand out to shake hands with Gazzar. 'You know me, mate. I've been keeping my neck clean, keeping under the radar so to speak. I got a bit of tomfoolery if you want a quick look?'

Gazzar rubbed his hands together and had a quick scowl around the area. This neighbourhood was full of do-gooders, people who would ring the dibble on you given half the chance. The door opened fully, and Jayden was invited inside. Despite the plain look of the house outside, inside you could see in an instant that Gazzar had the best of everything: white leather sofa, a thick creamy white sheepskin rug in front of the glass fire. Jayden sat down while Gazzar went into the kitchen to get his glasses. Jayden shouted after him, 'You've got a smart house here, Gazzar. As soon as I get back on my feet that's the first thing I'm going to do. Macy is always moaning about the state of our gaff.'

Gazzar was back in the living room, and he had his glasses held in his right hand. No more chit-chat, he was here to do business now, make some money. He sat down and Jayden passed him the ring. His eyes lit up as he tickled the end of his chin like Fagin. 'Decent, mate. How much are you looking for?'

Jayden knew this game better than anyone. He went in high and knew his pal would knock him down. 'I reckon at least three ton. I've got someone else looking at it too, if you're not interested.'

Gazzar smirked. 'Oh, that old chestnut,' he sniggered.

Jayden sat back and kept his face straight. 'Nah, straight up. Old Norman said to bring it over, but I always come to you first because I know you won't try and have my eyes out, and you give a decent price.'

Gazzar examined the ring further and licked his top lip slowly. 'I'll give you one and half for it, pal. I'm taking a chance with it because, if I'm just going on the gold price, I won't even get my money back on it.'

And here it was. Jayden put his poker face on and never flinched. 'Ah mate. Lowest I can go is one seven five.'

There was a silence and Jayden could see that Gazzar wanted the ring. This was going to be like taking candy from a baby. He just had to stick to his guns for a few seconds more. His pal looked at the ring again and dug his hand deep into his pocket.

'Go on, then. I'll tell you what, you drive a hard bargain, you do. A done deal.' He pulled his fist back out of his jeans pocket, counted out the money and passed the cash over to Jayden.

Once he'd pocketed it, he stood up. 'Right, I better scarper. I've got to see a man about a dog, so to speak,' he chuckled.

'Cheers, mate, for bringing this. Don't forget if you get anything else as good quality as this, always come to me first. Fuck old Norman.'

'As always, mate. Right, cheers for that. I'll catch up with you soon.' Gazzar was still looking at the ring and never looked up once when Jayden left. He knew he'd got a bargain.

Jayden went straight into the bookies and banged twenty quid on the first race. He'd never won big, but he always thought his luck was going to change one day. It never did. The race started and he shouted at the screen. The other punters laughed as they watched him chasing his money. Gambling was a fool's game and, even though these people knew the odds of them winning were slim, they all came back here every day to chase their fortune.

'Go on, you fucking donkey. Whip its arse for crying out loud, bleeding ride it, you fucking goblin,' Jayden screamed at the top of his voice. He moved closer to the screen; his heartbeat doubled as his horse was nose to nose with another one. A few punters cheered along with him. Then the cheers faded away. Jayden screwed his betting slip up and launched it at the TV. 'Wanker.' He marched over to the door without speaking another word to anyone, gutted.

As he stepped out of the shop, his eyes met a gang of the lads standing under a shelter. The Square was busy with shoppers now and a few kids were kicking a football to each other. Jayden nodded at the youths and dug his hand into his pocket as he walked over to them. 'Sort us a twenty bud out, mate.'

The youth looked him up and down and snarled at him. 'Go around the corner, and don't ever ask me when I'm stood here again, you muppet.'

Jayden curled his fists into two tight balls. Who the hell did this prick think he was talking to? He would one-arrow him if he carried on chatting shit. He walked around the corner and waited until one of the runners came to meet him.

'Next time ring the mobile, here's the number.' The lad passed a small white piece of paper to Jayden, then he took the twenty-pound note from him and passed him the weed. There were no more words spoken between them. Jayden checked his watch and headed back home. Macy would be clock-watching. He was being a good lad today.

'Fucking fifty quid, Jay? It was worth more than double that,' Macy spluttered.

'Babes, he weighed it as scrap gold, and he was only giving me forty quid, but I managed to get him to give me another tenner.'

'He's a cheeky git, he's had your eyes out with that. I should have sold it myself.'

Jayden gave her a shifty look and sat down on the sofa next to Alex. 'Fancy a game of Fifa?'

Macy jumped into the conversation before Alex could answer. 'No, he bloody doesn't. We need to go shopping and get some gas because Dozy Balls here forgot to. I can't believe you never got some while you were out. Thick, you are.'

Jayden coughed and gasped. 'Can't you go? I've been running about all morning.'

'Why do I even bother? Give me the bloody money. I'll go myself while you sit on your arse as per.'

Jayden smirked and winked at his son. He never said a word as he passed over the cash.

Macy was ready to leave. Before she left, she said to Jayden, 'It's my day off today, so you can clean the house. Get Leanne up too. The three of you can blitz this place.'

Alex dropped his head low. This was his weekend and there was no way he was spending it cleaning. No way in this world.

The front door banged shut and shook the house. Alex loaded the game and sniggered at his old man. 'Are you ready then?' Jayden nodded. 'Born ready, son.'

Chapter Eight

Terry Dolan sat in his black BMW as Jayden made his way towards him. His head was dipped low. Jayden started to jog faster as he spotted him. The car door opened, and he jumped into the passenger side. He blew his warm breath onto his hands, rubbing them together before he spoke. 'Yo Tezzar, how's it going pal?'

Terry grinned, and patted his shoulder. He was a big man and rigged out in designer clothing head to toe.

Jayden clocked the Rolex on his wrist straight away and smiled. 'Top watch that, mate. I bet that set you back a few quid?'

Terry looked down at his watch and nodded his head. Proud. 'Yep, ten grand for that beauty. I've had my eye on one for a few years.'

Jayden's heart missed a beat. What the hell was he doing wrong in life when everyone around him was making big bucks and he was barely surviving? Ten grand on a bleeding watch! What he would give to own something like that.

Terry cut the small talk and got straight to the point. His time was precious. He was here to make money today, nothing more, nothing less. 'Our kid said you are after some work?'

'Yep, what have you got?'

Terry looked at his pearly white teeth through his rearview mirror. He'd not long had the veneers done in Turkey and everyone on the estate was talking about his 'Hollywood' smile. A proper beamer it was and ten times better than his old not-so-pearly whites. 'A few runs to Blackpool and Leeds, if you're up for it?'

'I am, but what am I taking?' Jayden knew he wouldn't get too many chances to ask questions.

Terry licked his lips slowly and turned to face him. 'Well, that's up to you. I've got brown and white that needs shifting and some weed.'

Jayden cringed; it was not what he wanted to hear. Heroin and crack carried a big stretch in jail. A few of his mates had gone down that road and each of them were serving hefty sentences at HMP. He let out a breath and scratched the top of his head. It had better be worth it. 'So, tell me about the money.'

'Two ton for delivering the weed and five for the brown and white.'

Jayden looked Terry straight in the eyes. 'Fuck me, mate, that's not a lot for the chances I'm going to take. It's big time if I get caught with it.'

Terry sat back in his seat and gripped the steering wheel. 'It's up to you, kid. I've got lads ripping my hands off to do a few drops. And,' he paused and coughed to clear his throat. 'If you get caught with it then the debt is on your neck too. I find it tends to make my boys a bit more careful if they know what's on the line.'

'What the fuck, Tez, since when has this come into play?'

'Since some cheeky twats thought they could have me over.'

Jayden played with the black string hanging from his hoody. 'I'll take the brown and white this time, but the next time I take it I want the money raising. Come on Tez, you know me, and I know what you're earning. Hook a brother up, eh?'

Terry sniggered, looking straight at him. 'Mate, it is what it is. I'm only here because our Simon said you needed some work. It's up to you?'

Jayden sat thinking, looking from the passenger window. He had no other option. Maybe he could have done a bit of work here and there for friends and that, but the money would be crap and barely enough to put any food on the table. He was between a rock and a hard place. 'Right, tell me when and where, and at least you can give me a sub from my wages to help sort myself out?'

'Yep, I don't mind giving you a bit of cash until you start earning.' Terry reached over to the glove compartment and pressed the silver button. Jayden clocked the money straight away, eyes wide. Terry rolled five twenty-pound notes from the wad and passed them to him. 'That's off your first pay packet. The next drop is tomorrow night. Come to the lock up about five bells. It's best to go in rush hour traffic, nobody gets onto you then.'

Jayden gripped the money and patted Terry's shoulder. 'Sorted pal, see you then. Make sure the motor has petrol in it. I'm not supplying that too,' he chuckled. He was back in the game.

Chapter Nine

Macy walked down the main road. It was quieter than usual, not a lot of traffic on the road today. Not many people round here did a nine-to-five. It was all shift work, zero-hour stuff or, for plenty of others, they were probably still in bed after a late night on the piss. At least she had some money to get some gas and lecky. If the security guards were busy today in the stores she could always nick a few joints of meat and sell them too. Old habits, she thought. She walked past the row of shops on Rochdale Road and looked inside. The hairdresser's was packed out and from the corner of her eye she clocked a woman with bright ginger hair, the colour of Cilla Black's back in the day. She turned her head quickly, but it was too late, the woman was waving her hand in the air, and Macy knew she'd seen her. 'Fucking hell, that's all I need,' she muttered under her breath. The door opened and the woman stretched her arms out to cuddle Macy.

'Oh my God, I was just saying to everyone the other day, that I'd not seen you in forever. Where the hell have you been hiding?' Sheila Tierney let Macy out of the bear hug and stood back slightly. She dug her hand in her jacket pocket and pulled her fags out. She lit two and passed one to Macy.

'I've just been busy, Sheila. I've got a bit of a cleaning job now and I'm trying my best to stay on the straight and narrow.'

Sheila was a lovely-looking woman; her skin was glowing, and you could tell she took pride in her appearance. Macy took the fag from Sheila and stuck it straight in her mouth. She never refused a ciggie.

Sheila smirked and kept her voice down as she moved her away from the shop's entrance. 'Bloody hell, girl. You can earn with us lot instead. What the hell are you pissing about cleaning shitters for? We're earning at least five ton a day now.'

Macy swallowed hard. She knew that was money she could never earn doing what she was doing now. Anyone would be tempted. 'I know, love, but if I get lifted again then I'm going to jail. The judge told me last time. You know that. And I'm not taking any chances. The kids would be fucked if I got slammed. Imagine Jayden looking after them.'

Sheila sighed and blew a smoky breath. 'The risk goes with the job, love. Jail is something I don't like to think about. But even so, it's worth it with the money I'm earning. You must have heard that I got six months inside last year and, to tell you the truth, I enjoyed the break away from the kids. Honest, as bad as it sounds, when I was sent down I could lie and watch TV without any hassle and all my meals were made for me. It was like a holiday camp.'

Macy laughed and shook her head.

'Sheila, you're not right in the head. Who's running the show? Is it still Bobby?'

'Yeah, and he's chilled out a lot since you packed it in.'

'I could never go back grafting with him. Plus, I know he was having us over on the prices. He must think we're green.'

Sheila took a long drag of her cigarette before she flicked it onto the ground. 'You're right about that. That's why I go with him now to the buyers and make sure I never let the man out of my sight while he's doing the deal. Anyway, think about coming on a few runs again. I'm not saying every day like you used to. Maybe just a few days on the side to help you earn a few quid, because, I'm not being funny love, you look like you need a makeover. Since when have you worn trackies and trainers and your hair in a raggy ponytail? You were always dressed smart and classy. What has happened to you?'

Macy looked down at her dated trainers; her cheeks blushed. Sheila was right: if she was being honest with herself, she had let herself go. Every morning when she was grafting she would take hours on her hair and make-up. And her clothes were always neatly ironed and clean. She'd had to be smart for the line of work she was in. She had wanted to look professional, like a solicitor, she always imagined. She licked her bottom lip slowly. 'Sheesh, it's so hard. I've often thought of coming back, but Bobby and me – it's not a good mix. Plus, Jayden would start ballooning at me.'

'Listen love, that man hasn't got a day's work in him and, as far as I know, he's always on the cadge. You deserve more. Look at you when you were grafting and look at you now. Come on, even you can see how much things have gone downhill. Get back working with us and start earning again. Fuck cleaning. Put yourself first.'

Macy stood thinking for a few seconds. Her friend was right, she had let herself go, and for what? Nothing really. She didn't ever have any money and it wasn't only that her kids rarely got new clothes anymore, it was a struggle just to keep the heating on. Maybe she would be better off chancing her luck again shoplifting. At least then she felt alive. The buzz kicking in as she walked out of the stores, the feeling when she knew she had succeeded in her quest. Macy knew she had been one of the best shoplifters in the area in her day. Oh yes, everybody had placed orders with her. Especially the landlady from the Rook pub. She bought in bulk, good prices too. But it was Bobby who had upped the game by going out of town, going into all the top stores. He was a greedy bastard. Always wanting more. But he was right, and she knew it. Why should they take a chance on a fifty-pound dress when she could go in Selfridges and grip a coat for nearly a grand? It would still be the same charge at the end of the day if she got nicked. Bobby had changed her life and the money was rolling in when she was shoplifting with him and the team. Each of them knew their place and how it worked. They were the dream team, and a lot of shoplifters from other areas like Ancoats and Miles Platting were jealous of them and the stuff they got.

Sheila smiled softly at Macy again. 'Come and have a chat with us all later and see what you think. I loved working with you, and I always felt safe knowing you had my back. Please say at least you will think about it. Come on, say yes.'

Macy twisted about nervously: she was put on the spot. And she could see Sheila wasn't taking no for an answer. 'Right, I will think about it. I'm not saying yes, but I will think about it. I'm sick of being skint, and maybe going back grafting with you lot is exactly what I need to pull me out of this hole I've fallen into.'

Sheila rubbed her hands together in excitement. 'So you'll pop round and see us? Say about seven o'clock at Bobby's – I'm round there tonight to plan our next little trip.'

'Yeah, alright, see you then.'

Before Sheila made her way back into the hairdresser's, she grinned and said, 'Get scrubbed up too. Show Bobby what he's been missing.'.

Macy walked away, smiling to herself. This could be just what she needed to get herself back on her feet.

***

Not long after, Macy walked into the supermarket. There were screaming kids near the front entrance with a distressed mother ragging them about, trying to get them to behave. Macy smirked and tried her best not to laugh out loud at the mischievous kids – it felt like yesterday that she was that mum. She walked past into the store and clocked the security guard to the left of her. She pushed her trolley casually past him. The guy was in his mid-fifties, and she could see already it must have been a hard day for him, because he was sat on his mobile phone, scrolling through his messages. The store was busy, and the shoppers were out in full, probably nicking whatever they could too. She knew she wouldn't be the only one. Macy went straight to the meat section and started to look at the joints of beef and steak. She'd learnt a long time ago that if she planned any shoplifting she needed to be quick, not hanging about for too long and bringing any attention to herself. She picked up three joints of topside beef and plonked them straight in the front of the trolley along with four thick-cut sirloin steaks. Macy carried on shopping and before long she had a trolley full of other food. All within her budget. Smart price products. As she approached the checkout, she scanned the area quickly and picked her queue. She made small talk with the girl who was sat at the till. Laughing and joking with her, making sure she could not see the meat stashed at the front of the trolley, casually covered with her jacket, before she pushed it through. Macy stood in front of her trolley and started to place the rest of her shopping into bags. Her heart was pumping faster than normal, and the adrenaline was kicking in. She paid for her shopping and there was no turning back now: this shit just got real. She kept her head held up high and her eyes focused on the security guard near the door. If he so much as flinched, she would run as fast as she could out of the store and get on her toes. Five, four, three, two, one. She walked past him, her heart pounding inside her chest and small beads of sweat forming on her forehead. A group of shoppers walked through the exit at the same time as her and she knew this was the moment it could go tits up. She was through the doors and her speed picked up. In her mind, she was already spending the money she would earn from the meat she'd just stolen. Keep one for her family, of course, for a nice Sunday roast with steaming hot vegetables. Out of sight of the guard, she added the meat to the other bags, then quickly placed her trolley back and took her quid from the small hole in the handle.

A druggie was sat on the floor not far from her, with a blanket wrapped around him and a white plastic cup held in front of him. 'Any spare change, love?' he asked in soft tone.

Macy looked at him and her heart sank low. How cruel was this world when people had to beg on the streets for money? Macy knew she should have walked on, but she couldn't do it. Her fingers unfolded and she let the pound coin drop into the man's cup.

'God bless you, love,' he said.

She walked away and smiled. That was her good deed done for the day. Now for the not so good ones, she figured.

She walked down the road and called in at the boozer situated half-way along. There was no point hanging about. She'd have no problem selling the meat in here. Everyone wanted a bargain. And everyone was prepared to turn a blind eye to where things came from – if the price was right.

Chapter Ten

Her deals done, and money folded away in her purse, Macy had enough time to call in and see her mam. A nice coffee was just what the doctor ordered. Plus, it was hard for her to get there some days, what with family commitments and work. At least that's what she told herself. But it wasn't like her mam was alone. The door was always open at her mother's house and there was always a neighbour sat in with her, gossiping. Someone would be there telling her about the latest police raids and the who-was-sleeping-with-who sagas.

Grace Taylor smiled as she saw her daughter coming into the front room. She sat up straight and brushed her short grey hair back from the side of her face. 'Oh, you look perished, love. Do you want a drink to warm your cockles?'

'Love one, Mam, and put me an extra sugar in too, I'm cream crackered.'

Grace eyeballed the neighbour sat facing her in the room. There was no way she was moving herself, even for her daughter's sake; after all, she wasn't a well woman. And the doctor did tell her to rest so who was she to go against his medical advice? 'Go and bang the kettle on for Macy would you, Marj? My legs are playing up today and I want to try and rest. Doctor's orders and all that.'

Marjorie had lived next door to Grace for over twenty years and the two of them were as thick as thieves. Like an old married couple. Both of them were single and whenever they got a bit of a win at bingo they would pack up and piss off to Blackpool for the week. Marj told everyone she was single by choice and, even though she'd had a few dates back in the day, she'd never really had a relationship. No more than a quick knee-trembler. Grace often told Marj she'd been well out of all that. She herself had been on her own ever since Macy's dad had left the family when she was ten years old. *Sperm donor*, Grace called him, amongst other names. He had never sent birthday cards or Christmas presents; he only gave Macy the odd tenner when she saw him in the street. There had been no fatherly bond whatsoever.

Grace watched as Macy pulled her coat off. 'You look like you've lost a bit of weight, love. Are you eating properly?' Grace shot a look at Marjorie who was stood at the living room door.

'Of course I am. I'm tired, that's all.'

Grace examined her daughter more closely: dark puffy eyes, thin arms and legs, grey skin tones. 'You can take some stuff out of my freezer, if you want? I don't know why I buy half the stuff I do, I never bleeding eat it. There is a bag of sausages there, and steak and kidney puddings. I bought a parcel from the shoplifters a few weeks ago and banged it in the freezer. A bloody bargain it was too. You may as well take it home for you and the kids.'

Macy sat down before she replied, aware that her mother was worried about her. 'Thanks, I'll grab them before I leave. I'm not going to lie, our freezer is bare. I need to do a big shop when we get the next credit in.' She couldn't tell her mum that the next trip to the supermarket was going to be paid for with the money she'd just made selling the beef joints.

Marjorie was back in the room now. She placed Macy's drink on the table and plonked down on the seat next to her, a packet of cake in her hand. *Mrs Kipling*, Grace called her behind her back. 'Oh, I'm glad I've seen you. I saw your Leanne on the Square the other night and it was nearly eleven o'clock. She never spotted me, but I thought to myself, what the hell is she doing out at this time?' Marjorie raised her eyebrows.

Grace sat up straight and gave a concerned look; the oh-what's-been-going-on-here look.

'You need to get her in line, love. You know more than me that the Square is not the place to be. Cheeky bastards they are, the kids that hang out there, no respect for nobody. One of them lads who were on there the other day called me a fat slag when I only asked him to move out of the way. I mean, I've lost two pounds as well.' She patted her stomach down and twisted her waist.

Grace stared at Macy and held her look for a lot longer than she needed to.

Macy was unnerved and fidgeted about in her seat, aware her mother was going to have a go at her. 'I keep telling her to stay away from there. Maybe, she just called to the shop or something.'

Marjorie rolled her shoulders back. 'Nope, she was stood with a gang of lads. Smoking and drinking they were, and I could smell that wacky backy as I walked past them all. Nearly choked me half to death it did, got right on my chest.'

'I'll have a word, Marj. Thanks for the update though. I'll ground her if she's chilling on there with all of them head-aches.' Macy reached over and lifted her cup to her mouth. She could feel her mother's eyes still fixed on her. She could tell Marjorie was as proud as punch that she'd reported Leanne. Bloody super-grass, she was.

Grace rubbed at her arms, hairs standing on end. She knew more than anyone how much misery the Square could cause. Macy used to hang about there. Yes, drinking, smok-ing, underage sex. All the things you were warned about. But it had been much worse than she'd imagined – a bit of booze and bad behaviour she could have coped with. But the world had changed for her the night her daughter was witness to a murder.

Those days after had seemed to last forever. The police had been at her door every day, trying to get her daughter to tell them what she knew. And Grace could tell that Macy did know something. For months she had stayed in her room, awake most of the night crying her eyes out. Grace had tried to get her to tell her – not even the police but only her, her own mother. To this day Macy had never blabbed, never confessed what she had seen. But Grace had known then her daughter was up to her neck in it; she just couldn't prove it. Whoever she was protecting had got away with the murder, because nobody was arrested. The dust slowly settled. It had stayed like an invisible barrier between them ever since. Grace changed the subject before she said something she shouldn't. 'How's Alex, is he behaving? I've not seen him in ages. He keeps texting me, saying he will call soon, but tell him I'm still waiting,' she said in a sarcastic tone.

'You're joking, Mam. He never moves out of the house. He's always on that game though, to tell you the truth, that suits me because I know where he is. Most teenagers are like that these days. Harry the Hermit we call him at home.'

Grace pulled her dark blue cardigan together as another chill ran across her body. Marjorie had left the living room door open. She stood up and looked over at her. 'Were you born in a bleeding barn, woman? I keep the doors closed to keep the heat in. The bloody gas bills are through the roof and I'm struggling to keep up with all the rises. I'm a pensioner and the state should make sure we have enough bleeding money to live properly. Disgraceful, it is. The way I sweated my back out working all the hours I did. No wonder I'm practically a cripple now.'

Marjorie jumped on the bandwagon and agreed. 'We work all our bloody lives and pay taxes, and this is how they treat us, bleeding liberties, it is. They should let me run the budget for the country and I would make sure all us old ones are looked after. Fuck you, Chancellor of the Exchequer.'

Macy sighed. Marjorie could talk for England.

Grace changed the subject as soon as she got chance. 'Has that idle man of yours got a job yet?'

Macy had known it wouldn't be long before Jayden was brought up. It was the same every time. Her voice was low. 'No Mam, as I told you last time, he's looking but he has no qualifications and nobody is taking him on. He does try, you know, but no one will give him a chance.'

'That man sweats at even the word "work". Face it, he's a dead-leg and he'll always be the same.'

Macy raised her voice, sick of having the same conversation over and over again. 'Mam, stop having a go, will you? I don't come here to listen to things that I already know. He is who he is, so let it lie before we end up falling out again.'

Grace eyeballed Marjorie, giving her a look that said, *she knows I'm right*.

Marjorie started talking again. 'I've got some hair dye in the kitchen, love. I bought them from the shoplifters. Six for a tenner if you want any. Lovely colours too. There is a dark red one that would look nice on you. Take a look before you leave and give yourself a makeover.'

Macy looked down at her clothing and ran her fingers through her hair. Bloody hell, that was the second time today someone had mentioned her appearance. Maybe she should do more with herself, after all. Because if Marjorie had seen fit to pipe up, then she must look bad. 'Thanks, Marj. Let me have this coffee and I'll go and check them out.'

Grace started to flick through the channels on the TV. She and Marj always watched *Antiques Roadshow* together without fail. Marjorie rubbed her hands together and shot a look over at Macy as the theme tune came on. 'I bet your mam's knickers will be on here this week, they're that bleeding old.'

They all howled laughing, 'How do you even know what her knickers look like, Marj?' Macy asked.

Marjorie giggled. She pointed to the radiator behind her and there they were in their full glory, Grace's passion-killers. Big, white cotton briefs with small blue flowers on them.

Grace was blushing. 'I better watch you, Marj, if that's the way you're swinging.'

Macy was laughing her head off and it was nice to see her mam smile for a change. She sat and watched the TV show with her mother and Marj, all guessing how much the things were worth, shouting at the television. But, as the credits rolled, Macy sat thinking how she had nothing of any real value, nothing in her attic that in years to come she could pull out and pass to her kids. Certainly nothing she could sell for money. No paintings apart from the ones the kids brought home from nursery, no jewellery that wasn't knock-off, no old medals, nothing. Who were these people that had antique vases on their mantlepieces, precious heirlooms in a box under the bed? Not her, that was for sure. She was realising now that the life she had tried to leave behind was calling her back, the world that had been waiting for her all along. She could change her fortune, change all the things that were wrong in her life with money. New clothes, new furniture, gas and electric and food all the time. It looked like she had made up her mind already. She decided she was glad she was going to see Sheila and Bobby and going to get back to doing what she did best.

Leanne stood on the Square with Gino. She was quieter tonight and didn't seem her usual bubbly self. Gino had her dropping drugs off most of the night. As soon as anyone walked onto the Square, he nudged her and left her to do his dirty work.

He growled as he turned to face her. 'What's up with your mush tonight?'

'Nothing, just cold, that's all. I thought you said we were going to do something special, but all we ever do is stand here all the time, and it's me who's running about, not you.'

Gino's nostrils flared and he made sure nobody could hear him. He whispered into her ear. 'Keep that big gob shut and do what I'm telling you. Keep on pecking my head and I'll show you what I'm about.'

Leanne held her head back against the wall and tried to move him out of her way. He was aggressive and used force to keep her where she was, unable to move. 'Gino, fuck off, will you. Take your hands off me.'

He let out a menacing laugh and pressed his cold lips against hers. She was trying her best to push him away, but he was too strong. This was not what she signed up for, and over the last few weeks he was treating her more and more like she was just a piece of meat that he owned.

Gino stood back from her and looked her up and down. 'Fuck off out of my face while I cool down. I swear to you now if you don't do one, I'll kick the fuck out of you.'

She gulped and straightened her jacket. 'No need for this, Gino. I'm sick of the way you're treating me. You said we could go to the cinema or something, but it's the same each night, stood here freezing my tits off.'

Before she could even take a single step away from him, Gino ran at her and pulled her to the small alleyway out of sight from Jacko and Kyle and the others. He dragged her down to the floor and stood over her with his clenched fist pounding it into her body. 'Don't. Ever. Talk. Back. To. Me. Do you hear me?' he roared.

Leanne rolled into a small ball and covered her head with her hands, shaking like a scared animal.

Gino backed off. 'Look what you made me do. Stand up. I said, get up and get your arse here.'

Leanne stumbled to her feet. Thick brown mud clung to the side of her face, and along her legs. She stood in front of him with her head dipped low, snivelling.

'Don't think crying will make me feel sorry for you. Fucking sort yourself out, and go and get cleaned up. I'm going back on the Square. Sort your attitude out and be back in five minutes.' He booted a can as he left her side and disappeared out of her sight.

Her chest was rising frantically, and tears streamed down her cheek. What a bastard. He had said he loved her and here he was kicking ten tons of shit out of her. Kerry had been right: she wasn't the first girl this lad had battered. But what could she do? If she didn't go back to him, he would come looking for her, drag her back. He'd already told her she was his woman now and nobody would ever look at her again now he'd put his mark on her. At first, she had thought it was nice how protective he was of her, but she saw now it was all a sham. She'd been so desperate to believe the story she told herself that she'd buried the memory of his attack on her. But, as the days had gone by, she had started to feel different. Every time he'd demeaned her, bullied her or forced her, it was meant to make her feel smaller and weaker – but she knew now she had to turn that back on him. Leanne pulled her mobile phone from her pocket and stared at the screen. Maybe if she rang Jayden he would have been here in seconds with a baseball bat in his hand. But it could all go wrong and Jayden could get done in and then what next? Alex would be left without a father. Just like her. Perhaps she could ring Kerry and tell her what had happened, but then she might have said *I told you so*. Leanne reached down and started to wipe the dirt from her legs. She needed to be quick because he'd told her she only had five minutes to come back. How on earth had she let this guy treat her like this and get into her head? She felt her nerve grow. She straightened her hair and walked back onto the Square. She could see him straight away. His mates were there with him now and she could hear him laughing as she neared him. Leanne stood next to Gino and didn't say a word. She was in deep and didn't have an easy way out – but she would have to find one. He reached over and grabbed her hand, squeezing her fingers tightly. 'Are you sorted now?'

She nodded and that seemed enough for him. Then Kerry's loud mouth could be heard, even before anyone could see her. Leanne felt a sense of relief at seeing a friendly face. She went to walk over to meet her, but Gino held his hand out and blocked her path. 'Stay there. Don't be mixing with that slut.'

'Gino, she's my friend.'

He didn't have to say anything else to her: his eyes said it all. She didn't move a muscle.

Kerry walked over to the group, full of confidence and fearing nobody. Not even Gino. He was a waste of space in her eyes, a muppet. 'Leanne, are you coming to the shop? I've got some money so I'll get us a bottle of voddy. We can get steaming?'

Gino's eyes were burning into Leanne, fear riding through her body. 'No, I'm staying here. It's freezing. I can't be arsed.'

Kerry held her head to the side and placed a single hand on her hip. 'Don't be snidey. I always come with you.'

Leanne's eyes flicked to Gino. He had already turned away and was talking to his friend, completely at ease that his woman was under control. She clocked he wasn't watching her. It was a little thing, but it felt like a rebellion. She took her chance, never looked back once, but she knew immediately he was watching her. This wasn't escape – but it was something. As soon as she was out of his reach, she exhaled.

Kerry went into the shop first and, now they were in the light, she could see Leanne fully. 'You've got all mud on the side of your face.' She looked down at her friend's body sourly. 'It's all over your legs too. What's happened? Have you fell or something?'

Leanne had to think fast. She couldn't tell Kerry everything. Not now. Gino would come for them both. She needed to pick her moment. 'Aw, yes it was earlier when I was walking over the grass, a massive dog come running at me and I slipped over. I didn't know I had mud on me though. Eww, let me get it off.' She was glad how convincing she sounded.

Kerry walked down the aisle and went to the baby section. She opened a pack of baby wipes and pulled out three or four. 'Here, wipe the side of your face and legs, you scruff.'

Leanne checked where the shopkeeper was and quickly used the wipes to clean her body up.

Kerry was still watching her. 'I've just got back from bowling with Leon. We had a right laugh. You should have come. I thought you said you were going to watch a film or something, Leels?'

'We were, but Gino has been busy with work. The Square is his patch. You know what he's like when he's earning. A money-grabber, he is. He said we can go on another night, and he'll take me for a curry too, so I can't moan, can I?' Leanne almost believed her own story – enjoying adding details to it.

Kerry walked to the counter with the vodka held in her hand. She didn't speak to the shopkeeper and he never spoke to her, he just took her money. They both knew he should have been asking for some form of ID, something to prove this girl was old enough to be served, and the less said the better, it seemed.

Kerry stood outside the shop and unscrewed the red top from the bottle. She swigged a large mouthful from it and handed it over to Leanne. 'Why don't you come with me for a bit instead of standing there with Gino, doing his dirty work? You've gone a right miserable cow since you've been seeing him. I never see you anymore. All you do is stand next to him, running here and there for him.'

Leanne gulped and shot a look behind her. Where was he? Was he watching her, listening to her conversation? She could see Gino stood talking to his friends, his eyes off her. 'You are always with Leon so you can't talk.'

Kerry swigged some more vodka. 'Leon has a mate, you know, who's seen you around and he's mad for you. He's always asking where you are and if you're still seeing Gino. You should come and have a look at him at least and see what you think. He's a really nice lad, and I bet the two of you would get on really good.'

Gino started whistling over to her. Then his voice rang out loud. 'Yo, Leanne!'

Kerry snarled as she listened to him. 'And you're going to put up with the way he talks to you? Tell him you're not a fucking dog.'

Leanne was nervously biting her nails. Why didn't she just tell her best friend what was going on, and have this prick arrested for assault? She felt a stab of sympathy for other girls she'd heard complaining of dodgy blokes. Lots of their friends had boyfriends who knocked them about, made them hand over their passwords for social media, checked their mobile phones for call logs and messages. It wasn't right – and now she was in the same boat. But not for long, she swore to herself. 'I better go. We are going to his house to watch *Peaky Blinders*. It's good, you need to watch it.'

Kerry squirmed. 'Nah, I'm out living my life. Bleeding box sets,' she said in a sarcastic tone.

'I'll ring you later and we can arrange a girlie night,' Leanne said. 'I'll tell Gino, and he will have to deal with it.' There, that would keep Kerry happy for now, not too suspicious. She was still her best friend, and she knew she'd be there for her when she managed to get away.

Kerry swigged more vodka before she turned on her feet. 'Bell me then when you're free.' And she walked away.

Leanne smiled. *Free.* A little word for something that meant a lot.

Gino lay on the bed and looped his arms above his head, his bare chest showing, small beads of sweat across his forehead. 'It bugs me, you know?'

Leanne looked over at him. 'What does?'

'The way you sell me out to that slapper.'

She knew who he meant without asking. Was he really still going on about Kerry? What on earth was his problem with her? 'She's my best friend, Gino. She knows everything about me, and she's always there when I have shit going on.'

'And what, I'm not?' he growled.

'Yeah, but she's a girl, and sometimes it's nice to discuss personal stuff with someone who understands. Like, say I had bad period pains, then she would know what I was going through, wouldn't she?'

'I'm just saying, that's all. I want it to be me and you, nobody else. You know I love you, don't you? I'm sorry if I snap at you, but that's only me showing that I care.'

Leanne ran a single finger up and down his chest. 'I know you do, and I love you too.' The words stuck in her throat.

He sat staring into thin air and she knew he had something else to say. 'Are you on the pill and that? Because I've not been pulling out. I don't want any babies and all that yet.'

Leanne shook her head and blushed. 'I'm going to sort it out this week. My mam would shit a brick if I got knocked up.'

Gino nodded his head slowly. 'I think I would make a good dad though, not like mine who fucked off and left us. Violent twat he was too, always digging my mam and dragging her about the place.'

Leanne gulped. Like father like son, then.

Gino carried on, 'My mam doesn't know that I still see my old man. I have for a few years and he's sorted now. He puts work my way and he's said sorry for all that shit when I was growing up. He's got my back too. Any shit and I only have to get on the blower to him. He'll bring his team down to sort it out. He's sorting me out a nice little supply line. I'm thinking of growing my business on the Square. Something a bit spicier than just the weed.'

Leanne wasn't sure if she liked the sound of that. He didn't seem like the kind of guy she wanted Gino learning from. 'So is your dad local?'

'Nah, he's out of town, about an hour away.'

Leanne could see that Gino had respect for his dad – she'd not heard him speak that way about anyone else. The past was clearly the past and it looked like he'd forgiven his dad for all that had gone on when he was growing up. Or maybe he'd just realised the apple didn't fall far from the tree.

'One day, I will run shit around here, just like my dad used to. It's in the family.'

Chapter Eleven

Macy was ready and her hair looked nice. It no longer hung in rat's tails, and Marjorie was right, the new colour did suit her. Her skin looked fresher, and her eyes stood out. She'd even been into Leanne's bedroom and borrowed her straighteners. One last look in the mirror and she headed downstairs. She was ready to go. Jayden was still out, and she knew he would be out until late. A stray cat he was, never knowing when it was time to go home.

She walked into the living room. The noise was deafening, cars screeching, gun shots being fired. 'Bleeding hell, Alex, turn that shit down. I can't hear myself think with that crap blaring.'

Alex took a few seconds before he reached over for the tv remote and turned the television down. He side-eyed his mother as she pottered about at the side of him. 'Wow, where are you going all dressed up?'

She smirked and flicked her new hair colour over her shoulder. 'Going to see a few old friends. Pointless me sat in here all night, isn't it? You're on that game all the time, and your dad is out, God knows where. Need I say more?'

He sniggered. 'You look nice though, Mam. You should dress up more often. But don't let my dad see you all dolled up. You know how jealous he gets.'

Macy smiled and looked over at her son. He had such a big heart and, despite his fondness for a cheeky remark, he was always giving her compliments when she needed them the most. 'Aw, thanks son. I've told you, when you get a girlfriend, she's going to love all the nice things you will say to her. It's the little things that matter, remember that. The last time your dad gave me a compliment was about six years ago, and it wasn't really a compliment: he said *you look mint*. But, eh, it's better than nothing, I suppose.'

Alex's eyes were back on the video game. Macy stood over him, blocking his view, dodging one way then the other. 'Tell me what time Leanne came home. I don't know who she thinks she is lately, coming in at all hours, when she knows what time she should be in.' No reply. She booted his leg. 'Alex, did you even hear a word that I said?'

His body was moving from side to side, unable to see the TV. 'Yeah, tell Leanne not to be taking the piss, or something like that. Mam, move out of the way, will you? I'm going to crash if you don't.'

Macy knew there was no more chance of getting a conversation out of her son. She sighed, went to the dining table and picked up her coat. 'Tell your dad I've nipped out, if he comes in early. Tell him he can expect me when I arrive,' she chuckled. Yeah, he could piss off. It was about time she was out instead of staring at four walls all night, worrying about his whereabouts. She took one last look in the hall-way mirror and studied her reflection. There she was, the girl she used to be, make-up, hair done and nice clothes. 'Welcome back, Macy,' she whispered under her breath as she left the house.

Sheila opened the door and stood checking Macy out. 'Bleeding hell, did you finally find the soap, girl?' she chuckled.

'Cheeky cow, you caught me on a bad day, that's all.'

Sheila opened the door fully and invited her inside. This was Bobby's house. He'd lived here ever since she could remember. Her heart was racing and, all of a sudden, her mouth became dry. She'd not spoken with Bobby for what seemed like forever. Back in the day, Macy and Bobby were as thick as thieves – which was appropriate, considering their line of work. They had both hung out on the Square growing up and even then he was always the one with the bright ideas to earn them money.

Macy panicked and grabbed Sheila back by the arm, her voice low. 'He knows I'm coming, right?'

Sheila raised her eyebrows and kept her voice low. 'He's over the moon that you're here, but don't tell him I told you that. Now, let's get this show on the road.'

The panic was over. Sheila walked into the living room first, followed closely by Macy. The place looked like one of the big houses she was more used to cleaning than being invited into. The biggest television ever on the main wall, huge cream leather sofas that you could imagine relaxing into, lots of glitter and sparkle. This was a show house, nothing out of place, no clutter.

'Well, hello stranger,' Bobby said as soon as he spotted Macy. 'Take your coat off and park your arse. Sheila, grab her a cold one out of the fridge, will you? We have to celebrate.'

Macy was boiling hot, a rush of blood rising through her body, heartbeat pounding in her ears. She didn't want him to see her nerves and was relieved when Bobby's mobile phone started ringing. She knew she would have a few minutes to calm her speeding heart down. She sat back and listened to Bobby on the phone. He hadn't changed much in his look: pearly white teeth, Hollywood smile, tanned skin. His eyes – a feature she admitted she had always found attractive about him – looked bluer than ever. She stared at him, lost in those eyes. Quickly, she snapped out of it and was back in the moment.

She listened to his phone call. 'Yes Janey, yep, I've got a parcel for sale, all designer clothes, top of the range. You know me, I don't fuck about with high street brands anymore. Five ton, I want.' He was listening now and held his hand up mimicking a bird's beak opening and closing as Janey spoke. He smirked over at Macy. 'Well, give me a bell in the next ten minutes if you want it, because I'm ringing Steph too and you know she'll have it. I just thought I would give you first dibs on it.'

The call ended and Sheila said, 'She always pisses about, you know her. I bet she rings back in the next few minutes asking for a price drop. If she does, put me on the blower and I'll tell her to fuck off. I'm sick of her trying to get something for nothing.'

Sheila pulled two fags out of the packet and lit them both. She passed one to Macy and sat back.

Bobby turned to Macy. 'So Macy, nice to see you. You look good, girl. A bit thinner than I remember but we can soon sort that out when we start earning. We've changed our operation a lot since you were grafting with us.'

Macy took a breath. It was time to put her cards on the table and see how the land lay. 'I'll be straight with you, Bobby. I've been on my arse for a while now and I need to sort myself out. I'm not grafting for shite money like it was last time. I want an equal cut. I know I was your best girl.'

Bobby sat forward and his hands squeezed his knees. 'We have a new kid with us now. She's only sixteen but, fuck me, can she graft. She reminds me of you when you was top of your game.'

Macy squirmed. She was still a top shoplifter, she knew that, and just because she wasn't out every day nicking stuff it didn't mean she had lost her knack.

Bobby tilted his head. 'We split the take four ways. Everybody gets an equal share. We have a few different buyers now too, according to what we're selling, and we have a great money scam going where Diane takes the clothes back to the store for a full refund. I'll explain that more when Di comes to meet you. She was supposed to be here tonight but she bailed out at the last minute. She's on the piss I think. You'll have money to burn on nights out too when you're back with us.'

Sheila had been trying her best to let the two of them talk, but she was finding it hard to keep her mouth shut. She blurted it out, 'So, Macy, are you back in or what?'

Bobby was watching Macy. She stuttered, 'Yep, as long as we are all equal?' She burned her eyes into Bobby, letting him know that she knew what she was doing. A leopard never changed its spots, and she knew what a robbing bastard he was and that he would have had her eyes out and come back for the sockets given the chance.

'Like I said, everyone gets a cut.'

The deal was done. Macy was back in the world she was familiar with and it was like she had never been away.

'Sheila, order some food. We can get a curry. I'm starving. I could eat a scabby horse.' Bobby had barely finished his sentence before his mobile phone started ringing again. He smiled from cheek to cheek when he spotted the name of his caller. 'Eh up, Janey has seen the light,' he chuckled. 'Yo Janey, have we got a deal or what? Don't even try and have me over on this bundle. We both know you'll earn a butty on it.' He shot a look over at the girls and nodded his head before he punched his clenched fist into the air. 'Nip around in ten and I'll load it up. Bell me when you're here. Come the back way, though. Too many nosey cunts on the front. That Mrs Evans is like a fucking plant pot. She never misses a trick, the bleeding curtain twitcher.'

Sheila rubbed her hands together. 'Ch-ching,' she chuckled. 'At least I can get some bills paid now and piss the debtors off. One day, I will learn to manage my money. It's in one hand and out of the other at the moment. Right, I'm going to get off and sort the kids out. I'll leave you to have a catch up.'

Macy wriggled about in her seat. The thought of being left alone with Bobby was hitting her full on. Bobby was staring at her, and she could feel his eyes burning into her. There was no way she was locking eyes with him again. The last time she'd done that she'd ended up in bed with him. A secret she still kept close to her chest. A drunken night of passion and the less said about that the better. Dawn, Bobby's other half, was on a hen do and away for the weekend when it happened. In her bed too, nothing to be proud of. Macy would be the first to slag anyone off for sleeping with some-one's boyfriend, and having sex in their bed was on another level. But did she regret it? She wasn't sure. It was something that she tried to forget about, but every now and then it raised its ugly head. Bobby and her went way back and the tension was always there – she just usually managed to keep a lid on it. Most of the time she didn't want to reminded of the girl she used to be, back when she was a teenager on the square. But sometimes, the past kept calling her.

Bobby had been shit-hot in the bedroom. He was adven-turous and probably the best lover she had ever had. Oh my God, why was she even visualising that night in her mind? She was blushing again and quickly she brought herself back to the present moment before she exploded with embarrassment. 'So, how's tricks then, Bobby? Are you and Dawn both alright?' She cringed after she spoke, such verbal diarrhoea. Why on earth was she asking about his relation-ship? Like she gave a flying fuck if he was happy or not. She was here to earn a wedge, not to play happy families.

'Yeah, it's not been bad at all. Money's been flowing, so can't grumble. Anyway, are you still with that Jayden? I've not seen him flying about like I usually do.'

Macy squashed her cigarette out in the ashtray and sat back. Her mind was doing overtime. Why was he bothered if she was still in a relationship or not? She kept her cool. 'Yeah, we're still together. Just about, though. He's been doing my head in lately. You know, with work and that?'

Bobby let out a sarcastic laugh. 'He's never worked. I've always thought you were too good for him, you know that, don't you?'

Her mind cast back to that drunken night again, the words he'd spoken to her while he was ravishing her body. The words she had never forgotten. She had to change the subject. Talking about her private life was something she was not willing to get into.

Luckily, Bobby changed the subject for her and told her about the shops they currently targeted and how it all worked. Shoplifting was a fast-moving business and he classed himself as a professional. Plus having a few contacts on the inside helped. Bobby knew a dodgy security guard in Selfridges who, when he was on duty, would give them the heads up on all the blind spots in the store. Of course, he wanted a bung for his part in this. Everyone always wanted a piece of the pie when they were involved in any kind of scam.

The front door slammed shut and Bobby was alert. A voice rang out from the hallway. Dawn.

'Bobby, Janey is out the back. She's been there for over ten minutes, waiting for you, she said.' Bobby jumped from the chair, and sniggered. 'I thought she might have rung me when she got here, the clown. Fancy just waiting there in the car and not giving me a bell.'

Dawn was in the living room now and, as she put her keys down on the glass table, she clocked Macy. It was clear there was no love lost between the two women, but she put on a front and acted like she didn't have a problem. 'How are you, Macy? Bob tells me you're getting back in the mix again. I can't say I blame you. You were on good dosh when you were all working together. I bet it's been hard for you losing all that money each day, hasn't it?'

'You can say that again. I can't wait to start earning again and get myself a few new rig-outs while I'm at it.'

Macy was paranoid about the way she dressed now. Looking at Dawn made her aware that her clothes were shabby and old. Dawn was a stunner, for sure. She'd had the look of a glamour model in her day. Bobby had had her on his arm for a few years now but even though she was good-looking, she could talk a glass eye to sleep. Macy looked her up and down; maybe a bit of the green-eyed monster was creeping in. Dawn kicked her Jimmy Choo shoes off and walked into the living room further. Her figure was perfect and anyone could see this was a woman who liked to take care of herself. Acrylic nails, curly blow, and her make-up was on point. She sat down and kicked her legs up behind her. She fanned her long talons out in front of her and admired them. 'I've just had an infill, a new bright red.'

Macy hid her fingers away. She was a nail biter and, whenever she got stressed, she ended up nibbling at them. It was so surprising how a set of nails changed the way your fingers looked. Macy's looked thick and stumpy, cuticles sore and inflamed.

There was a silence now, neither of them talking. What did they have to talk about? Their worlds were so far apart and they had nothing in common apart from Bobby. They both sat watching the television, glad to have a reason not to speak. Bobby came back in through the back door and rubbed his hands together as he flashed the cash, fanning it out. 'Lovely jubbly, a nice little earner as always.' He stashed the cash and plonked down on the sofa. 'I've ordered some scran, Dawn, if you're hungry. Macy is going to stay for some too, so crack open some beers or wine and we will have a few drinks.'

Dawn looked like she'd smelt a bad odour, her nose twitching; a bitter expression she couldn't quite hide quickly enough for Macy not to spot it.

'Yeah, that's fine. But give me a few minutes and let me chill out. I've been rushed off my feet all day. Not stopped.'

Bobby shook his head. He knew his woman was lying. She had probably been sat in some salon all day getting pampered. She lived off her man and never earned a penny to her own name. Bobby turned back to Macy and got down to business.

'So, are you ready for graft tomorrow? We can hit the Trafford Centre. It should be hammered on a Saturday. I will break you in slowly and show you a few new things.'

Dawn was listening. Her face was still watching the TV, but Macy could see she was interested in their conversation.

'Yes, what time are you thinking?'

'About twelvish. Give it time to get the shoppers in.'

Macy smiled and rubbed her hands together. She felt alive again at the thought of it and already she was planning a makeover for herself. Fuck cleaning up other people's mess. This was where the money was. She was back in business. All she had to do now was tell Jayden.

Chapter Twelve

M acy opened her eyes and lay still for a few seconds. The wind was howling outside and there was a cold draught seeping in through the top window. She looked around the room and her heart sank. The bedroom was in desperate need of a refresh: peeling wallpaper, black mould creeping along the top of the ceiling like it wanted to leave the house too. Maybe now she was going to be grafting again she would finally be able to pay someone to paint it all. There was no point in asking Jayden to do it, she'd wait forever. Lazy bastard. She stretched her arms over her head and shot a look to the side of her at the empty space. Jayden was probably kipping on the sofa again, hungover. She sat up with the duvet tucked under her chin. It was freezing. No doubt the gas had ran out again. She had to tell Jay her plans, tell him she was going back working with Bobby. He had told her to but she knew he still wasn't going to like it. But she had no choice.

The smell hit the back of her throat as she walked into the living room. There he was, as per usual, sprawled along the sofa. She pulled her dressing gown tighter and stood looking at the lifeless heap. She studied her other half closely. Trying to find things about him that she still liked, things that still turned her on, made her heart beat faster. He'd aged, his skin tone grey, dark circles under his eyes. She wondered whether, if he'd had a decent job, he would have looked different, had ambitions, life goals. All this man cared about was getting stoned and wasted whenever he had the chance. He didn't worry like she did, he couldn't care less. She tugged at the black crusty sock hanging over the edge of the sofa.

'Oi, lazy bollocks, wake up. I want to speak with you.'

Jayden stirred, moaning and groaning. His head lifted slightly, and it took a while before he could focus. 'Wow, what time is it? Leave me alone and let me get back to sleep, I've hardly slept a wink. Piss off, will you?' He rolled onto his side and her eyes widened as she clocked the red scratches on his back. She poked her finger deep into his white flesh.

'What the fuck are those on your back?'

Jayden sprang up from his seat, eyes still not open, hair stuck up. 'What the fuck, Macy, what are you going on about?'

She ran at him and turned him around again to get a better look. '*These*, and don't even bother saying you fell or something stupid like that because I'm not buying it. It's not the first time you've come in here with dodgy marks over your body.'

'You need medical help you do,' Jayden slurred. 'What the fuck goes on in your head is beyond me. If I've got a few scratches on my back, why do you always think the worst?'

'Because you are a lying cheating fucker. Do I have to remind you about the slapper you got caught kissing, or what?'

He knew this was a road he didn't want to go down and he tugged his hands through his hair. 'Oh, here we go again. It was a drunken mistake. I've said I'm sorry how many times to you? But, here you are again, throwing it in my face. Get over it Macy, no need.'

Macy swallowed hard. Her blood was boiling and she was ready to scratch his eyes out, to bin bag him. She backed off, still not convinced there was no foul play here today. 'I'm going back working with Bobby.' She fired the words out of her mouth.

Jayden froze on the spot and slowly his head turned like an owl. He spoke through clenched teeth. 'What did you say?'

This time her voice was lower, not as aggressive. 'I said I'm working back with Bobby. I'm sick of being skint and having nothing.'

His ears pinned back, nostrils flaring. 'After all you said about that guy and now you're licking his arse. I've got a bit of work on with Terry this week, so you don't need to worry, we'll have some money.'

She sat down on the sofa and looked up at him. 'My mind is made up. I've tried my best to keep on the straight and narrow but I can't do it. I want nice things, the kids need stuff, and they all cost money. I'm sick of borrowing, sick of having no food in. No gas or electric…' Her eyes clouded over and a ball of emotion filled her throat. Months of desperation, tears all rising to the surface.

He edged closer to her and bent down so he could look into her eyes. 'Babes,' he said in a quieter voice. 'Just hang on in there. I've got work now and, if it pans out, we will have regular money coming in each week. I don't want you going back grafting, risking your freedom, especially with Bobby. The guy is a wanker, you've said so yourself how many times before?'

'My mind is made up, so don't waste your breath. I'm sick of broken promises and all the things I could have won with you. I need to get us out of this mess and I'm doing what I know best. And don't think I've forgotten about the scratches on your back, you wanker. Dodgy, you are, through and through.'

He stood up fully, growling at her, hating that he had no control over her. He bent down again and went nose to nose with her, his stale breath spraying into her face. 'Do what you're doing, but when it all goes tits up, like I know it will, don't fucking come mithering me. You can jog on.'

She dropped her head. She'd said what she had to say and that was that. She could hear him grunting as he left the room. It wasn't as bad as she thought it could have been, if she was being honest. He couldn't exactly get on his high horse when he'd been a dirty stop-out.

Leanne walked into the room now. 'Wow, what's up with him? He's just barged past me on the stairs.'

'Nothing that concerns you. And you can sit here for a minute. I've got a bone to pick with you.'

Leanne sat down next to her mother and folded her arms tightly across her chest, already rolling her eyes. 'Go on then, say what you have to say and get it over with.'

This girl was full of attitude this morning. 'I've heard you've been knocking about on the Square. Marjorie has seen you. She said you were stood with a gang of lads who were blazing bud. You better not be smoking that shit, let me tell you.'

'How can you dictate to me when Jayden smokes it all the time? You need to have this chat with him too if I'm getting my ear chewed off about it. And, for your information, I'm not smoking anything.'

'Who do you think you're talking to Leanne? Have some bleeding respect.'

'I do have respect, but I don't like it when nosey people start chatting shit about me.'

'They are just keeping you safe, that's all. And why have I not seen Kerry as much these days? Have you fallen out or something?'

Leanne went bright red, pulled her legs up onto the sofa, tucking them under her bum. 'She's hooked up with her boyfriend now. We've planned a girlie night this week for a catch up. But that's what happens, Mam, you meet a guy and your mates go on the back burner.'

'Well, it shouldn't be like that. Men are ten a penny, friends are for life.'

'And where are all your friends, Mam? You don't bother with anyone anymore.'

Macy was shocked, stuck for words. It was true but there was no way she was telling her daughter that. 'I still see

Zara every now and then. I've been working all the time and not had time to meet up.'

Leanne chirped in. 'Oh, I forgot to tell you Joanne called last night. Fuming she was, saying something about a ring going missing from one of the houses you clean. I told her to call back when you're in. I didn't understand what she was going on about.'

Macy went white, colour draining from her skin. She stuttered, 'What the fuck is she going about? What ring?'

'I don't know, Mam. Go and see her and she'll tell you. But, like I said, she was fuming.'

Macy sighed. 'Anyway, back to you. I want you in on time every night from now on and there will be no more staying at Kerry's when I know you are up to something.' Macy stood up and shot a look over at the clock. 'Right, I better get ready.'

Leanne had her mobile phone out now, watching Tik Tok videos. Macy was just glad she'd stopped asking about the ring. It was like talking to a brick wall when her daughter was on her phone. She got no sense out of her.

Before long, Macy was dressed and decent. Jayden was laid on the bed and his eyes never left her. 'Where you off to all dressed up?'

'I told you before, I'm going to earn some money.'

He bolted up from the bed. 'What, today? Are we not even talking about it? I'll tell you what, you can fuck right off. Go and see if Bobby will have you, because if you choose him over me then we're over.'

Here it was again, him threatening to leave her. If she had a pound for every time he said he was packing his bags she would have been a rich woman. It was an idle threat and not something that bothered her anymore. Anyway, it would do him good to get a bit jealous, maybe now he might pay her more attention. She snarled over at him, eyes narrowed. 'Whatever.'

Chapter Thirteen

Macy flicked her cigarette butt before she knocked on the front door. She was nervous and forever looking down at her clothing. Was she over-dressed, were her jeans too last season? She wasn't sure. Her heart was pounding inside her ribcage, and she was all hot and clammy. Maybe she'd not thought this through enough. She should forget this daft idea and go back home.

But it was too late: the front door opened. Dawn stood gawping at her and then she slowly opened the door as if there was a lead weight behind it. This woman had the knack of making Macy feel like a dollop of shit on her shoe just by looking at her.

'Bobby's just getting ready. Do you want to come in and wait?'

Macy squirmed. What she wanted to say was, 'No, I'll stand here like a prize prick, shall I, and wait in the cold for him?' But she kept schtum. 'Yes, I will come in and wait, thank you.'

Dawn had no make-up on, her hair not yet brushed. Macy smirked to herself and, once she had sat down in the living room, she couldn't wait to make her feel the way she made other people feel.

'Have you had a bad night? I've never seen you without any make-up on. You are always dressed to the nines.' First point to Macy.

Dawn pulled her hair back from her face and tried to pat it down with the palm of her hand. Her nostrils flared slightly. 'I always make sure I take my make-up off for bed. I have to look after my skin. I'll jump in the shower when Bobby's gone and doll myself up. I hate not looking my best when I go outside. I don't know how you do it.'

The gloves were off and point two went to Dawn. Macy's mouth was moving but no words came out. She had to bite her tongue, otherwise she would say something she'd regret. Silence again, both of them looking around the room.

Bobby walked in and Macy's eyes widened. He was dressed in a grey suit with a crisp white shirt and tan brogues. He looked like he'd just stepped from a photo shoot.

Dawn smiled over at her other half. 'You look amazing, babes, as always. I'm not being funny or anything, but do you want me to go upstairs and dig something out for Macy to wear? I mean, you look tip-top and she looks like she wouldn't belong next to you, if you know what I mean. I'm thinking a black pencil skirt, white blouse and a blazer, plus heels?'

Bobby shot a look over at Macy. Dawn was right, but he could see by her face that her cage was rattled.

'Yes Macy, let's get you changed. I want us to look like we are rolling in money. Like I said, we've upped our game and I want us both to not look out of place in the best stores. You look decent, don't get me wrong, but we can improve.'

Macy stood up, her cheeks bright red. She did have to admit that she looked like the poor relation stood next to Bobby. She had to swallow her pride. 'Yeah, I don't mind shoving something else on if you have anything that might fit, Dawn?'

Dawn stood up and stretched. She couldn't resist a grin, aware she had settled the score with Macy. 'I'll take her upstairs and give her a quick makeover. She needs some colour in her skin, she looks near-dead.' Dawn chuckled as she left the room.

Macy hissed at Bobby through clenched teeth. 'What the fuck is she going on about? *Near-dead?* Bobby, let her carry on with her snide remarks and watch, I'll bleeding one-bomb her.'

Bobby sniggered. 'Go with the flow. She'll jazz you up a bit. That's her thing, isn't it, make-up and clothes and all that.'

Macy stomped past him and headed upstairs. 'Fucking Barbie,' she mumbled under her breath.

Dawn had laid a few outfits out on the bed already. The wardrobe doors were both wide open and she had her head inside. 'Look through those clothes on the bed and see what you think. Corporate look is what I'm going for.'

Macy looked down at the outfits. Some even still had the price tags on them. Dawn was stood looking too now and she picked up a fitted black pair of trousers with a white polka dot shirt. 'They will look good together. Hold on a sec, let me grab you some heels. I think you would look better in pants, unless your legs are tanned?'

Macy shook her head. When did she have time to tan her body like this bimbo did? The last time she had been on the sunbed was yonks ago. Dawn opened another cupboard. Macy tried hard to hide her amazement: Dawn had an array of different-coloured shoes, flats, heels, trainers, boots, sandals. Macy couldn't wait until she could build a collection even half as impressive.

The outfit was quickly sorted, and it was just Macy's make-up to do now. Dawn pulled the silver chair out from under the mirrored dressing table and switched on her ring light. 'Right, park your arse here and let's have a look at your skin tones.'

Macy didn't have much to say and plonked down on the chair. Dawn opened a big black case and out of it unfolded three levels of make-up. There were blushers, foundations, eye shadows, lipsticks, eyebrow pencils, everything you could think of. Dawn had a serious look on her face now. She had been on a few courses, and she seemed to know her stuff, Macy had to admit. She put a white headband on Macy and started her work of art. You could see the concentration on her face as she pulled one brush out after another, dabbing them in different products. Macy didn't sit facing the mirror. She simply remained still and let Dawn work her magic.

A voice from downstairs. 'Are you nearly ready or what? She's not getting bleeding married, Dawn. Finish off now. I want to get going.'

Dawn used a big fluffy brush and fanned it over Macy's cheekbones. She stood back and smiled. 'My work here is done. I'll go downstairs. You shove them clothes on and have a look in the mirror.' Dawn kept turning back looking at Macy, proud of her work. She'd always said she wanted to open her own beauty salon, but up to now all she ever did was spend hours on her own appearance and had never earned a carrot from any qualifications she had gained.

Alone now, Macy slowly turned to face the long mirror on the wardrobe. Her hand came up and she covered her mouth. She was amazed. Was this really her? She looked so fresh, beautiful, even. She neared her reflection and examined her eyes. The bluey grey shadow suited her. She stood back now and rotated her body. She looked mint and just like the women she had seen in the town centre walking about. The ones who had a career, the ones who were having lunch with their work colleagues. Macy wobbled out of the room; it was ages since she'd worn heels. The last time she could remember was at her mother's birthday party about two years ago. It had been held at a local pub and she had made an effort that night. Everyone there had told her how stunning she looked. It was a shame the night had been ruined by a gang of lads fighting, throwing chairs about, launching bottles. Plus Jeanette Barnes had been in, staring at Macy all night, ready to kick off, so it was a blessing in disguise that the night was cut short.

Jeanette was Nathan Barnes' little sister and she hated Macy with a passion. It might have been years since

Nathan's death but, for Macy and Jeanette, it could have happened yesterday. While Macy coped by staying silence, Jeanette was the opposite. She always shouted insults.

'You know who killed my brother, you bitch, and one day I will find out, and when I do God help you and whoever you are protecting. Justice will be served, mark my words, justice will be served.'

Macy never stayed long wherever this woman was. The minute Macy turned her back, Jeanette would have attacked her.

Macy walked into the front room now and Dawn rubbed her hands together with excitement.

Bobby was taken aback, and he took a few seconds to speak. 'You look good, Macy. Bloody hell, I've not seen you looking this good for time.'

'Cheeky get. Bloody hell, you are both going on like I am a scruff or something.'

Dawn didn't think before she put her mouth into gear. 'You were – how shall I put it? – *weathered*, love. I said to Bobby the other night how much you had, well, not made the most of yourself.'

Macy screwed her face up: this woman was going over the top.

Bobby checked his wristwatch. 'Right, I'm here for a good time not a long time,' he chuckled. 'Wish us luck, Dawn.'

Dawn walked over to him and wrapped her arms around his neck. Her lips pressed against his. Macy looked the other way, embarrassed. She was never that big on public affection and struggled even to hold hands with her man, even when they were walking in the street. She walked out of the door, shouting behind her. 'Thanks, Dawn. I'll drop your clothes back off after. Cheers for the makeover too.' She opened the front door and stood waiting for Bobby, who sauntered out a minute later. 'Wow, lover boy, how long does it take to say goodbye? Any longer and I would have been asleep.'

Bobby sniggered. 'What can I do if she loves me?'

He walked past her and out to the car. Macy followed, wobbling slightly as she tried to get used to the heels she was wearing. Bobby opened the car up and she got into the passenger side. This was their time now, time to catch up, have a proper chat without anyone listening. Bobby reached over and opened the glove box. He grabbed his *Savage* after-shave and sprayed it over his body. It was a lovely soapy, fresh clean, aroma.

Macy coughed slightly. 'Bloody hell, no need for all that. I bet it only lasts you a few weeks if you're spraying it like that?'

'I know, but I love it. I earn enough to buy more, so it's all gravy, isn't it?'

Macy rolled her eyes as he started the engine up. He oozed confidence, loved himself. He pulled out of the drive and straight away he put the tunes on. Macy smiled. This was just how she remembered it: happy times, him and her singing in the car on the way to earn some money.

He reached over and turned the volume down a little. 'So, is your arse flapping or what?'

'No, just because I've not been grafting with you it doesn't mean I've not been doing my own bits.'

'Habit of a lifetime and all that,' he giggled as he reached over and gave her a playful punch in the arm. 'I must say you look mint. I didn't want to say too much in front of Dawn, because she would have seen her arse, but yeah,' he paused as he stared over at her. 'You look gorgeous.'

Macy turned to face the window. A real compliment: she'd not had that in a long time, and it felt good to hear it. She turned back to face him, her cheeks blushing. 'Thanks, it's nice of you to say that.'

There was a silence for a few seconds until he spoke again. 'I've missed you. I don't just mean working with you, I mean I've missed you as a person. We had some great times, me and you, and when we fell out it gutted me. I felt like someone had died.'

'Shut up,' Macy blurted.

'Honest, you ask Dawn. I took to my bed for days. I had an ache in my heart that wouldn't go away.'

Macy burst out laughing. He was pulling her leg for sure. 'You can't half tell a good story, Bobby. On my life, I almost believed you then.'

He kept his eyes on the road. Was he telling the truth or pulling her leg?

Bobby had already given her the talk about how things were going to run, and she was ready for it. He and Macy looked the part; rich professionals, definitely not the kind of people you would have down as shoplifters. The first hit was Selfridges - lots of perfumes and aftershaves there for the taking and, at two-hundred pound a bottle, the high-end ones were on their hit list. It was showtime.

Bobby walked into the store with Macy at his side. He placed some gold-rimmed glasses on and smiled at her. 'It's all about the look.'

He went to the *Creed* perfumes and aftershaves, and clocked the young girl working behind the counter. He needed to be sharp today and on the ball. Just behind where she stood was where the stock was kept. The plan was to get her to open the cupboard and keep her talking while Macy bagged as many bottles of it as she could. Bobby stood at the counter and already the girl was flirting with him. She had long blonde hair and bright red lipstick on. An easy target for Bobby's charm offensive.

'Good afternoon, sir, how can I help you today?'

Bobby moved in closer to her, looked her in the eyes and began his script. 'Hi there, I'm looking for some *Creed* after-shave for myself and the lady's version for my daughter and sister.'

The girl's eyes opened wide: a potential sale of at least three bottles. That would be a great result for her today, and it would keep her line manager off her back with her pressure to sell, sell, sell. The assistant wasted no time. She ducked behind the counter and got out some boxes. She put the testers on the counter and started to spray them on strips of white paper. 'This is the latest fragrance, sir, and very popular with the ladies.'

Bobby took a deep breath and smiled at her. 'I hate testing them on those cards. Any chance I can smell it on you?'

The young girl smiled and looked around her. This wasn't a usual request but she had to make a sale. Two spritzes: one on the side of her neck and one on her wrist. He neared her neck, aware how close he was getting to her. Macy wasted no time whatsoever. She moved quickly and within seconds she was gone. This was fast. No one had an idea what had just gone down. Bobby kept the assistant talking for a few more minutes until his phone started ringing.

He answered it straight away. 'Hello? Oh no, when did this happen? I'm on my way, please don't panic, just stay there and I will be there as soon as I can.' Bobby looked at the girl and spoke in a distressed tone. 'I'm so sorry, my daughter has had a bad fall. I have to leave.'

'Erm, no worries. I hope she is alright,' she said as he left her side.

Job done. Macy was smiling when he met her at the car. Everything had gone to plan. He clicked the button to open the car boot and Macy put the stolen goods in the back of it. There was no way they were carrying the perfumes around with them. This was the rule. Once they had copped for anything, it was stashed away immediately, away from the police if they were to get searched. Macy rubbed her hands together. Six bottles she had gripped. So, even selling at half price, that was six hundred quid already earned, three ton take-home for each of them. She was already spending it in her mind and thinking about how the money would be welcomed in her family.

The two of them worked well together. They were on another level, professionals, not petty shoplifters nicking booze, razor blades or batteries. They knew what could earn them the money and headed straight for it. Today was a good day.

Bobby started the car up and kept checking his rear-view mirror. He knew he wasn't safe until he was out of the car park. The rozzers could swarm him at any second. Macy sat nibbling her fingernails, just as nervous as he was. The music was on low, his eyes looking one way then the other, aware of his surroundings. Just a little bit further and they would hit the open road.

Macy's phone started ringing and she could see Joanne's number flashing across the screen. She had to answer it, get the call over and done with, there was no way she wanted her turning up at her house shouting the odds.

'Hello,' she answered. She held the phone from her ear as the abuse came flying down the line.

Bobby looked at her and raised his eyebrows.

'Listen Joanne, I never touched the fucking ring, so get off your high horse and shut up accusing me. I'm not working for you anymore because I'm sick of cleaning up other's people's shit.' She held the phone to her ear and listened for a few seconds more. 'Whatever, Joanne. You know where I am if you want to say anything more but, trust me, if you turn up at my gaff where my kids are, I'll make sure you are stretchered away. So, before you carry on making threats, be mindful that that's what will happen.' Macy ended the call and let out a ragged breath.

Bobby burst out laughing. 'Wow, who the fuck was that?'

'Oh, just this girl I used to work for, she's a crank.'

'What is she saying about a ring?'

Macy moved about in her seat, there was no way she was admitting to Bobby how low she had sunk that she was stealing out of people's houses. 'A ring has gone missing in some house that we clean and that slapper is accusing me of taking it. The woman has probably mislaid it or something. Honest, there was stuff all over the place in that house. It's a wonder they haven't reported each other missing.'

Bobby never delved deeper. He was on a high now. Today had been a good day and their pockets would be lined with money later that evening when the stolen goods had sold. Bobby patted her on the arm. 'A few beers before we go home? There is a nice little pub down this road, we could grab some tea too if you want?'

'Yes, alright, my stomach is doing somersaults. A few drinks is just what the doctor ordered.' Macy looked over at Bobby while he was driving, studying him, digesting every inch of him. She was away with the fairies until a message alert flashed on her phone. She opened the message and squirmed.

It was from Jayden.

Hope you are enjoying being with Bobby, you dirty cow.

She quickly closed the text and shook her head. Jayden was a jealous man and she knew now her phone would be pinging all night long with abuse from him. He wouldn't settle until she was back at home. She stared out of the window, debating cancelling going to the pub. But, why should she go home? Jayden was likely out doing God knows what, and she would only be sat in the house bored out of her head. Today she'd earned more than he had in a few months so, why shouldn't she celebrate her own success? He could take a run and a jump if he thought she was rushing back home to him. She was back in the mix and, if today was anything to go by, then she wouldn't need him and his poxy dole money anymore. She could stand on her own two feet and tell him to piss off. She had been questioning her love for him for a long time now anyway. What was he really bringing to the table? Nothing. The sex was crap, and even that wasn't very often. The bins went out more times than she did, and he was constantly sponging off her. She didn't need him, she never had.

Macy had been around the block with men in the past. She had had the nickname the 'bike' when she was growing up because everyone claimed they'd had a ride on her. Even Leanne's dad was just some guy who had turned up on the Square one night when she was steaming drunk. She didn't even know much about him, he was a friend of a friend. When she found out she was pregnant, she got one of his mates to let him know, but he never got in touch with her, never offered to support Macy. He just vanished from the area. She knew his name and age and that was about it. But the night Nathan Barnes died changed all that. She sorted her head out after that: no drinking, no more drugs. They were her dark days, times that she never wanted to remember.

Bobby parked the car up and smiled over at Macy. 'Come on then, let's go and get some scran. I fancy a steak, what about you?'

Macy licked her lips as she walked at the side of him. Steak was something she had not had on the menu for a long time. She'd nicked pieces of it to sell but she never bought it for her family for tea. It was so expensive, nearly a fiver for a slice that would shrink to half its size after she cooked it anyway. No, she always made family teas like shepherd's pie, potato hash, chilli con carne: food that everyone could eat and some be left for the next day.

Macy walked into the pub with her head held up high, smiling. She was like a business woman, a lady the staff would run around after and talk to with respect. She'd never had that, never had anyone looking up to her. The couple sat down in the corner of the pub and within seconds the staff were at their side.

'Macy, red wine?' Bobby asked and she nodded her head.

'Can I have two red wines please, and can we have the menu?'

The assistant reached over to a shelf at the back of her and pulled out two black leather menus. She placed them carefully on the table. 'I won't be long, I'll just get your drinks. My name is Debbie if you need anything.'

'Thanks Debbie,' Bobby smiled.

Macy looked around the boozer. It was such a lovely place. Dark red walls, cream seating area. It felt so welcoming, a place you could sit for hours chatting. Bobby made a quick phone call to his buyers and told them the price he wanted for the goods. The deal was done in a few minutes, no messing about. Everyone wanted to earn a crust and Bobby knew how to move hot items quickly.

The waitress was back and she placed the drinks on the table. 'Are you ready to order food, or do you want me to come back in a few minutes?'

Bobby slipped his jacket off and placed it on the back of the chair. 'I'm having the rump steak, darling, with all the trimmings. Medium rare.'

Macy had not even looked at the menu. 'Can you make that two steaks, love? I would like mine well done. I can't stand the sight of blood.'

Bobby moved closer after the waitress left and whispered into her ear. 'I'm buzzing with today. I know I keep saying it, but I've missed you.'

'I'm back to earn money, Bobby, no other reason.'

His expression changed, the corners of his mouth dropping. 'I still think about us, Macy.'

She had to shut him up, stop him from reminding her about their past. 'Bobby, wow, that was a drunken mistake. I've grown up a lot since then. Older and wiser and all that.'

'You're not fooling me, Macy Taylor. I can see it in your eyes, like I did when you was younger. You still fancy me?'

'Get over yourself, mate. Like I said, we've had a few drunken nights together.'

Bobby sat back in his seat and licked his bottom lip. 'I'm just saying, that's all. No need to bite my bleeding head off.' There was a silence for a few seconds before he spoke again. 'I'm thinking about fucking the other grafters off. Sheila and Mary are great, but we can earn as much on our own in half the time, if we only do top level stuff. I know you might think it's shady and all that, but think about it. Why should we split everything four ways when we can split it two?'

Macy shifted in her seat. Did she really want Sheila on her case calling her a sell-out when it was her who brought her back into the group? She'd tell everyone too, blab to the world and his wife about how she had double crossed her. 'Bobby, you can't do that. The girls would go sick. I've been back two minutes and you are talking about carting them. How would Dawn feel too? You know she can't stand me.'

'You leave Dawn to me. A few new handbags and she will quieten down.'

'I want a quiet life, no drama.' Macy ran a single finger around her glass. 'I've changed, you know. I think about things more these days. I suppose I've grown up. Jayden says I've turned into my mother, and sometimes I think he's right.'

Bobby laughed out loud. 'How is our Grace? I've not spoken to her in yonks. She's a right rum fucker. Is she still gossiping and laughing with Marjorie? Your mam always liked me, didn't she? When we were growing up she always thought we would end up together. I swear down to you, she always said to me she would have loved me as her son-in-law.'

'Oh, ignore my mam. She said that about every boyfriend I had. The minute they left the house, she was slagging them off, telling me how much of a waste of space they were.'

Bobby sat up straight, alert. 'Did she say that about me too?'

Macy smirked. She could see he was really bothered. 'Yes, probably, so get down from your high horse. You were no different than the others.'

Bobby was wounded. He spat his dummy out. 'She liked me more than Jayden. I think you got with him just to have a father for Leanne. I told you I would have stepped up and helped you, but you carted me and ended up with that plonker.'

'Jayden is an alright kind of guy when he's got a job. I'm not going to lie, it's been crap lately between us, but that's because we have been arguing about money all the time. They say money does not buy happiness, but it does, you know.'

Bobby nodded. 'I have to agree with you there. I hate not having any money. If I was skint, Dawn would do a runner for sure. She thinks I'm green but I know her inside out. She's with me to line her purse, get gifts. I know she loves me, but take the money out of the relationship, would she still be with me?' He sighed, 'I doubt it.'

Macy shot a look over at him. She knew better than to voice her honest opinion.

Bobby smiled and took a large gulp from his glass. 'I'm not arsed to tell you the truth. She knows how to treat a man, and does my washing, so it works for me for now.'

Macy slapped him playfully on the shoulder. He loved the whole Neanderthal bit but the way he'd agreed to cutting her in equally showed what he really thought of women.

She rubbed her hands together as Debbie came back with the food, and wasted no time in tucking in. She was starving. As she cut into her food she said, 'I've missed having things like this, Bobby. I've missed feeling the way I do now. I suppose I bottled it the last time I was in court and got spooked. It's hard when you have kids, Bobby. If it was only me, then I wouldn't care about Jack shit. But it's not, I have Leanne and Alex to think about. I mean, if I got sent down, who would look after them? Because Jayden can barely look after himself, never mind the kids.'

'I think we all got spooked the last time we had our collars felt, Mace. I don't think I could handle jail. Not at my age. It's a young man's game in the nick. I've told you before my fear about being in jail. I've got used to the finer things in life. Inside, I wouldn't last two minutes.'

'And. What makes you think I would? I would cry every bleeding night being away from my kids.'

Bobby reached over and touched her hand. 'I will look after you, Macy. If it's on top and you get arrested, I will make sure your kids are sorted. We are friends, and friends have each other's backs, remember.'

All of this talk about going to prison was no good. They were meant to be celebrating. She poked a few chips onto her fork and dipped it into the creamy peppercorn sauce. 'This is amazing food.' She picked her glass up and raised it to Bobby. 'Cheers, here's to making money.'

'To money,' said Bobby.

The glasses clinked together and they smiled at each other. Some people called it the root of all evil – but Macy figured you only said that if you'd never looked true evil in the eye.

Chapter Fourteen

Leanne stood behind the bathroom door with her body placed firmly behind it, her eyes wide open, sweat forming on her forehead, a hand resting on her chest. She looked flustered and kept walking to the bathroom sink and peeping over at something. Slowly, she picked up the white plastic stick and looked at the two red lines in the square box.

'Fuck, fuck,' she hissed as she threw the pregnancy test back into the sink as if it was diseased. Her body melted behind the bathroom door and her head dropped onto her knees. A single tear ran down her cheek and landed on her rosy lips. This was not the result she wanted and she could have kicked herself for ever letting this happen. So, that's why she had been feeling sick and dizzy. Her period was over a week late. What a fool. She'd wondered at other girls who had been pregnant at an early age, and here she was in the pudding club with them. She could picture them now, hear them whispering behind her back. For weeks she'd said she was going to the family planning clinic to get the pill, but she'd never made it. How many times had her mam told her she needed to be on the pill if she was sleeping with lads? But she'd always denied it, told her mam she was still a virgin. That ship had well and truly sailed. But, what now? Would Gino even want a child? Was she even ready to be a mother? She was still a kid herself. No, no way, she couldn't have a kid. Her nana would disown her. She was always commenting on young girls having babies when they were still babies themselves. Macy had joined in that conversation too. *There is no reason for girls to be having babies when the pill is available these days,* she could hear her nana say. *In my day there was none of this contraception about, we just had to keep our legs shut and our knickers on or deal with it, but you lot have a choice.*

Her nana's words echoed throughout her mind, strangling her thoughts, crippling her breathing. Leanne stood up and walked over to the bathroom mirror. Thick black tears ran down her cheeks, last night's mascara smudged all around her eyes. She neared the mirror and used the edge of her grey jumper to wipe her panda eyes. She'd fucked up big time and she knew it. Who could help her?

Kerry sat on the edge of the bed and shot a look down at the white stick Leanne had just passed her. Kerry lifted her head up slowly and looked down again at the test result. The penny dropped and so did her jaw. 'Fucking hell, no way.'

Leanne plonked down on the bed next to her and wrapped her arms tightly around her body. 'I don't know why I have let myself get in this position. I need to think straight. My head is going a thousand miles per hour. If I carry on like this, I will have a heart attack.'

Kerry was still in shock. 'Don't even tell me you're thinking of having it. It's a no brainer. Get rid, and as soon as.'

Leanne rocked her body slowly to and fro. 'I have to tell Gino and see what he thinks. It's up to both of us to sort this out, not just me.'

Kerry snapped, 'Are you for real? Gino needs to know nothing. Just get the clinic booked and sort it out. Nobody needs to know. The less people know the better.'

'Gino is the father and what if he says he wants us to set up a home together, you know, be a family?'

'For fucks sake, girl, what planet are you on? This is the rest of your life we are talking about. Who wants a kid with a psycho prick like Gino?'

'Kez, I know you don't like him, but it might be what he needs in his life to sort him out. He has some good traits, you know, he's not as hard as he makes out.'

Kerry had heard enough, sick of listening to her friend and the perfect world she was creating in her head. This was real life here, not a soap she was watching on the television. 'I'm your best friend and my advice would be to get on the phone now and get it sorted out before it's too late. Imagine it. No more chilling on the Square. A baby crying all the fucking time. Think about it, Leanne. This is not a doll we are talking about, it's a kid that needs around the clock attention.'

Leanne retaliated. 'I know what a baby needs. I'm not thick. I've told you, so you can help me, not give me a lecture. I need to sort myself out and quick. Honest, my head has been pounding all morning.'

Kerry sat back on the bed and kicked her legs up. 'I need a cig. Get me something to flick the ash in. Where's that bottle top we used last time?'

Leanne shot a look about the bedroom and pointed to a drawer near her bed. 'In there, and make sure you empty it, it stinks my room out.'

Kerry lit a fag up and passed one to Leanne. She held it there for a few seconds and watched her best friend hesitating. 'For crying out loud, don't tell me you are not smoking now. It's the size of a baked bean, Leanne. My mam smoked all the way through when she was carrying me and I'm alright, aren't I?'

Leanne gripped the cigarette and flicked the lighter underneath it, sucking at it with force. She sat back and blew a mouthful of grey smoke through her lips.

'Seriously, on my life. This is a no brainer and as your best mate I'm giving you some sound advice. I'll ring the clinic if you want, just get it over with. Fucking hell, you won't be the first and won't be the last.'

'I am still thinking, Kez. It's not like this is a one night stand with some guy I've only just met. Plus maybe a baby is what I need – something to love. Something pure.'

Kerry sprawled back on the bed and chugged on her fag. 'It's up to you. But I'll tell you now Gino will have you chained to the kitchen sink. It was only last week when you was saying to me that we needed to spend more time together. What happened to us both getting jobs and going working away? Remember, Leanne, our dream for years, me and you licking the lid of life in the sun?'

'I know, I can hear everything you're saying. Only let my mind calm down. We will go away still, I just don't know when. We made a promise to each other, didn't we, and I have not forgotten.'

'As long as you haven't. I want out of Harpurhey and I want to see the world. If you don't come with me, I'll go on my Jacks.'

Kerry reached over to her mobile phone and searched through her playlist. Times like this needed some good tunes on, something to change the mood. The music played and Kerry watched Leanne from the corner of her eye. She watched her typing out a message and reading it and reading it. 'So, you're telling Gino then?'

Leanne lifted her head from her phone and nodded slowly. 'Yes, I've asked him to meet me at his house in an hour. I've got to tell him. You know I couldn't lie to him.' She pressed the send button and held her mobile phone close to her chest.

Kerry was singing her head off and she no longer seemed bothered about her friend's predicament. After all, it wasn't her who was tubbed, the one who every girl on the estate would be slagging off once the cat was out of the bag. Leanne sat back and folded her arms tightly in front of her. She bit down on her bottom lip. 'My mam will hit the roof. If I decide I'm keeping the baby, I know she will throw me out. I'll probably end up at my nana's.'

'Nah, you're mam is sorted and, I'm not being funny, she was a young mum herself. You said yourself she didn't even really know your dad, so how can she slag you off and throw you out when she's done the same thing? It's like history repeating itself, isn't it?'

Leanne scratched her cheek, a red rash already starting to appear. 'I've never thought about it like that. You're right, Kez, I'll remind her of that if she starts dictating to me.'

Kerry closed her eyes for a few seconds. Despite what she'd just told her friend, Macy was a snapper when her cage was rattled, and she didn't want to be in Leanne's shoes when she told her she was pregnant.

Leanne had been clock-watching and biting her fingernails for over forty-five minutes. She jumped off the bed and started to look for her trainers. 'Right, I'm going to Gino's. Are you walking me there, or what?'

Kerry pulled a face and hauled her body up from the bed. 'Nah, can't be arsed. I'm going to meet Leon soon, so I want to go home and wash my hair. He's coming to meet my mam tonight and he's bricking it.'

'Check you out introducing guys to your mardukes. You must really like him, because nobody ever gets to come to your house.'

'I'm taking things easy with him. But up to now he's passed all the tests, and he's really nice, you know, treats me good and he's always giving me compliments. I like that about him. I think he's a keeper.'

Leanne held a sadness in her eyes, but she couldn't let on that she was jealous her friend had found a decent lad, one who treated her with respect. 'I'm so happy for you, Kezza. You have dated some right pricks in the past and I suppose you have to kiss a few frogs before you meet your Prince Charming, don't you?'

Kerry stretched her arms over her head and yawned. 'You sure do. And I've got myself on the pill and made sure I'm never in the same boat as you are now.'

Leanne hissed, 'Wow, rub salt in the wound, why don't you. Who needs enemies when I've got a friend like you?'

'You know what I mean. Don't be a mard-arse.'

Leanne examined her reflection in the mirror and turned to the side, looking at her stomach. She held her flat palm over her belly and looked over at Kerry. 'There is something growing inside there, isn't there? A baby.'

'So stop fucking about and get round to Gino's and get it sorted out. One way or another. Remember, we have plans and, kid or no kid, that can't stop us. We are party girls, loving life girls. Don't forget that.'

Leanne took a deep breath and opened the bedroom door. 'How can I forget when you are constantly reminding me?' she replied. But she was in a world of her own, working out what to tell Gino. She knew that whatever she decided to say to him would change her life forever.

Chapter Fifteen

Gino opened the front door and stood looking at Leanne. 'Are you coming in, or just standing there watching me freeze my bollocks off?'

He was such a cocky bastard. Being nice never cost anything, thought Leanne, and someone should have told him to use his manners when he was talking to people. 'I'm coming in. I was waiting for you to move out of the way.'

Gino led her into the front room and slumped down on the sofa. He waited until she had sat down and jerked his head over at her. 'So, go on, what's up? I hope it's not a load of shit, because you've just got me up out of my pit. I'm knackered.'

She gulped, cheeks going bright red. She needed a moment. 'Brew up and I'll tell you. I'll have a milky coffee.'

He burst out laughing and reached over for the TV remote. 'Like that will ever happen. What do you take me for, some sort of pussy? Do one and go and make your own brew.'

Leanne's fists rolled into two tiny balls at the side of her, and she could have easily run over to him and pummelled them into his face.

He asked her again. 'Wow, don't keep me hanging on. Tell me whatever it is you've come to say.'

'Hold your horses, will you? I'm trying to word this properly.'

Gino sat up straight in his seat, ears pinned back, nostrils flared. 'Have you come to tell me you're binning me? Because, if you have, you better start running. You know me and know I don't like shit like that.'

She flapped. 'Gino, no, it's not that. Come over here and sit next to me. I need a bit of support at the moment. I'm going under here. I need you to give me a hug or something.'

Gino cringed. Needy, she was, always craving affection, attention, his time. He stood up and plodded towards her. There were no hugs, no comforting words. 'What, spill then. Tell me, because you are winding me up now, playing with my head.'

'There is no point going around the houses, I'll tell you the way it is.'

His eyes were wide open, and he never budged. He held his breath for what seemed like forever, waiting for the news.

'I'm pregnant. I done a test and it's positive.'

The silence was deafening. His chest was rising frantically, and his eyes closed slowly. The vein at the side of his neck was pumping with what looked like blue blood.

'Say something then, don't leave me hanging here.'

His eyes flicked open, and he stared at her, no blinking, no sounds.

She prompted him again, took hold of his warm hand in hers. 'I said I am having a baby.'

Gino moved away from her, back to his seat. He started to roll a spliff before he spoke. 'Standard, I'll tell my mam and she can start buying some clothes and that.'

'So, you are happy about this? I mean, you want me to have the baby?'

He twisted his head to her and snarled, 'What, you think I would have you get rid of my bloodline? This is my kid, my genes. I want more too. About six or seven, I reckon.'

Leanne sighed and started to smile. 'I didn't know how you would react. I thought you might have gone ballistic and told me to get an abortion.'

'You thought wrong then, didn't you. But you better not start piling pure timber on and all that.'

Leanne was just happy that he wanted a baby. She sat playing with her fingers. 'I have to tell my mam now. She won't be happy, she will lose the plot.'

'No worries. Tell her you are moving in here with me. I'll tell my mam and she can get things sorted.'

She was confused. 'What, me leave home and come and live here with you?'

'Are you going deaf or what, girl? You heard what I said, so stop having me repeating myself.'

'My mam won't let me leave home, Gino. She hasn't even met you.'

'Listen, you are having my kid so I want you here where I can see you. You're seventeen, there is fuck all she can do about it. Go home, tell her the score and bring your stuff here. It's not rocket science, why do you always make things seem like hard work?'

This was all too much to take in. Macy loved her mother and, no matter what, she knew she wouldn't turn her back on her. So what, she would shout and scream for a bit, and say things that she didn't really mean, but she would calm down and then everything would be sorted. Moving in with Gino wasn't something she wanted to do. But how could she tell him that? She knew how angry he would get if he thought she was going against him.

She took a few minutes to calm her heartbeat down, and coughed to clear her throat. 'Gino, I like living at home. It would be different if we were moving in together and it was just me and you, but I'm not into moving in with you and your mam when I've got my own mam at home.'

She flinched as the long black remote control hit her head. The batteries fell out from it as a warm trickle of claret-red blood started to roll down her forehead.

'What the hell did you do that for? Look at my head now, you've cut me.' She patted her fingers on the wound and looked down at the bright red.

He was in her face now, spit spraying from his mouth as he roared into her face. 'You do as I tell you, you daft bitch. What, you don't like my mam or something? She's done everything for me, and you expect me to leave her on her tod. What kind of person are you?'

She backed off, moving her face away from him. 'I didn't mean it like that, Gino. I meant that I want my own place in time. I like living at home and I would miss my family if I moved here with you.'

He was in her face again. 'I'm your family now, the one who will protect you and the baby. Do you think I would sleep at night knowing you are not here with me when you're carrying my baby?'

She started to sob. This was supposed to have been a happy memory, the moment she told him he was going to be a dad, a memory she would treasure, the thing that made him change his ways.

'Oh, here comes the tears again. You're like a baby yourself, woman. I swear to you now, if you wasn't pregnant I would have told you to fuck off home. I can't be arsed with tears. Tears show weakness and nobody must ever see you are weak. Sort it out now. I can't even look at you. Honest, you are making my skin crawl.'

Leanne used her sleeve to wipe her eyes. He was right, she needed to toughen up. She had never felt so defenceless in all her life, and she couldn't understand why all she was doing lately was crying all the time. Maybe it was her hormones, but surely it was too early for all that to be kicking in. She took a deep breath, and her chest shook slightly. She wanted this baby and she was going to have to get used to standing up to Gino.

Chapter Sixteen

Jayden hid the cash deep in his pocket before he went inside the house, wobbling, staggering one way then the other. The less the Mrs knew about exactly how much he earned the better. He'd bung her a score or something, that would shut her up. He shoved his key into the lock and twisted it slowly. It was late and he was in no mood to have Macy pecking his head about his whereabouts. He was a man after all, the king of his castle, and he wasn't having no woman telling him when he should be home. He was one of the lads. He closed the front door slowly, checking behind him. A ray of yellow light seeped from under the living room door and lit up the hallway slightly. He crept near the door and popped his head inside as he held onto the door-frame. He could see the TV was still on, but couldn't see anybody. He opened the door fully and walked in as he slid his jacket off and flung it on the back of the armchair. Alex was asleep on the sofa and the top of his legs were hanging over. He always fell asleep here. Usually he would have given him a nudge and sent him up to bed, but tonight he ignored him, walked over to the television and switched it off. No wonder there was never any electric left when his son was up all hours playing on his games. He looked at his lad for a few seconds more, wondered if he was finally going to be the kind of dad every kid deserved. Then he turned away. The room was in darkness now.

Jayden went up to the bedroom, and he could see the shape of Macy in bed. She was sound asleep, like she always was at this time of the night. He studied her for a few seconds too, a cunning look in his eye. He quickly stripped off and jumped in bed next to her, his cold hands all over her warm flesh.

'Macy, you awake? Come on, babes, wake up and let's play hide the sausage.'

Moaning, groaning, she rolled on her side.

He spoke again. 'Babes, do you fancy a bit of slap and tickle? I won't be long; I'll be in and out like a ninja.'

Macy's eyes opened and she dragged the duvet back over her shoulder. 'Fuck off Jayden, I'm tired. Leave me alone.'

He tried again. 'Just give it a feel, then, anything. I'm horny as fuck here, hook a brother up. A wank will do.'

'Fuck off and go to sleep, you drunken bastard.' Macy was awake now, fuming. She could smell the alcohol on his breath, tell by his eyes that he'd had a skinful. 'Inconsiderate bastard, you are. You're wasted, so leave me be.'

His eyes changed, a look she had become familiar with over the years. 'You don't want sex with me because you've probably been getting shagged by Bobby. Don't think I don't know about you, slut,' he hissed.

This was her warning sign, her time to get as far away from him as possible. She hoped he'd pass out here so she could get out of his way. 'Go to sleep. I'm not arguing with you tonight.'

Before she managed to get up, he pinned her down, his nose touching hers. 'Go on, admit it, you want Bobby, don't you? If it's not him then it's someone else, because you are not interested in me anymore.' She wriggled about, trying to break free. He looked in her eyes and spat in her face. 'Like I need you anyway. I have women falling at my feet. And,' he paused. 'They all tell me to leave your sorry arse. I deserve a decent woman, one who wants sex with me, not some frigid bitch who lies there like a sack of spuds when I'm giving it her.'

Macy never flinched; she knew better. She kept her mouth shut, no eye contact.

He released his grip and plonked back down on the bed. 'Go on, do one. I'll have wank, like I always do when you're not giving me any.'

She darted up from the bed, looking around the room for a weapon. Anything that would knock the bastard out if he came after her. She stood shaking at the doorway. Her chest rising, words stuck behind her teeth, things what she wanted to say to him, to tell him to get his stuff and leave her alone. There was no love lost here and she didn't know why she had let him treat her the way he had been doing over the years. When she was younger she would have given anyone a run for their money, but these days she felt weak, as though life had knocked the fight out of her. She slammed the bedroom door shut behind her. He was going nowhere. He would roll over and go straight to sleep. The usual story.

Macy stood with her back to the wall on the landing, breathing calming now but still wanting to go back in the bedroom and smash his head in, go for gold and show him that she was not the weak woman he thought she was.

But before she could decide on her next move, noise from the bedroom opposite distracted her: sobbing. Her eyes shot to Leanne's bedroom door. There was a soft light creeping from underneath the door. Macy flicked her hair back and stood outside listening. She could definitely hear crying. She knocked gently, pushed the door open and stood looking at Leanne sat on the floor folding clothes that she had taken from her wardrobe.

'What on earth are you doing at this time of the night messing about sorting clothes out? You should be asleep.'

Leanne's shoulders were shaking as she continued crying. Macy walked over and sat on the floor next to her, moving her hair away from her face so she could see her properly. 'What's wrong, why are you crying like this?' Macy dragged at her hand, needing answers, needing to know what had upset her. If it was that Kerry upsetting her again she would be around at her house first thing in the morning. She'd bang her out if she'd been nasty to her baby.

'Mam, I have to tell you something. You're going to hate me.'

Now, this was serious. Macy sat back and folded her arms tightly across her chest, bracing herself. 'Go on, I'm listening.'

Leanne dropped her head again, still not ready to deliver the news. Her hands trembled as she started to bite her nails. She needed a few seconds, time to go over in her head what she was going to say. She fidgeted about, breathing rapid. 'Mam, sometimes things happen and we just have to deal with it. There is no point in shouting and screaming, because it doesn't make it any better, does it?' Macy was losing her patience now, eyes wide open, the mam look, the one that told her she'd better hurry up before she swung for her. 'I'm pregnant.'

You could have heard a pin drop. Leanne blinked as the words left her mouth. She half covered her head with her arm. She was a sitting target and almost expected a belt across the head. But nothing: no shouting, no abuse, just silence. This was not the normal Macy. Leanne was scared, bottom lip trembling as she spoke again. 'Well, say something then, because I know you want to.'

Macy blew a breath through tight lips and eyeballed her daughter. 'So, what was it? A drunken one night stand, a quick roll on the fields?'

'No, it wasn't.' Leanne paused. This was her chance. She could tell her mother the truth about what Gino had done to her. If she didn't have him arrested, she'd go round there and skin him alive herself. But she knew, in that moment, that if she sent her family to war with Gino's family, they'd all be in an early grave. She'd told the lie so many times now it came more easily every time. 'I love Gino, Mam, and he loves me. I've been seeing him for ages.'

'So why have I never heard his bastard name mentioned in this house before?' Macy was blood-red now, fingers curling up at the side of her legs, her voice getting louder. The news sinking in. 'Go on, why have you never told me about him?'

Leanne had to come back with something, to keep her mother from picking up the truth. 'You've been stressed with work and that, and, to be fair, when you are home you're always tired and we never get chance to have a chat anymore. You're always a million miles an hour, here one minute and gone the next. How could I have spoken to you? The only words you speak to me lately are orders to clean up and cook tea.'

This was the truth and Macy knew it. Sadness filled her heart. Regrets. Everyone had them. Some more than others, she thought. Leanne was right: she'd had no time for anybody lately, and it was all work, work, and work. And it was even worse now she couldn't let on to the kids exactly what kind of work she was doing. She dropped her head into her hands. This was history repeating itself, but at least Leanne was saying she loved her boyfriend, not like she herself had been. She'd been a lost soul willing to take her knickers down for anyone who was giving her a bit of attention.

Macy lifted her head up. 'Right, we can sort this out. Nobody needs to know. I will get you booked in somewhere and get this mess sorted out, sooner rather than later.' She stood up, pacing about the bedroom. 'You don't tell nobody about this. The less people know the better.'

'Mam, I'm keeping the baby. Gino wants it too, and he wants me to move in with him and his mam.'

Macy nearly choked. She stood tall, shoulders back. 'Over my dead body are you moving anywhere. I don't even know this guy, never met him, and you think I'm going to let you fuck off with him? No, give your head a shake, girl. You're going nowhere. You're staying here with your family, people who care about you.'

'Mam, Gino cares about me too. And if we are having the baby, it makes sense we stay at his for a bit until we get our own place.'

Macy was tearful now. Life came at you fast. 'Oh, you've got this all mapped out, haven't you lady. Well it's not happening, no way in this fucking world is it.'

Leanne remained silent. This was best for now, let her mother calm down. She stroked her hand over the pile of clothes and kept her head low. Noises from behind her.

'I can't believe this, when it rains in this house it bleeding pours. I thought my worries were about you smoking weed and hanging out with the wrong sort at the Square, not getting caught pregnant.'

'I'll bring Gino to meet you. He's nice, you'll like him.'

'I'm not ready to meet anybody yet. I need time to digest this, get my head in gear.' Macy shot a look down at the clothes on the floor. 'So, this is you packing your stuff ready to leave home?'

'I was going to tell you. I wasn't just going to leave.'

'Thanks a bleeding bunch for that. It's like we mean nothing to you. You love your family. Why would you give us up for some random guy?'

'He's not random. He's the father of my child.' Leanne stood up and held her open arms out to her mother. 'Can you just hug me? I've been in bits and I just need a hug.'

Macy had never been the best at showing her feelings, and she didn't rush towards her like Leanne wanted her to. It was more a slow walk, apprehensive.

Leanne squeezed Macy tightly in her arms. 'I'm so glad I've told you now. Everything is going to be fine, you wait and see.'

Macy stared up at the ceiling. It was never going to be fine, never again. She knew from experience.

Chapter Seventeen

Macy sat sipping her strong black coffee. She was knackered and had only slept a few hours. Dark circles under her eyes, small red veins on her eyeballs. She sat smoking and looked over at her son spread across the sofa. Was she a bad mother? She should have made sure he was in bed at a decent time, not leaving him downstairs when she knew he would be up all night long. Maybe if she had been home more she could have spent more time with her kids, but she had to work, put food on the table. Her head was a mess. The damage was done, no point in crying about spilt milk, was there. Worse things happen at sea, or so her mother had told her. How was she ever going to tell Grace, though? Her precious granddaughter having a child with God knows who.

The living room door opened and Jayden walked in with eyes like piss holes in the snow, hungover, and clearly coming down from something stronger, too. 'It's cold in here. Is the heating on?'

As if she was even talking to him. What a clown, did he not remember how he had treated her last night, or what? She watched him make his way to the sofa.

He gripped Alex's foot that was hanging over the arm and yanked at it. 'Yo, come on lazy balls, go and get in bed. I need the couch. Man's got a bad head.'

Alex stirred, face like a smacked arse. 'Wow, just leave me here. Go and sit on the chair or something.'

Macy could see this was going to end in blows. Alex was a right bad-tempered so-and-so when he'd just woken up. His hair was stuck up too, and that meant he was in a bad mood, or so Macy used to say when he was growing up. She shouted from where she was sat. 'Alex, come on, I want to clean up and I can't do that if you're spread all across the sofa.'

He darted up and headed straight for the door. 'I hate this house, you don't get a minute's peace,' he ranted.

Jayden plonked down on the sofa and folded the cushion under his head. 'You doing a drink, or what, babes?'

Macy stubbed her fag out in the ashtray. 'I'm doing nothing for you, mate. You can go and get your stuff packed. Go and treat someone else the way you do me and see how long you last.'

He lifted his head up and looked sourly at her. 'What's up with you now?'

'Last night, spitting in my face, manhandling me again, thinking you're some fucking gangster. I'm not having it. I told you last time if you ever laid your hands on me again it would be over and nothing has changed. Horrible, you are, when you've had a beer. Honest, you need to see yourself and you'd see what I'm talking about.'

He drew a breath. 'So where are the bruises, cuts, if I've manhandled you?'

'It's the mental abuse that you don't see. The worse kind, if you ask me.'

'So, I never slapped you about then, or smashed the house up like I used to do?'

'No, but it doesn't make it right, does it? You have a horrible mouth on you when you're drunk. I can't stand you. Honest, you make my skin crawl.'

'Aw, Macy, stop blowing this up. It was me being a dick-head. You know to ignore me when I'm like that. End of.'

She started to clean up. It was the end for her – but she couldn't tell him that now. Not with everything Leanne had said. 'Just don't lie there all day like always. For me, you can go and live at Simon's and live the single life.'

Jayden sniggered. 'Be careful what you wish for, love. And look, you say you want me bringing home the bacon, I've got twenty quid here for you. See, I'm always thinking about you when I could have easily been and got a bud with the money, couldn't I? So, I'm not all bad, am I?'

She wasn't listening. She had to be ready soon to go and see Bobby and Sheila. But she would never be able to focus on the job in hand with her daughter's bombshell still ringing in her ears. She had to tell Jayden. He would love this, say I told you so, say he knew she was up to no good.

Macy stood over him. 'I found Leanne upset last night. She's pregnant. So, don't you go shouting the odds at her. I've already spoken to her and, like you always tell me, she's not your blood, so I'll deal with her, not you.'

Jayden squirmed. 'Tubbed? How old is she, seventeen years old? She should be playing with dolls still, not babies. Bleeding lovely, just what we need on our plate: a hormonal girl and a crying bastard kid.'

Macy was furious. 'Like I said, it has nothing to do with you, so keep your snide comments to yourself.'

He twisted onto his side and reached for the remote. He had a few drops to do later and until then he wasn't going to move a muscle. 'Fucking pregnant, like I need this,' he mumbled under his breath. He couldn't wait until he had some decent money in his pocket. Another drop and he'd be quids in. Maybe he'd follow his mate Simon's example – invest in a bit of growing gear, forget this family-life crap. He didn't want to be raising some other kid's baby – he was ready for the single life. He just needed the money to get there. And you didn't get rich caring about other people, he knew that much.

Chapter Eighteen

Macy had left by the time Leanne walked into the living room, still dressed in her PJs. She curled up in the armchair and looked over at her step-father. She squirmed as she felt his eyes all over her, a look of disgust, a look that told her she was in his bad books.

'What's up with your mush, why are you staring at me like that?'

'You know why, so less said the better.'

She looked sheepish. Did he know? Had her mam told him her secret? She wasn't sure. Poker face. 'I don't know why, so stop beating around the bush. Just come out with it and stop being such a tool.'

Jayden rolled on his side, so he had a full view of her. He licked his lips and ran his fingers through his hair. 'You're having a kid, aren't you?'

She gulped. But who was he to judge her? Her shoulders went back, ready to tackle him. 'Yes, I told my mam last night. So, God knows why you have a problem with it.'

Jayden sat up, eyes wide. 'I have a problem with it because this is my house too. I pay the bills, or are you forgetting that? As if we need a kid screaming all night long, shitty nappies all over the place.'

'You won't hear any screaming kid, Jayden, because I'll be moving out. I'm going to live with Gino and his mam.'

He let out a sarcastic laugh. 'Thank fuck,' she heard him whisper under his breath.

Her temper was rising. 'I heard what you just said, you idiot. I'll be glad to get away from your sorry arse too. I don't even know why my mam hasn't got rid of you. You're such a cling-on, a needy prick who she's better off without.'

He moved forward, bare-chested, speaking to her through clenched teeth. 'You're a little slag. Everyone's probably had a go of you. I told your mam ages ago that you was up to no good, and I was right, you dirty sperm bank.'

Leanne launched the cushion at him as Alex walked into the front room. He stood there listening.

'Truth hurts, Leanne. Good luck with having a kid. You'll be on benefits all your life and end up like your mam did, a moaning cow, begging it from anyone who would have her.'

This was war. Time to stand up to him. 'As I understand it, you begged it from my mam. She had loads of men chasing her back in the day and God only knows why she picked you. You've held her back for years. She's worked her arse to the bone while you have been lay on the sofa watching her. You're not a man, you're a prick, and the sooner she gets rid of you the better.'

'Get your stuff packed and do one if you don't like what I have to say. I brought you up when your dad was nowhere to be seen, so have some respect, you bitch.'

'Respect! All my life I've heard you going on about how you brought me up when I was younger. You've never been a dad to me, so stop playing the martyr.'

Alex came and sat on the arm of the chair and patted his sister's shoulder. He glared over at his dad, no need for this kind of talk. 'Ignore him, you know what he's like when he thinks he's right.'

Jayden darted up from the sofa. 'Go on, tell your brother your dirty little secret. Tell him you'll be the talk of the estate soon. That's if he's not already worked it out for himself. All his mates will be talking about how easy you are.'

Alex looked down at his sister for answers.

'I'm pregnant, Alex.' She shot a look over at Jayden. 'There you go, muppet, he knows now, and what?'

'He should disown you just like I'm doing, dirty cow.' Jayden stormed out of the living room, slamming the door behind him. They could hear him still shouting as he bounced up the stairs.

Alex sat looking at his sister. 'So, you're having a kid. Not a bad thing, is it?'

She smiled softly, her eyes clouding over. 'Thanks Alex. He's horrible to me, you know. My mam never sees it, but he's always been like that. If she knew the half of the things he'd said to me over the years, she would have kicked his sorry arse to the kerb. Horrible he is, fucking horrible.'

'Ignore him, like I do. I know he's my dad, but there is something wrong with his head, I'm sure. One minute he's as nice as pie and the next he's a fucking head-the-ball.'

'Tell me about it. But, eh, one thing for sure is that I'm not living here no more. I know where I'm not welcome.'

Alex let out a breath. 'So, who's the dad? Anyone I know?'

'Gino Gallagher.'

Alex gulped. 'Wow, Leanne. I've heard some right stories about him. He's a crank. Heavy with his hands, I mean.'

'It's just hearsay. He's as right as rain with me. He loves me.' She almost believed it now, she'd said it so often.

'And, he's loved all the other girls too, but it never stopped him whacking them in, did it? Just think about this before you go and live with him. At least, while you're here, we can look after you.'

'It's sorted. I can't stand another second living under the same roof as that weapon.'

'Listen,' his voice low. 'If he ever raises his hand to you, you let me know. I know he's a big guy and all that, but I'll stab the bastard up. Honest, I will cut him up. I'm not arsed by his tough guy act.'

Leanne patted her brother's arm. 'Check you out getting all hard and all that. I'm fine, stop worrying about me.' Leanne got up from her seat and left the room.

Alex growled to himself, and shook his head. His sister was making a big mistake and he knew it. He only hoped it wasn't a fatal one.

Chapter Nineteen

Jayden put his foot down as he speeded onto the motorway. Another drop would line his pockets today. Four boxes of weed he was carrying this time in the boot of the car. He'd watched Terry place it all into a bigger box and cover it with a red tartan blanket. His job was to get the package there safely, nothing more, nothing less. The music was blaring as he positioned himself in the fast lane. He should have dressed in a suit, glasses, something that would have made him blend into the traffic. But no, he had his car window open, tunes blaring. Jayden looked into his rearview mirror, clocking any suspicious movement behind him: nothing. He reached over and popped a joint into his mouth. This was the life: earning, getting stoned and listening to music.

He pulled into the services and filled the tank. Terry couldn't be arsed doing his part of the job this morning and had bunged Jayden forty quid to get him to his destination and back. Jayden put the pump back and went to pay at the kiosk. He'd only put thirty quid in. The rest was his treat, his snidey little earner. Jayden shot his eyes to the left of him. Two guys were crossing the forecourt, heads dipped low, dressed in black. He couldn't see their faces. He nodded at them and carried on about his business. He was being paranoid, he told himself. He walked back to the car but kept glancing back.

Jayden was about ten minutes away from Blackpool. He rang his guy and told him to be ready for his arrival. His eyes were all over the place, looking one way then the other. Something had unsettled him. There was no longer any music playing and his windows were securely closed. Jayden hated this part of the job, meeting new faces, handing over the goods. He pulled slowly into a dark layby. This was the place he'd agreed to drop the boxes. Once he'd parked up, he turned the engine off and sat looking around. 'Fuck this,' he whispered under his breath as he sparked a fag up, his hands shaking as he flicked the lighter underneath it.

In a heartbeat, Jayden's head went west, glass firing around the vehicle as the window went in. Darkness. His head smashed one way then the other, voices blaring, his body being dragged from the driver's seat. All over in an instant.

Jayden lay in a pool of blood, thick claret dribbling down the side of his cheek. He didn't know how long he'd been there. His fingers unfolded slowly as his eyes opened. He tried moving, crawling along the cold grey gravel, but he was weak. Reaching into his pocket with trembling hands he tried to make a call but lost the grip on his mobile phone. A car was coming towards him, headlights on full beam. Two men got out and stood next to him.

'Get the twat up from the floor and get him in the car,' the man's voice said.

Jayden's eyes flickered; words trapped behind his lips.

The man's voice came again, his hot breath in his face. 'Where's the fucking weed?'

Jayden's eyes were wide open now, his voice barely audible. 'Dunno. One minute I was sat there waiting on you guys to arrive, and then I know fuck all. They attacked me.'

The man dragged him to his feet, his legs buckling. 'Don't give me that shit. You set it up, didn't you? Fucking rat.'

'No, honest, I was nothing to do with it. Tez has been good to me, a good mate and all that. I would never piss on my own doorstep.'

'Nah, I don't believe a word the runt is saying,' the taller of the two men said to his friend. 'Shove him in the boot and we'll soon see, when he's got a shooter to his head, what he knows. Because, trust me, I'll blow your fucking head off, mate.'

Jayden was dragged by the scruff of his neck by the men and flung into the boot of the car. His voice was a whisper, no energy to protest his innocence.

Darkness again. His breathing shallow. If he carried on like this he was going to have a heart attack for sure. He could feel wetness around his head, cold shivers down his spine. Was this his time to meet his maker? The car started and he dragged his knees up to his chest, twisting in the narrow space as a pain surged into the back of his eyes. His eyes stared into the darkness but he found no answers there.

Chapter Twenty

Bobby smiled over at Macy. Today had been a good day and they'd had a great haul. These two were the dream team, or so Bobby said. Bonny and Clyde had nothing on them. Decent stuff they'd lifted, Armani jeans, Gucci tops. The cream of the crop.

'Shall we go for a few drinks on the way home? I'm gagging for a pint. Dawn's out, so it's pointless me going home to an empty house. And sack that cooking lark, I'd rather get some scran in the boozer.'

Macy hunched her shoulders and smiled. 'May as well. Jayden's not even replied to my text, so he can do one. The kids will have grabbed something, so I'm in the same boat as you, if the truth was known.'

Bobby chuckled as he turned the music down a touch. 'So, how's things with Jayden? I know the last time we spoke you didn't really say much about him. You know I've always thought that he's a tosser but, eh, he's your man and who am I to call him? I've been not always been straight to

Dawn over time, and I'm no angel, as you know.' He raised his eyebrows and gave her a cheeky wink, the one that told her he was remembering their drunken night of passion.

She blushed and jumped straight into conversation. 'Exactly. I know you think me and Jay are an odd couple, but I'd never put you and her together.'

Bobby didn't look at her, but put his indicator on to turn right. 'Dawn has a big heart, and she looks after me.'

'So, you're with her coz she cooks and cleans for you. Out of order, that. What happened to saying, "I'm in love with her", or "she is my everything and I can't live without her"?'

'Nah, sack all that shit. I don't do love; it only ends up in tears.'

Macy knew this conversation was taking them back into their past. Back onto dangerous ground. 'Oh, are we talking about Justine, your first love? Because, bloody hell, you were done in when you split up with her.'

'I loved her and I'm not afraid to say that out loud. Yeah, when she said it was over I was on my knees begging her to stay. I made a right twat out of myself when I think back. I was belling her phone out every minute of every day, and when she never answered I went around to her mam's gaff and terrorised the fuck out of her until she told me where she was. You know me, love, I was willing to stay there for days until she told me where she was. I knew she knew.'

Macy knew Bobby had a different side to him – a switch that flicked – and she was glad he'd learnt to control that part of himself as he'd grown up. She covered her mouth with her hand. She was hanging on his every word as he pulled into the car park. Forget any soap she'd watched on the TV: this was real life, real people. Hearts, and lives, at stake.

He continued, still angry at the thought of his woman with another man. 'I tracked her down and found her with this other guy. I said to her, "who's this then?" She panicked and stepped in front of him, because she knew he was getting it. "Bobby, we stopped loving each other a long time ago. I told you if you didn't stop partying with the boys I would go, and you never listened." She was sobbing. That was it, I saw red. I dragged her out of the way and steamed the bloke she was with. It wasn't really his fault but I didn't care then, I only wanted to do him in. I was hurting bad and wanted to make sure he was feeling the pain I was. She got a slap too, I'm not going to lie. She's lucky I never kicked the fuck out of her for the way I was feeling. It done me in big time, sick to the stomach.'

Macy shook her head. 'And you wonder why Justine didn't want to stick with you? You were like a wild animal when we were younger – law of the jungle it was for you, back then. You must have really gone for him.'

'Yes, like I said, I lost it. I leathered him and, if she hadn't pulled me off him, I would have been on a manslaughter charge. I went to town on him. You should have seen the state I left him in. I sat waiting for the rozzers to come for days, expecting the knock at the door, but they never came.'

'I remember you vanishing for a bit – was that then?'

'Yeah, I was gutted. On my life, I even thought about ending it all. I was low, honest. All I done each day was smoke my head off, pop pills and get steaming drunk. My head was all over the place, nothing made sense anymore. But I got through it, and from that day forward I promised myself I would never let any woman get under my skin again. I met Dawn not long after that, and it's right what they say, what makes you ill makes you better. Dawn did just that. She fixed me and got me over that slapper.'

Macy was intrigued. 'So, are you faithful to Dawn now then, or do you still fuck about on her?'

His cheeks blushed slightly. He tapped the side of his nose and winked at her. 'Now that would be telling, wouldn't it,' he chuckled. 'Come on, let's get a few drinks down our neck and you can fill me in on your life, now I've opened up to you.'

Macy shook her head. 'Shut up, I'm never telling you my private stuff. Why do you want to know about me anyway?'

'We're mates, that's why. And we go way back. I can be your therapist, try and sort shit out with you. A problem shared and all that.'

'Can I have two more red wines, love?' Bobby smiled at the waitress as he pushed away his plate.

Macy had been glad of the distraction of the food coming. She didn't want to dwell on the past. Or the present, even. Jayden still hadn't called her back.

Bobby moved in closer to Macy as the drinks were brought. He waited until they were alone and kept his voice low. 'I still think about us, you know...'

She went bright red, fidgeted about, unable to look him in the eye. 'Bobby, we said we would never talk about it.'

'But it did happen. And we are both adults. There's only me and you here, so why can't we talk about it?'

'Because it's embarrassing. We're not kids anymore that share everything. You are in a relationship, and so am I.'

'But, just admit, it was cracking sex, wasn't it?'

She picked her drink up and gulped a large mouthful. Deep breaths, she needed to calm her racing heart. 'It was a good night, Bobby, and yes, we had a great time, but we both said it was a mistake. No point in going over old ground, is there?'

He whispered in her ear, his breath creeping down her shoulder. 'You still make me hard. When I first saw you again after all this time you stirred something inside me, had me thinking what could have been.'

She shoved him away. He was winding her up for sure. 'Bobby, you're like a dog on heat. Sort it out, you have a girlfriend.'

'But what if I didn't?'

She stuttered, lost for words, trying to think of her answer. 'But, you do, so no point pretending, is there.' He looked deep into her eyes. He wanted more, she could see. A warmth rose through her body, a feeling that she had not felt in a long time. If she'd have been a bit more drunk she would have kissed him and taken him somewhere for hot, passionate sex. After all, she'd not sex for months: no kissing, no touching, zilch. Her love life was as stale as the loaf she had in her kitchen cupboard.

Lost in the moment, she wasn't thinking straight, the wine clouding her judgement. 'It was a great night, and yes, I have thought about it more than once. Maybe we missed our way, maybe we didn't. We have had two chances at each other and, if we were meant to be, then maybe that was all it was meant to be.'

Bobby sat back and necked his drink before he shouted over to the waitress again to bring them more drinks. 'You have always been in my life, Macy, and what you did for me I'll never forget. We have a bond, something more than friendship, and given the chance I would have wifed you off years ago. We went our separate ways – we had to – but we have always ended up back together somehow. It could be fate, you know?'

The wine had loosened both their lips tonight and, even though she should have gone home hours ago, the past was dragging them back together. They came from the same place, had seen the same things, spoke the same language. But did they want different things?

Bobby nudged her, sensing a chance. 'Shall we get a room and have a few more drinks? I'll make something up to tell Dawn. I'll say we got chased and have to keep our heads low for a bit. I've done it before, and she has never bothered.'

Macy snapped out of her daydream. 'No, I have to go home. The kids will wonder where I am. I'm not arsed about Jayden, and he probably won't even know I'm not home, but the kids will.'

'It's a shame that, Macy, we could have had a good time.'

She folded her arms tightly and sat back in her seat. Was that all he thought she was? A good time for a night? Her eyes were wide open now as reality hit home. She was weak, vulnerable and didn't want to make another mistake with this guy. She couldn't look him in the eyes anymore. His big blue sexy eyes, come-to-bed eyes. She quickly checked her watch. 'Are we ready to make our way home then?'

Bobby picked his keys up and nodded his head slowly at her, knowing she'd knocked him back. 'Yep, let's get that lot sold, and get some cash in our pockets.'

Macy walked out of the pub first and she could feel his eyes burning into the back of her head. She wobbled, couldn't wait to get in the car. She held her mobile phone to her ear, one last try calling Jayden's number. No reply.

Chapter Twenty-One

Leanne lay on the double bed. Gino had told her to wait at his place for him. Hours he'd been gone, and she was getting restless. She was in two minds whether she should piss off home but after some thought she'd come to the conclusion that it wasn't worth upsetting him. He'd only go on and on for hours that she didn't respect him, or claim she took the piss out of him. No, it was much easier just to stay put and keep him happy. Anyway, she was going to be living here soon, so she may as well start getting used to the place. She flicked the TV station over and lay with her hands wrapped over her stomach. Already she loved her baby, planned so much in her head, how happy the three of them would be. So what if her boyfriend was a bit wild? This was his chance to have a fresh start, and who couldn't love an innocent baby? That was all that mattered.

Alex sat on the edge of the sofa, shouting at the screen. His mam was late tonight. Usually by this time she was home. A plate lay next to him with a crust of bread on it, an empty bag of crisps. He screamed at the TV as his character got shot down. 'Wow, fucking hell, bro,' he ranted. Lost in the game, he didn't hear the loud banging, voices coming nearer. He froze as the living room door swung open, banging into the wall. Three men sprinted to his side, balaclavas concealing their identity. He was dragged from the sofa and pinned up against the wall, his legs not touching the floor.

'Where's the food? Tell me where the fucking food is. Don't fuck me about because I'll wet ya up,' the tallest of the men screamed at him.

Alex's wriggled about, his breathing laboured, his lungs screaming, as his airways were restricted. 'I don't know what you mean,' he croaked.

'The fucking food, tell me where it is,' his attacker growled into his face again. The other men were running about the room, searching, throwing things all over the place. One sprinted into the hallway and went upstairs. The man went nose to nose with Alex, a cold metal blade pressing deep into his cheek. Seconds away from cutting the flesh. 'Money, drugs, where is it?' The man didn't wait for him to reply. His clenched fist pounded into the side of Alex's face.

This was no playground fight. No video game. No, this shit had just got real. If he'd been fighting a kid the same age as him, Alex would have given as good as he got, but these guys were strong, powerful. As the man released him,

Alex dropped to the floor like a sack of spuds. He tried to scramble to safety, but they gripped him again, booting him, punching him until he was still. Alex's eyes started to swell, his lip pouring with bright red blood. He was dragged up again by the scruff of his neck, his body limp. 'Think about this, kid. If you tell me where the cash is, then you will live, but if you give me shit then I'll slice you up and feed you to the fucking pigs.'

Alex spat a mouthful of blood out. 'We don't have any money, we never have. My dad smokes a bit of weed, but he only buys ten-buds.'

The first man dropped him to the ground and stood up tall, his chest expanding, ears pinned back. 'Where's ya mam?'

Alex answered with desperation in his voice. 'I don't know, she should be home by now. My dad should too.'

There was whispering between the men, all looking over at him. His body was shaking, lips trembling, a wetness spreading between his legs. So, this was what fear felt like, to see his life flashing before his eyes. He'd always thought if ever he was attacked he would have fought back, picked something up and used weapons to defend himself, but this was on another level, he had never expected it, never stood a chance. The man came back over to him and bent down so he could see the whites of his eyes.

'Who does your old man lick shot for?'

Alex shook his head, he didn't have the answer. His voice trembled as he replied. 'He doesn't sell drugs, he smokes a bit of weed, that's all.'

The man was losing his patience realising that there was no money at this gaff, or drugs like he'd expected. 'So, what's your name, kid?' the man asked.

'Alex, my name's Alex.'

'Listen up, Alex. Your dad is in a lot of trouble and, if I don't get the information I'm looking for, your dad will be in a body bag the next time you see him.'

Alex gulped, hands shaking as he held them up to the side of his head. Pleading with them, knowing this was his last chance to convince them. 'I don't know anything. If I did, I would tell you. Where is my dad? Please don't hurt him.'

'Too late for that, you wanker. He has tried to have us over and he'll pay the price. You all will. We'll be back. Do you get me? The next time we come, the lot of you will be ended unless this is sorted – fast.'

Alex shuddered. Every bone in his body was shaking, coldness filling him, blood rolling from the gash at the side of his head. His attacker turned his head and studied a family photo at the side of him. He looked at it a lot longer than he needed to before he launched it into the wall, shards of glass spraying around the room.

He let out a menacing laugh and kicked the coffee table before he jerked his head over at the others. 'Come on, let's do one. This rat knows the score. Remember, four boxes you owe us for, so get it fucking sorted.'

Alex didn't take his eyes from them as they left. His ordeal was over for now. He sat in the corner of the room with his knees held up to his chest. His breathing was rapid and the side of his head was still pouring with blood. He heard noises from the hallway, convinced they'd come back to finish him off. He covered his head with his hands, ready for the worst.

'What the hell has been going on here?' His mother's voice echoed through the hallway. He wanted to shout her name, jump up to his feet and run and tell her what had happened, but his body was weak, the pain coming through in waves now the adrenaline was fading. The living room door creaked open, a spray of yellow light seeping in from the hallway. He could see her, see her looking one way then the other, but still his words were trapped behind his teeth.

'Fucking hell, what's gone on here?' she mumbled as she started to pick things up from the floor. Rustling behind her. She froze, squinted and looked into the corner of the room. Slowly she stepped forward, eyes focused. 'Alex? Alex, son, what's happened?'

His bottom lip quivered and his head sank. He could see her feet now. She bent down and lifted his head up softly in her hands. The second she spotted blood, her jaw dropped. 'Alex, are you OK? What's gone on, tell me, son, please?' Her fingers stroked along the side of his bloody cheek. He was properly hurt and she knew it. She sprang to her feet and ran into the kitchen. Panic set in and she was shouting at the top of her voice from the other room. 'If he's laid a single finger on you, then he's gone from this house. How many times have I told you not to back-chat to your father?'

She was back at his side now. A bowl of hot water and a tea-towel. Dipping it into the warm water, she started to clean away the blood.

He cringed as the water touched his skin, every inch of him filled with pain. 'They've got Dad. Mam, do you hear me? They have got him. I just don't know who they are. They wanted money or drugs. I couldn't follow everything they were saying but I thought they were going to kill me. I told them Dad doesn't have any money or gear, but they never listened. Three of them, there were, and they said they want the money for the weed. What weed, Mam? He's never got anything more than what he can cadge for a spliff. We need to help him. They said he will be in a body bag if we don't pay the money or get the drugs back.'

Macy was still cleaning her son up, her eyes welling as she looked at the swelling under his eyes. 'I should have been here with you. I should have been here,' she whimpered.

A ball of emotion burst from the back of his throat, he could cry now. He sobbed his heart out, held by his mother. 'Like I said. There were three of them, ballied up so I couldn't see what they looked like at all. The main one said he would slice me up, they just burst in here and done me in, Mam. I couldn't move, I was outnumbered.' Alex struggled and placed his flat palm on the wall behind him to get up.

She helped him up and guided him to the dining table. 'I'll go and get you some clean shorts and a T-shirt. You've got blood all over you.'

Alex sat slumped over the dining table, no strength to hold his body up. He could hear his mother rummaging about upstairs.

Half an hour later, Alex was cleaned up and refusing to go to the hospital. The cut at the side of his head had stopped bleeding, but both his eyes were nearly shut, purple-black bruises forming.

Macy sat down next to him and rubbed her eyes. 'Fuck, fuck, fuck,' she mumbled. 'Where is Leanne, why wasn't she here?'

Alex replied softly, 'I'm glad she wasn't here, Mam. She's pregnant, isn't she? Imagine them slapping her about too?'

Macy gulped; how did he know? She stared at the wall facing her as she listened to her son.

'She was staying at that guy's house tonight, said you knew about it?'

Macy jumped up from her seat, pacing about the living room. 'No I bloody did not. She's taking the piss, that one is. But, like you said, it would have been worse if she was here. So tell me again what they said to you. What were they looking for? Are you sure they have Dad? They might have been blagging you?'

'They called it food, *where is the food*, they said?' His eyes closed, reliving every second of his ordeal.

Macy wasn't wet behind the ears. She knew straight away he was right and that they meant drugs. But nothing else was making sense in her head. She was putting two and two together and coming up with six. Yes, Jayden had said he was doing a few drops, but she never had him down for being any big time drug dealer. He was a foot soldier, a mug who took all the risks. She rammed her hand into her pocket and pulled out her mobile phone. She'd try his number again, keep it ringing until he answered. Macy looked at her son as she put the call on speaker. No answer. Still. She paced about the room, what the hell was she going to do now? Even after grafting with Bobby again, she only had a few hundred quid to her name, not bleeding grands like they would be talking. Who had that kind of money around here? Bloody nobody. She sat down next to her son and draped her arms around him.

'All this is going to be sorted, son. You should have never had to go through this. It's that daft bastard's fault for getting his ugly head mixed up with people he knows can hurt us. But I'll sort this. I know the guy he was doing the drops for. I'll march round there now.'

She shot a look at the clock on the wall. It was late but surely Terry wouldn't mind her calling. After all, her man was missing and three geezers had rushed her house; he had to help her, put a stop to it all and make sure her Jayden was back home with his family where he belonged. The clock was ticking now, and she had to step up and protect her family any way she could.

———

Terry's gaff was around twenty minutes from where Macy lived. She paid the taxi and stood opposite his house. There were still a few lights on, so at least he was still awake. She zipped her coat up and walked into the garden through large black iron gates. So, this was how the other half lived. She took in everything around her. The garden was as big as her whole house. Her step quickened, scared she was going to set off an alarm or something. The security lights were on now, beams of lights spreading over every inch of the garden. She pressed the door bell and stood back.

A man's voice. 'Hello, what do you want?'

Macy gulped and stepped closer to the speaker. 'Is this Terry?'

'Who's asking?' the voice enquired.

'My name is Macy, I'm Jayden's girlfriend. I need to speak to you, need you to come and talk to me.'

A light went on behind the door but it didn't open.

'Who's sent you here?'

'Nobody's sent me here. I've had men through my door saying they have Jayden; they have battered my son within an inch of his life and said they want money from us to pay for the weed they think Jayden has had away. They've got him, so you need to sort this out, get him back home, end the fuckers if you need to.'

Terry, bare-chested, quickly stuck his head out of the door at that. Was this woman mad or what? She couldn't go around suggesting a hit.

'Get your arse in here, woman. Fuck me, like I need this. How do you know where I live? If any trouble comes to my door, I'll do your useless boyfriend in myself, never mind them doing it.'

Macy went into the house and followed him into the front room. He pointed to the black leather sofa and told her to sit down.

He sat facing her. 'Jayden rang me earlier and everything was going fine, so what the fuck has gone on?'

'Don't be asking me. I only know he was doing a few drops for you, that's all. I know nothing more. You know what Jayden's like. He's a shady fucker and only tells me what he wants me to know.'

Terry looked into space, thinking. 'So, you're here because he didn't come home and someone's decked your boy?'

'I'm here because three men have boomed my front door down, attacked my son, and they said they have my boyfriend. Are you not getting this, or what? The men will be back. They want money from us.'

Terry chuckled. 'This seems like a *you* problem, not a *me* problem. Once the drugs left me then it was his shout, he is responsible for everything after that until they've been safely delivered. How do you know he's not set all of this up as a stunt? He's a dodgy twat, you've said as much. I only gave him a bit of work because Simon asked me to help him out. Nah, fuck all I can do. It's his problem now.'

Macy jumped up to her feet. 'Terry, get a grip, man. I've told you the score and you're looking at me like I'm a bleed-ing lunatic. Yes, Jayden likes a bit of ducking and diving, but he's hardly going to arrange to have his own kid beaten to a pulp. These men know where I live, they said they have Jayden, and they want more money than I earn in a year. So,' she sucked in a large mouthful of air before she continued. 'If you're closing your door on me, I'll tell them who the fucking big man is, because they asked, you know, oh yes. I'll tell them where you live and see how *you* like men coming through your door, smashing the place up and battering your family.'

He was up on his feet too now and he growled at her, 'You keep my name out of your fucking mouth. Anybody turns up here because of you and your prick of a boyfriend, and I'll make sure none of you fucking breathe again. Do you hear me? Keep my name out of your mouth.'

Macy barely even flinched. She stood tall and watched as he sparked up a cigarette. 'I'll have one of them, if I can?' She needed it to steady her nerves.

He flung one over at her, still angry that she was ready to sell him down the river and didn't seem to have folded at the sound of his threats. She walked over to him with the fag hanging out of her mouth and got a light from the lighter he was holding.

He took out his phone, walked just outside the door. Macy shot her eyes around the front room. It sickened her to see how many luxuries this man had. Selling drugs paid well if you were near the top of the tree, and this man had reaped the rewards. He preyed on the poor people around him, people who were skint and wanted to earn a few quid. He paid them barely anything and creamed a healthy profit from them all. And here he was, sat pretty without a worry in the world. No, he could do one. He was going to help her, if he liked it or not. She got her poker face ready for him; she had already decided that she wasn't leaving this house tonight without him sorting something out. She would burn his world down if he refused to help – for her kids' sake, if not for Jayden. Whatever Terry said, this was his problem too and, if he refused, then she'd make it his problem.

Terry stormed back into the room. He spoke through clenched teeth, fists in tight balls at his sides. 'Jayden must have been set up. When our boys he was delivering to got to him, he was battered and on the floor, barely breathing, saying he'd been had over. So this is his mess. He's either blabbed his mouth off or he's not kept his eye out to see who's following him. But the question is, who the fuck is playing games here?'

Macy shrieked, 'As if Jayden would have you over, Terry! Come on, you know as well as me that he is happy with a few quid for his beers and his weed. He's not a top dog. He has no contacts to sell drugs to anyway. Don't start chatting shit, thinking he's the fucking King Pin here.'

'I don't know what to think. All I know is that he had four boxes on him and, if he's not delivered them to the people my guys sold it to, then who the fuck has the stuff? Now forget Jayden: the boxes are my real problem. Some cocky bastard out there is fucking my shit up and when I find out who, heads will roll. Go home, woman, and let me sort this shit out. If you're lucky, I'll find who's robbed me and end them before they finish off Jayden.'

She squashed her cigarette out and stood with hands on hips. 'And what about us, my family, are you going to sort us out too?'

Terry's phone pinged and he read a text message. It was like a jolt of electricity through him. He grabbed his car keys from a small glass table. 'Turns out the people who have him aren't trying too hard to cover their tracks. That's a bad sign – and they are fucking ruthless. The money man behind the deal is a guy I know from back in the day. He's dangerous. I need to sort this shit out before they come knocking on my door. Go home and, if Jayden turns up, tell him to bell me as soon as – they might let him go as a warning. The sooner this is sorted out the better. You speak to nobody and keep my name out of your mouth. The last thing I need is the dibble knocking on my door while I'm fixing this.'

Macy realised this was the best answer she was going to get tonight. She followed him out and headed down the garden path. Moments later, his silver Range Rover screeched past her and headed onto the main road.

Macy continued trying Jayden's phone all night. Nothing. It was nearly four in the morning now and she hadn't slept a wink. She'd looked in on Alex, sleeping now, but there was no rest for her. Every noise she heard, she was up out of her seat, checking. She'd patched things up as best as she could, but her front door was still half-off its hinges, just balanced on and braced shut with a few chairs. As soon as the housing office was open in the morning she was going to report it and get it fixed. She would have to say it fell off with wear and tear; she'd never tell them the truth. Round here they were used to stories like that. People who couldn't say what had really happened. She couldn't report it as a burglary either – or an assault. The police were the last people she needed knocking at her door. Instead, Macy sat smoking in the darkness. Despite her son upstairs, she felt more alone than ever. All she had was the sound of the clock ticking, the moon shining in from the window to keep her company. And a terrible sense that, despite everything that had gone down tonight, worse was to come.

Chapter Twenty-Two

Jayden lay sprawled on an old sofa. He was black and blue. Voices sounded outside the room. He knew they'd be back in soon, asking him more questions, slapping him, kicking him, in the hope they would get some names. He could hear them talking, deep voices. One of his attackers popped his head inside the room. Jayden kept as still as possible, hoping they would leave him alone. No such luck. The man kept the door open, the others stood at the side, ready to steam in if they needed to.

'Yo bro, listen up, and listen good. I suggest you start talking and quick. I've been to your yard and left a little message with your son. I hope he loves you enough to use his head and sort this shit out. We want our drugs back, end of.'

Jayden's eyes widened. 'I don't know what happened to them. I was hijacked, had over, set up. What have you done to my son? Please, not my family. I don't know who you think you're buying off, but I'll tell you where you can find

175

the big man. He runs the shows down our ends. He gave me the drop, but I know fuck all else.'

The man smirked; this was music to his ears that made his life much easier. He stood over Jayden and looked down at him. 'So spill, no bullshit, straight to the point.'

Jayden licked his dry cracked lips, dried blood still visible on his face, eyes swollen. 'I get my gear from Terry Dolan. He's the biggest supplier in our area. I only do the drops, I do sod all else. I don't know where he gets it from, I'm just the daft git who transports it. A couple of hundred quid he pays me, fucking peanuts. I swear down, on my kid's life, I was set up. Somebody must have known where I was dropping the weed off and got there before you did.'

'So, let's hope you are being smart here. Think before you answer me.' His words were slow, each one echoing in Jayden's blood like a cold knife stabbing into his heart. 'Where does he live?'

'I don't know the address, I only know where he lives. I can show you.'

The man looked behind him. 'I've heard of this Terry geezer, heard a few tales about him. I'll use my guys and give him a visit. Because, let's face it, he is our prime suspect up to now – giving a shitty foot soldier the gear, getting more senior boys to nick it back off you and selling it on again. Prick. Well he's messed with the wrong buyers this time. Jayden, you've seen how quickly we found out where you live, so don't fuck with us, because the lot of your family will be punished if you are leading us up the garden path. We'll pay Terry a visit – see if your story checks out. You're going to show us where this Terry lives. If I get what

I want from him then you owe me fuck all – cash or weed, either's good, and it sounds like he's got more of it than you have. But you're my security. I need cash and plenty of it before you see the light of day, mate.'

Jayden tried to keep his cool, there was no way he wanted to antagonise these men. Not only was he beaten to a pulp, but he was outnumbered, unarmed. If he tried anything now, the next beating would likely be the one that killed him. And he certainly didn't feel like dying to protect Terry. Especially now he'd heard his captors theory that Terry might have set the whole thing up.

The man walked away and closed the door behind him. Jayden heard talking again outside the door but couldn't hear what was being said. A single bulky tear ran down his cheek. He was up shit street, and he knew it. 'Please, not my family, please,' he sobbed. He'd really done it this time.

Macy stared at the clock. The noise was doing her head in now and her eyes were near closing. She'd finally had a few hours' sleep but even those had been full of nightmares. Her mind was doing overtime. What could she do for the best? It was still too early to call and report her door, but not too early to call on friends. She picked up her phone and rang Bobby. She had a pang of disloyalty as she remembered how close she'd come to giving in and sleeping with him last night – cheating on Jay while he was being set up, thinking about the past when in the present her boy had been beaten up. But who else could she call? Bobby would know what to do. He was connected and he would give her real advice, the honest answers she needed.

'Hello Bob, it's me, Macy. I need your help. I don't want to say too much over the phone but, fuck me, Bobby, I'm near breaking point here.' She listened to the voice at the other end of the phone and nodded. 'Thanks, get to mine as soon as you can. My head's falling off here. I'll explain everything when you get here.' The call ended and Macy reached for her fags. 'Fuck, fuck, fuck,' she mumbled as she lit up.

Alex hobbled into the living room and she flinched at the sight of him. 'Oh my God, look at the state of you. Go and get back in bed, you need to rest. I'll string them bastards up myself when I get my hands on them. Who the fuck do they think they are coming in here and doing that to a fucking kid? Piss-takers, they are. I swear down to you now that they won't get away with this, not an earthly. An eye for an eye and all that. Since when has beef been brought home to your family? The rule of the street used to be that you fought each other. Never, ever, did they come to where your family was. They've crossed the line here. Trust me, heads will roll.'

Alex sat down on the sofa. 'Don't be daft, Mam. It's Dad you need to worry about. I'll be fine. It probably looks worse than what it is.'

Macy looked unconvinced. She took a long hard drag from her ciggie and blew out a puff of grey smoke. 'Your dad is fucked in the head getting us involved in this. How many times have I told him to keep his shit away from our door. He's fucked it this time. He's getting bin-bagged. I don't care if they do him in, it will save me a job.'

'Mam, you don't mean that. We need to find him. I'm scared what they will do to him. These men are animals.'

'I know son, I'm trying my best here. I've got Bobby, my friend, coming around. He will know what to do.'

'Who's Bobby?'

Macy was glad she'd always kept her work with Bobby on the down-low. 'Just someone I've known for a long time. An old friend.' She needed to get off this line of questioning. 'I'll ring someone over that door soon. I don't know if I should phone the housing, or just get old John from across the way to have a look at it. He's good at fixing stuff, and if I tell housing it was someone else who did it, they want to know the ins and outs of a cat's arsehole.'

Alex sat with a cushion in front of him, hugging it, holding it close to his aching body. Feeling comfort from it.

'Hello,' a male voice shouted from the hallway.

'Bobby, in here, come in.' Macy flicked her hair over her shoulder and tried to straighten her clothing. She didn't want anyone to see her looking as defeated and vulnerable as she felt right now – especially not Bobby. She sat up straight and took a deep breath before Bobby popped his head inside.

'What's gone on with your front door? And what's all that?' He gestured to the broken glass and broken pictures she'd left in a wastepaper bin.

Macy raised her eyebrows. 'Sit down. It's been a nightmare, Bob. On my life, when it rains in this family, it bleeding pours.' But she wasted no time pouring her heart out. 'That plonker of a boyfriend of mine has got himself in some serious shit. He's been doing a few drops, like I told you, to earn a few quid. And all I know is that some meatheads came through the door last night and messed our Alex up. They said they want money from us for missing drugs. They have got Jayden. And if you look at the state they left Alex in, I can't imagine what they've done to Jay.'

Bobby winced. He knew, if it was involving drugs, guns and knives would be the weapons of choice. His days of messing about with shooters were far behind him now and goosebumps appeared on his arms at only the thought of it. There was a reason why he'd chosen shoplifting as his line. Sure, he and his girls risked their freedom – but not their lives. Drugs were another level. It was a dangerous world where drugs were mentioned, and not one he ever wanted to get sucked into. But, yes, he was in the know, knew who could help, who could sort this crock of shit out.

He sat forward in his seat, hands cupped. 'So, why do they want money?'

'Jayden was doing a drop and apparently the drugs didn't reach the right people. He's saying he was set up and somebody had nicked the lot from him.'

Bobby screwed his face up, fidgeted, scratching at his head. 'You don't fuck about with people's shit, Macy.'

'I know that, Bobby, I'm not daft. And they want us to pay for it now. Like we have that sort of money hanging about the place. I've got about three hundred quid stashed upstairs, but that's it. I don't even know where to start. I went to see the guy he drops for last night, and he more or less told me that it's not his problem. He was more arsed that someone is messing about on his patch, challenging him. Taking his grafters down. He wants his merchandise back, wants to neutralise any threats – but he's not bothered about his workers.' She paused. 'Jayden could be in a ditch, lying dead somewhere.'

Bobby tried to hide the fact that he too couldn't give a flying shit where Jayden was. But he had to show some concern, show he was willing to help – he didn't want his best girl hurt. 'So, give me the name of the supplier, and I'll sort something out. You need to stay put, stay here in case he rings you or something.'

Macy sighed and ran her fingers through her hair. 'Bobby, they messed my lad up, but it could have been a lot worse. Look what they did to him. We're not talking about playground gangsters here, these men are fucking animals.'

Bobby looked around the front room, his first chance to see how Macy was living. Scruffy dated furniture, punch marks in the doors, old wooden flooring that had lifted up. It was clean enough but still it wasn't what he was expecting. Getting shut of Jayden might be the best thing that could happen for her. She deserved more than this.

Macy froze as her mobile phone started ringing. No caller ID. 'Fucking hell, Bobby, this could be them.'

Bobby sprang to his feet, ready to get on his toes if there was any danger lurking. He wasn't prepared to get cut up if the big boys were involved. 'Answer it, see what they are saying because, if they are saying they're coming here, we need to be gone. Fuck waiting about here, waiting for it to happen. Nah, we need to be smart with these guys. Macy, take Alex to your mam's and make sure he's safe.'

Macy's face dropped, panicking. Why on earth had she not done that last night? Why had she let her son be at risk again? She answered the call with a trembling voice. 'Hello.'

There was a male voice on the other end of the line. 'Tick tock, tick tock. I hope you have got my money ready, bitch. You're living on borrowed time.'

The call ended.

Macy felt her heart race, panic escalating. 'You're right. I need out of here, Bobby. They want money, they will be back, I know it. I need to get Alex out of here. Help me, Bobby. Give me a minute, let me grab some stuff together. I'll tell my mam the bailiffs are knocking, threatening to boom the door in, she should buy that.'

Alex looked unimpressed. 'I'm not going to my nana's. She won't let me take my PlayStation and I'm going nowhere without it.'

'You'll do as I say, cheeky bollocks. I'm not letting you stay here to get killed over a bleeding game. Stop giving me more pressure when I'm trying to keep you safe. These men will be back and, if they can do that to a kid, imagine what they are capable of next.'

Alex rubbed at his cold arms, hairs standing up on the back of his neck. Their voices still fresh in his mind, the destruction, the punches, his life flashing before his eyes. He knew it made sense to go. He was a sitting duck here. 'Well, phone my nana and tell her I'm allowed to bring my PlayStation. The last time I was there with her she made me watch all the soaps.' He raised a faint smile.

Bobby was curtain-twitching, uneasy. 'Right Macy, if you two are following my advice and shifting, I'm getting off too. Who's the guy who Jayden's working for?'

She followed him into the hallway, her voice low. There was no way she was letting her son know any names. The less he knew the better. 'It's Terry Dolan, I bet you know him.'

Bobby nodded; of course he knew Terry. A flash bastard who drove around the estate in his new whips and always dressed in designer clothes. 'Leave it to me. Let me ask around. Just get out of here and I'll bell you later.'

Macy walked him to the door. 'I'll get Alex gone, but then I'll get the door fixed before I go anywhere. I'm in no rush to get to my mam's, it will be like the Spanish Inquisition once she gets wind of this. Plus if they come for me – I'll show them never to come near a mother who's kid they've hurt…'

Chapter Twenty-Three

Leanne sat downstairs waiting for Gino to get up. He'd come home late, buzzing, and she'd had to pretend she was asleep. And now it was morning he hadn't stirred. All she seemed to do these days was sit about twiddling her thumbs waiting for him to say *jump*. This was no life, just sat in this house all the time. How on earth she had let herself get in this position was beyond her. She was a strong, hot-headed young woman who'd had a voice once, but he'd silenced it. Made her timid, made her weak. She'd lost who she was. She was fuming inside, wondering where he had got to the night before. A few hours, he'd told her he would be, not all bloody night. Plus, there were new girls knocking about on the Square lately, and she knew he'd have clocked them. If she heard one little whisper that he was playing about, she would leave his sorry arse, she told herself. Yes, she would tell him straight that she was nobody's fool. That was the trouble with the girls these days: they had no respect for nobody. They didn't even care if the guy was in a relationship, they seen them as a meal ticket for anything they could get out of them. So she'd got free booze from lads, and cigs and even weed, when she'd been single. But since she'd met Gino she would never do that again.

Gino's mother walked into the room and smiled at her. It was nice to see her when she wasn't rushing about to get ready for work, or cleaning. She was like a stick insect, cheeks drawn in at the sides. Usually, it was a quick hello and goodbye, never a full conversation.

But this time Leanne was eager to talk, to have a conversation with a person instead of sitting here watching TV on her own. 'Is it your day off today, Jean?'

Jean joined her on the sofa and pulled her light blue housecoat around her body tighter. She was all skin and bone. 'It sure is, and I'm not moving a muscle. I'm going to watch a film on Netflix and eat crap.'

Leanne chewed on the side of her nail, not sure what else to say. It's not like she'd met her more than three times. There was an awkward silence, neither of them speaking.

Jean lit a fag up and turned to face Leanne. 'Where's lord of the manor? Still in bed, I bet?'

'Yeah, he didn't come in until late and you know he likes his kip,' Leanne chuckled.

'You can say that again. I think he's bleeding nocturnal sometimes. He's always been a sleeper, late to bed and late to rise. Mind you,' Jean raised her eyebrows. 'He won't be doing that when the baby comes along, will he? Babies need twenty-four-hour care. You can't take the batteries out of them when you've had enough.'

Leanne placed her flat palm on her stomach, rosy-cheeked, smiling. 'I think Gino will be a great dad. He's not really said a lot about it, but I think he's getting his head around it, like I am.'

'I hope he's better than his own dad was at the father role. Waste of space, that wanker was. He was never there when I needed him, always out on the town. A womaniser too, always some tart hidden away.'

Leanne's eyes were wide. 'I'm so sorry, Jean. Gino hasn't really mentioned a lot about his dad, only that he never saw eye to eye with him when he was growing up.' She didn't know how to tell Jean she knew about the beating her ex had given her. She couldn't even think of the words without thinking of what Gino had done to her and she'd sworn to herself that, now the baby was on the way, she mustn't even think about that night. He was her man, wasn't he? He couldn't have forced her – she told herself she'd been over-dramatising things. Then blinked away the panic that always rose in her when her thoughts wandered that way.

Jean took a long hard drag from her ciggie. She kept her voice low, checking the door was closed behind her. 'He was an evil bastard. He liked to see me suffer, sick in the head, he was. I'm so glad I got away from him. Our Gino helped me do that.' She chewed on her bottom lip, nodded her head slowly, fist curling. 'I should have finished him off when I had the chance. He was on the floor once, pissed out of his head. Our Gino had punched him a few times to get him off me and had put him on his arse. It would have been so easy to whack the twisted sod over his head. It would have been goodnight Vienna then, wouldn't it?'

Leanne tried not to feel shocked. She wanted to know more. 'Does Gino still have contact with him?'

Of course she knew the truth but wanted to know if his mother knew.

'He did a few years ago. He turned up on the Square, Gino said, with his cap in hand trying to build bridges, saying he could help him make money.' Jean squashed her fag out in the ashtray and flicked her strawberry blonde hair over her shoulder. 'The man is all about himself, he's never given a fuck about anything else. I knew that if he wanted Gino back in his life it would be for his own selfish reasons. Anyway, let's talk about you and the baby. A little ray of hope this baby will be. Have you got any morning sickness yet?'

Leanne snuggled into the sofa. She'd not really had chance to open up to anyone about how she felt about being pregnant. Cooped up here at Gino's house, there was no one to chat to normally. There were so many questions she wanted to ask. And she wanted to talk about giving birth and what it felt like. 'Yeah, I've spewed up a few times, especially in the mornings. It can be anything that sets me off too. I hope it passes.'

'And what does your family think about you being pregnant?'

'My mam was shocked at first, and I suppose disappointed I'm so young, but I'm sure when she gets her head around it she will be buzzing for me. It's not like she was any different. I'm dreading telling my nana though, she'll go to town on me. She's like that, she holds nothing back, she says what she sees.'

Jean sniggered. 'Yes, once you get older you have no filter. My mam's the same. I think it comes with age, because some of the things my mam says to people, I could curl up and die.'

Leanne twiddled her hair at the side of her face. 'I just want us all to be happy. Me, Gino and the baby.'

Jean pulled her shoulders back in surprise. 'Erm, and me. Our Gino has already said you will be staying here long-term. He'll never leave home; he likes to make sure I'm safe.'

Leanne went bright red. 'Yes, we will stay with you until we get our own place. But we will want to start out on our own once we get enough money saved for our own place.'

Jean folded her arms tightly in front of her, sour expression. 'Not on my watch, lady. This is the first I've heard about my son moving out. I'll pull him about this later, shocked I am.'

Leanne realised she'd put her foot in it and tried to backpedal. 'Jean, we are staying with you. I'm only saying we can't live with you forever. No need to speak to Gino, is there? We don't want to upset him.'

Gino got up about three o'clock in the afternoon, the day already half gone. Leanne had ended up watching films with Jean and she was doing her best to get on the good side of her. She'd rubbed her up the wrong way for sure and she wanted the beef forgotten before Gino got wind of it.

Gino sat on the sofa and yawned. 'Mam, do me a brew please.'

Jean sprung up from her chair and headed to the kitchen. 'Do you want a bacon sarnie while I'm up on my feet, son?'

'Yeah, go on then, plenty of brown sauce on it too.'

Leanne's stomach rumbled and hoped her name might be called, but it never came. She was eating for two, but no one ever offered her anything and she knew Gino would think she was trying to get away if she went to the shops herself. Although it wasn't like she had two pennies to rub together, even if she could get out somewhere. So much for living the life of luxury. She was surrounded by all this show home bling, a world away from her mam's kitchen – but at least no one ever went without there. Macy would have gone without rather than not offer a guest something. To be fair, even Jayden and Alex would have been ashamed at that – there was no way any of her family members would make something to eat and sit there filling their faces when someone else was sat there with nothing.

Gino flicked the TV over and started to watch the boxing. He loved Tyson Fury and Leanne knew he often watched him in the early hours of the morning when he was fighting. He was like him, she thought: unpredictable, driven, ready to do anything to win. The smell of bacon lingering in the air distracted her. She licked her lips. Jean marched into the front room holding a plate in one hand and a cup in the other.

'There you go, son. The bacon is just how you like it, crispy.'

Gino didn't thank her or even take his eyes from the TV. He just reached over and took it from her hand. She went back into the kitchen and came back holding another plate. Leanne looked hopeful but Jean walked past her and sat down. Leanne didn't know where to look. She couldn't watch them eat, could she? Her temper was bubbling, and she wanted to say something – but she didn't know if this was a deliberate dig or whether they both just saw her as unimportant, not even worth noticing.

Gino licked his fingers and slid the plate onto the coffee table near him. 'Mint that, Mam.'

Leanne was still fuming, eyes fixed on the television, wondering whether, if she offered to wash up, she might be able to sneak herself something.

Jean coughed and thumped her chest which sounded like an old boiler, rattling and spluttering.

Gino was alert, watching her. 'Mam, you need to get to the doc's with that chest, it's not right. And smoking like a trooper isn't doing it any good either.'

She was gasping to get her breath. 'Nothing wrong with me. My food went down the wrong way, that's all.'

Gino smirked over at Leanne. 'On my life, she would never admit that she needs to give up smoking, it's always something else that's causing her to cough.'

Leanne agreed. 'Yes, everyone will have to watch their habits when the baby comes along, I suppose. I can't believe people didn't use to think twice about smoking near babies.'

Gino shot a look at Leanne. A look that told her he wasn't happy. Jean was taking deep breaths and getting ready to reply, but Gino beat her to it. 'Oi, don't ever tell my mam what she can and can't do in her own gaff. My queen does what she wants, isn't that right, Mam?'

'That's right, son. I smoked in the same room as you when you were a baby and it never done you any harm, did it?'

It was only Leanne who didn't see the funny side of it. There was no way any kid of hers was inhaling smoke and tobacco fumes all day long, not an earthly. She felt more trapped than ever in this place.

When Jean went upstairs, Leanne snuggled closer to Gino. 'I need to go home and get some stuff. My mam will be going sick trying to reach me, check on how the baby is doing. My battery has died and I don't have a charger for my phone here. I think it would be nice for you to come and meet her anyway. After all, you are family now.'

Gino looked down at his hands and cracked his fingers. 'Nah, not today. I'm busy.'

'Gino, you have to meet them sometime, so it's better sooner rather than later. My mam said she wants to meet you before I move out, so it's polite, isn't it? To come and tell her you are going to look after me and the baby.'

He bolted up, staring at her. 'Are you deaf or what? Man's got places to go, people to see. And tell your mam straight you don't need her permission to move out. You're not a kid.'

'Gino, I'm not saying things like that to my mam. I have respect for her, you know.'

'You don't need her anymore. You've told me yourself how much hard work she is – giving you curfews, calling up to see where you are. Forget it – I'll get you a new phone, new number. You're free of her. Plus it's me and the baby you should be thinking about now – not your old life.' His voice was firm, told her not to carry on speaking.

She twisted away from him, trying not to let him see how much his words stung. He got up out of his seat and stretched his arms over his head. 'Right, I'm going to get ready. Work calls. You better give my mam a hand cleaning up. It will be nice for her to get a bit of help around this place.'

Leanne turned to face him, words pushing from behind her teeth. 'I'm supposed to be resting. I've read it on the internet.'

He span round to face her. 'You cheeky bitch. Here's my mam running around after us and all you want to do is sit on your arse. I'll tell you something for nothing, should I? Things are going to change if you are living under this roof. There will be no more sitting down being waited on. In this house, the women look after the men, and the young look after the old. That puts you at the bottom of the heap but you'd better deal with it. It's time to grow up and fast.'

She hesitated, trying to get up the nerve to challenge him, tell him she was going home and never coming back. Her mouth was moving but no words came out. Her heart was beating like a speeding train. It couldn't be good for the baby. No, she backed off, not ready to pull the pin out of the grenade this time. He slammed the door as he left the room. A ball of emotions climbed up her throat and her eyes flooded with tears. She collapsed back onto the sofa and held her head in her hands. She was trapped, not just by him, but by his mother now too.

Chapter Twenty-Four

Alex sat in the chair with his arms folded tightly. 'Nana, you are not watching the TV, so why can't I set my game up? I'm bored out of my head sat here doing nothing.'

Grace wobbled over to him and snarled. 'Laddy, I want to know what really happened to your face. Until you tell me the truth, you're not getting any favours under my roof. Because I wasn't born yesterday. You would have to get up early in the morning to get one over on me, sunshine. Been there and worn the bloody T-shirt.'

'I've told you. I fell off my bike. I come in with a few scratches and black eyes and you're like bloody Vera, wanting to know the ins and outs.'

Grace studied her grandson, and she knew he was lying: no eye contact, shuffling about and messing with his fingers, like he always did when he was trying to pull the wool over her eyes. She sat down, leant forward with her old hands on her knees. 'And why has your mam sent you here? Come on, I'll get to the bottom of this, so you may as well tell me everything before she gets here. If I hear you've been giving your mother a hard time again then I'll bloody flatten you myself. I might have a walking stick, but I can still give you a clout. Your mam said something about the bailiffs coming but I'm not buying that story. I believe in tough love – so come on, spill…'

Macy locked the front door behind her. Her neighbour had fixed it the best he could, and she'd bunged him twenty quid for his time. She started to walk down the path and she could hear a car pulling into the close. It screeched to a halt at the end of the path and the back door opened on a black Mercedes. Whoever it was didn't wait about – dumped something, revved the engine and sped off again. Macy couldn't even catch the number plate; her eyes shot to what they'd left on the grass verge. It didn't look like the kind of usual white van you saw dumping rubbish, or someone offloading an old mattress. Her eyes squinted as she tried to make out what it was. Slowly, she approached it with caution. Her jaw dropped, her heart in her mouth.

She ran to Jayden and rolled him onto his side. She could see instantly he was in a bad way. Dried blood clung to his cheeks, his nose still trickling blood, even his knuckles were full of cuts and bruises. But he was still warm to the touch and breathing, even if shallowly.

'Jayden, can you hear me, Jay, who did this to you?' she sobbed. She'd cursed him for bringing trouble to their door but she'd never wanted to see him hurt.

Jayden moved slightly. His voice was low. 'Get me inside, hurry up before they come back.'

She scooped her arms under his and tried her best to move him. He was like a dead weight. 'Jay, you're going to have to help me. I can't move you on my own. Wait here and I'll see if anyone's about to give me a hand.'

'No, don't get anybody else. I'll try and move, just give me a minute.'

Macy stood over him, quivering, bottom lip trembling. 'You're in a right state. I need to get you seen by someone.'

His voice was shaking. 'No, I'll be fine.' His body moved and, with every bit of strength he had left, he got onto his knees. Macy was by his side now, helping him up, looking around, making sure the men who did this to him weren't parked up, watching. Slowly, slowly, she took him back into the house.

With shaking hands, she locked the door behind her. 'Tell me who did this? They came here last night and wasted Alex, he was a mess. He's black and blue, but thank God he's going to be ok. I've sent him to my mum's. Jayden, you need to speak to me and shine some light on this. We are not safe, none of us. Whoever these people are, I know they want the drugs, or the money.'

Jayden sat propped upright in the armchair. His head drooped. 'I was dropping off the stuff and from nowhere they ambushed me. A man, tattoos down his arm, don't remember anything else about him. More men were with him and they wanted to know who I was working for, who the big man was. They kicked the fuck out of me, saying I had set it all up. Fuck, Macy, I swear down to you, I was set up. I don't have a clue what happened.'

Macy sat on the coffee table facing him, stressed. 'And what did you tell them?'

'Nothing at first, but they kept going at me, punching, kicking, held a knife to me. I seen my life flash before me. On my life I thought I was a gonner.'

'So, why did they let you go?'

Jayden's voice dropped to barely more than a whisper. 'I had to show them where Terry lived, grass him up. I'm a Judas.'

Macy covered her mouth with both hands. So, he'd grassed? She never had him down for that. She always thought that, if someone had held a gun to his head, he would still keep his loyalties to his boys. This was bad. Terry was a name, not someone you messed around with. Sure she'd threatened Terry with doing the same but she knew well enough that if she'd actually gone through with it she'd be a marked woman. And of course, she'd been to see him, told him they had Jayden. Once the gang came knocking on Terry's door, it wouldn't take him long to put two and two together to know that Jayden was the one who sold him out. The shame, everyone would know sooner or later, and their family home would not be safe. Grasses were seen as the lowest of the low in the area and under no circumstances could you snitch. It was the law round here, street rules.

Macy sighed, realising that Jayden was living on borrowed time, a dead man walking.

'I'll go and see Terry again. Tell him you had no choice, remind him he would do the same in your position.'

Jayden froze, held his head to the side. 'Again? Why, have you been to see him, you daft cow?'

'I knew the drops were for him, and if someone comes through our door, kicking ten tons of shit out of our son because of him, then he can help sort it out. It's his mess, not fucking ours.'

Jayden closed his eyes. 'Are you fucking right in the head? You've fucked it all up now. He'll know it's me. I could have blended it, said I knew fuck all about it. But now he'll know for sure. You just don't think, do you?'

Macy went bright red, temper bursting. 'Our son was terrified. I didn't know if you were even coming back alive. I'm not having anyone coming to our house threatening any of us. You know Terry takes the piss out of you anyway. What, he pays you a poxy couple of hundred quid and he sits on his arse raking in the cash, while it's you who's taking all the risks. I told you not to get involved with him, but did you listen?' she gasped. 'Did you 'eck.'

Jayden gripped the side of the sofa and shakily got to his feet. His legs nearly buckled, and he had to take a few seconds before he found his balance. 'Fuck off, will you. Like I need you pecking me head. Look at me, Macy, look at the fucking state of me and you don't even care.'

'If I didn't care, I wouldn't be here. If I didn't care, I would not have gone to Terry's to tell him to sort this out.

The man is big enough to sort anything out that comes his way. You live by the sword; you die by it.'

Jayden limped out of the room, and she could hear him stumbling up the stairs, banging against the walls. She sat looking at the wall, thinking. This was a nightmare and the sooner it was over the better. But some nightmares only got worse when you opened your eyes. She knew she couldn't sort things out alone. And if she wanted any kind of future, it was going to mean going back to her past again. She reached for her phone, and dialled Bobby once more.

Chapter Twenty-Five

Bobby sat on the road facing Terry's house. He'd been there for over an hour and watched what was going on. Shit was going down and the moment he spotted the black Merc speeding down the road he knew exactly where they were heading. Even when the men left the gaff only a few minutes later he still kept his face low and stayed well out of sight. He'd had his taste of this life many years ago and he promised himself he would never go back into that world again. That world was dangerous, could end your life in the blink of an eye, and it put anyone and everyone you loved in the line of fire too.

Slowly, Bobby opened his car door. Always looking over his shoulder, making sure he was safe. After all, he was only here for a favour, this wasn't his mess and, if it wasn't for Macy, he would have given this beef a wide berth. The sooner Jayden was out of the picture the better. He brought nothing to the table, and Bobby couldn't stomach him. He walked up to the front door and inhaled deeply, his chest expanding. You couldn't show a moment's weakness with guys like this. He and Terry had seen each other around for years. He knew Terry would respect the fact that he'd always stayed out of his business. They were two professionals in different games. But if Terry thought Bobby was sticking his nose in where it wasn't wanted, then he'd not think twice before turning on him. He gave a quick knock on the door and stood back.

Terry opened the door and he looked flustered. 'What's up, Bobby?'

Bobby gulped and coughed to clear his throat. 'Can I have a word, mate? A friend of mine needs a bit of help and I'm hoping you can sort it. Her fella Jayden has got himself in some shit or so I believe.'

Terry jerked his head forward. 'Come in. Yeah, I know all about that useless turd. I've just had a few heavies here at my door demanding money and all that. That prick lost the gear, so it's his debt, not fucking mine. He must have sent them here, give them my address. I'll slice him up now myself for that, watch this space.'

Bobby shook his head, followed him inside and looked behind him as Terry closed the front door. He led him into the front room. 'Park your arse there, mate. Do you want a beer?'

'Yeah, go on then,' Bobby replied.

Terry passed him a bottle of cold Budweiser and sat down. 'The guys that took Jayden are the ones that were buying my gear. Of course, we'd arranged it all on WhatsApp – never by number, no route back to me. You know how it goes. I trust my deputies to find new clients. These ones are pricks from Blackpool. Apparently, they have foot soldiers working down here in Manny – they're the heavies who showed up just now. You should have heard the shit they were saying, telling me they want money from me. I told them straight they were getting fuck all, and when I pulled the shooter out they were out of here like rats from a drainpipe.'

Bobby swigged a mouthful of beer and nodded. 'Yeah, I agree Jayden needs filling in, especially if he's grassing you up, but Macy is a good friend of mine and I would ask for you to keep her out of the picture. We go back years and she's a good girl. Do whatever you want to that wanker, but please keep it away from her door.'

'Yeah, she came here. She seemed alright, but you know how shit rolls, mate. I won't put a price on her head, I'll tell my lads she's straight, but still, if she's involved with him, then I can't promise she won't get hurt in the crossfire.'

Bobby knew when to keep his mouth shut. Terry was a force not to be messed with. He'd heard stories about this man that would make your toes curl. No, there was no way he wanted to get on the wrong side of this man. After some more chit-chat, Bobby stood up and offered his hand to Terry. He'd done his duty by Macy, the rest was down to Jayden's poor choices. From the corner of his eye, he could see a silver pistol on the side. A chill crept over his body, and he wanted gone from this house. His life was nothing like this now and the world Terry was living in was not a place Bobby ever wanted to be back in. 'There's my hand Terry, there's my heart, take it easy mate and thanks for sorting this shit out. Just think on about Macy and her kids. It's not her fault that wanker has fucked up. By all means kick the fuck out of him but let her have a bit of peace. She's had a hard time lately and she's sound.'

Terry shook his hand and walked him to the door. 'Seems like you have a bit of a soft spot for this girl, Bobby. Keep it real, mate, stay safe,' he chuckled as he let him out of the front door.

Bobby sat in his car and got on his mobile phone. 'Hiya Macy, come and meet me at the King's Head. I've been to see Terry.' He listened to her reply and was clearly masterminding something as she told him Jayden had landed at the house.

Once the call was over, he got back on the blower. The phone rang and he could see Terry in the living room going to answer it. 'Tez mate, I'm still outside, just heard from Macy. Jayden is back at his gaff. Macy is coming to meet me now at a boozer and nobody is in the house. Ideal time to capture the grass, isn't it?' The call ended seconds later and Bobby looked at himself in the rear-view mirror. 'Bye bye, dickhead,' he sniggered.

Bobby sat thinking for a few seconds and sent a text message:

Hurry up with the cash

He pressed the send button and smiled again at his reflection in the mirror. It was all turning out pretty damn nicely.

Terry had wasted no time in gathering his boys together. He met them in a café in Harpurhey. A place he felt safe, a place he could trust people in. He could see the surrounding area through the large window, see anyone coming, be prepared. Not that many people would risk trying something when you looked at who Terry was surrounded with. These men looked as hard as nails and not people you would like to meet on a dark night. One guy, who sat next to Terry, had a large scar running down the side of his right cheek. A sign that he was game as fuck for anyone who stepped in his way.

Terry hushed his men down. 'This firm need teaching a lesson. Who the fuck do they think they are, coming to my manor and shouting the odds off at me? It's a good job I was armed, otherwise I dread to think what would have gone on. They said they will be back.' He glared as he smashed his clenched fist onto the table. 'But I'm not going to sit about waiting for that to happen, no way. I want to sort this out as soon as possible. We use our contacts in Blackpool, find out who these muppets really are. The lackeys that came to threaten me were only their local boys – I want the guys at the top. Not just who was expecting to receive the delivery – I need to know who the money men are. And when I find out, I will take all their doors from their hinges, batter their mams, batter their dads. Scare the fuck out of their whole families. Who do they think they are, sending shit to my home? The gloves are off and I'm not taking any prisoners. My job was to send the food to them. Not my problem if someone has them over, is it? But first, we have got a call to make. Get me Jayden from his gaff. Drag the bastard by his hair if you have to. I want to know what he told them, see if his time in their company means he knows who these pricks are and who is their main man. Nobody fucks with Terry Dolan, fucking nobody.'

Chapter Twenty-Six

G ino walked onto Tavistock Square and looked around with his head held high. This was his domain, his manor, and God help anyone who tried to take this away from him. His dad ran the area back in the day, or so he told him, and it was now up to him to keep up the family name. Since he'd been back in touch with him, his dad had made a couple of plays for taking this patch back, saying he could help make the drugs sales bigger. But Gino had told him straight, he needed no help, this was his Square now, his rules. His old man had told him straight: trust nobody. Money was power and there would always be someone ready to take him down. But Gino liked the fact that people underestimated him, wrote him off as little more than a kid. It had given him a streetwise head, always on the lookout for trouble. He'd had to come up through his world by himself, and he was the man now. He'd show anyone that he was a force not to be messed with. This was what it was about, this was the life he'd chosen, and selling drugs was only the start of building his empire. A text message made his phone buzz in his pocket. He ignored it. Probably another message from Leanne chatting shit, asking him how long he would be, who he was with. The girl was becoming a pain in the arse. He stopped as he saw her friend Kerry walking across the Square on her own. He smirked and whistled over at her. Kerry turned to him and looked puzzled. He jogged towards her, smiling. This was a turn up for the books and she looked confused.

'Yo, not seen you in time. Why haven't you been chilling with Leanne?'

Kerry huffed, looking him up and down. 'Like she's not already told you?'

'Nah, she's not said a word. What's gone on? Have you two fell out or what?'

She placed her hand on her hip before she began. 'What's with all this being nice to me then? I thought you hated my guts, hated Leanne being anywhere near me?' This was a different Gino than she was used to seeing. He was actually breaking a smile, using a softer voice.

'I never said I hated you, just hated the company you were keeping. I don't like Leon and he doesn't like me, no love lost.'

'Well, you don't need to be worried about him anymore. We have broken up. He liked chilling with his mates more than me, so I told him to make a choice, and he did. So I'm riding solo now. Men can piss right off for all I care. I'm done with them all.'

Gino chuckled. 'I'm not going to say sorry for hearing that. The guy was a tosser and word on the street was he was sticking it up anyone who would have him anyway.' Gino checked he was still alone and moved in closer to her. 'Leanne is doing my head in too. Too fucking needy, wanting to be with me all the time. She's pregnant, not on a life support machine. Every two minutes she's belling my phone out.'

Kerry tried to hide the sadness in her eyes. She missed her best friend, needed a shoulder to cry on, and yet Leanne was at the beck and call of this tosser. Three weeks she'd been split up from Leon, and all she'd done was sit in her bedroom moping about. Heartache was the worst kind of pain ever and, if there was a pill for it, she would have overdosed on it. She and Leanne should have been hanging out, making each other laugh – instead they'd let two boys who thought they were men break their hearts.

Gino lifted her hair up and looked at her, aware she was upset. 'Can we start again, Kez? I mean Leanne is your best friend and we should be able to get on. What do you think?'

Well, this was a surprise, but still she didn't trust him, she didn't trust any man anymore. 'Where is Leanne? Is she at her house? I might go and see her, see if we can straighten this shit out. It was only a daft argument. One we should have been able to sort out, but it got out of hand and we both ended up saying things none of us meant.' She didn't let on that the reason they'd fought was her real opinion of Gino himself.

Gino rubbed his hands together. 'Do you fancy grabbing a drink? We can go in the café down the road. If you're lucky I will treat you to some dinner.'

Kerry raised a smile. Taking a few seconds, she nodded her head. 'Yeah, you can make up for the way you treated me. I'll have a cake too, a big chocolate one to help heal my broken heart.'

Gino patted her shoulder. 'Come on then, I might be able to stretch to a cake too.'

Sat in the warmth of the café, finishing off the huge slab of cake Gino had bought her, Kerry leant back in her chair. Gino was staring at her; she'd caught him a few times now just looking at her. She had to say something: he was spooking her out. 'Why do you keep gawping at me? Have I got food on my chin or something?' She fidgeted, wiping her hand across her mouth.

'No, I just never noticed how pretty you are.'

She didn't know where to look. 'Stop messing about, Gino. I know I'm a bit down but you don't have to throw compliments at me. I'll bounce back, I always do.'

His voice was low, making sure the two lads on the next table didn't hear him. 'Being serious. You should put in for modelling or something. Your eyes are amazing. I've never noticed them before.'

She joked. 'You won't when you are hating on me, will you?' She flicked her hair over her shoulder and took a sip from her drink. 'So, how're things with Leanne? I bet you're dead excited that she's having a baby, aren't you?'

'Erm, so-so.'

'Wow, you should be more excited than that. Leanne was over the moon. Personally, I would never want a kid at this age, and I told her that. I want to travel the world, live my life, not be tied down with a crying baby, changing shitty nappies all the time. I couldn't think of anything worse.'

Gino nodded. 'You have got your head screwed on, haven't you? If I'm being honest, I was not ready to be a dad, but now I'm getting my head around it, it is what it is. Leanne is moving in with me too. I want her where I can see her, make sure she's safe.'

Kerry examined Gino in more detail. He wasn't fooling her. 'You need to chill out with Leanne. She's a good girl, you know, and I know she will look after the baby. I'm not going to lie, I told Leanne I thought you had her on a tight leash. You know, a bit too controlling.' She watched his reaction, waiting for him to blow but he never did.

'Maybe I am. I'm just a protector, that's all. I have my reasons.'

Kerry nodded. 'Well, that's good to hear. She's my best friend and I would hate anyone to hurt or upset her.'

'I'm not that kind of guy, Kerry. I hope you can see that after today?'

Kerry wasn't going to be won over that easily. 'My days of listening to men are over, Gino. I thought I could smell a rat a mile away. But I'm blinded lately, maybe that's why I never have any luck with the men.'

Gino laughed out loud. 'Why don't you come around to my yard tonight and chill for a bit? I'll get us a few beers in, and we can have a smoke if you want?'

Kerry was over the moon that she was going to see Leanne again, and that Gino had ended his beef with her. Maybe today was a good day after all. 'That would be great. I've got so much to tell her. What time, or should I come with you now?'

Gino shook his head. 'Nah, you're better off coming later. She's tired a lot lately so let her have a sleep and that. I'll tell you what, meet me on the Square about ten bells and I'll take you to mine. Here,' he dug his hand into his jacket pocket and pulled out a twenty-pound note from a wad of cash. 'Here, get some beers in, meet me here at ten like I said, and I'll sort some nice weed out for us. You do blaze, don't you?'

Kerry held her head back laughing. 'If it's free, I'm smoking it.'

'Right, I've got to get going, I've got shit to sort out. I'll catch you later.' Gino stood up and nodded his head at her. He was gone.

Kerry didn't leave the table straight away. She sat there looking about, digesting everything he had said to her. Could a leopard change its spots?

Leanne sat watching the television, bored as ever. Jean walked into the room, shot a look over at the TV and snarled, 'Oh, turn this load of shit off, will you. I don't know how you watch these reality shows, they do my head in. Showing their tits and arses all over the screen, they need to bleeding cover up.'

Leanne clenched her teeth. There was no pleasing her. She passed the remote over to Jean.

Jean turned to face her and made sure she had her attention. 'Me and Gino have been a team for a very long time. Just the two of us. I know by your face that you don't like that fact, but that's the way we are. If things are going to work out with us both, then we need to work together. My Gino is all that I have in my life and I'd bend over backward to make him happy. I hope you will do the same?'

'Yeah, of course I will. It's hard for me too, Jean. I wanted to stay at home, but it was Gino who said I have to live here with him.'

Jean rolled her eyes. 'And that's right. You are having his baby and he needs to make sure you are looking after his child.'

'Of course I will look after the baby, but he does not own me, Jean. I should be free to come and go when I want. I feel like he wants me to stay in all the time, lock me away from the world.'

'Does he hell. Our Gino is not like that, he's not controlling, so don't let me hear you saying he is. Maybe you're a bit touchy because your hormones are all over the place. Pregnant women are like that. One minute they are up in the air and the next they are down in the dumps. You need to get plenty of rest, so enjoy putting your feet up while you can, because when the baby comes along it will be hard work. You will be cooking, cleaning, and looking after a baby too. You won't get a minute to yourself.'

Leanne slumped, reality seemed to be hitting home. If this was a glimpse of her life in the future, she didn't want it. How on earth had she let herself be dragged into this kind of relationship? When she'd imagined it in her head, she was happy, nesting, spending hours and hours with Gino and he was forever touching the child growing inside her stomach, planning their lives together. When, in fact, he didn't give a toss. She was stuck at home with his mum, and his life was all about him and what he wanted. Once, she'd mentioned going back to college after the baby and he'd snapped at her telling her that no stranger was going to be watching his baby while she was out all day galivanting. So, what did she have to look forward to? Nappies, sleepless nights, a boyfriend who never let her go out and a mother-in- law who thought the sun shone right out of her son's arse. And even this miserable prospect was a best-case scenario. She'd tried to forget Gino's violent side, hoped he'd stopped that as he thought about fatherhood. But what would happen when the baby was here – crying, not sleep-ing? She knew everyone found it hard adjusting – what if he snapped?

Panic set in, the colour draining from her face. She bolted up from her seat and took long deep breaths. She hadn't had a panic attack in years but remembered all the signs. She knew she couldn't explain to Jean or even ask permissions. She had to go. Now.

'I'm going to see my mam, Jean. If Gino comes home tell him I'll be back later.'

She grabbed her coat from the back of the sofa and darted into the hallway, trying to get her breathing under control, to stop her pulse racing. She needed to be out of here, as far, far away from Jean and her son as she could possibly be.

Leanne ran down the street, never looking behind her, never turning back once. Tears streamed down her face. Once she found a place to sit, she sat down and sobbed her heart out, curling her arm over her stomach. This was a big mess. She needed to tell her mam what was going on. Tell her the truth about her abusive partner. She would protect her, tell her how she could fix her life. Gino was not who he made out to be, and she had got in deeper and deeper before she knew what was happening. And now she was trapped in a big sticky web, unable to escape. Leanne wiped the tears away from her eyes with her sleeve. She had to move from here, people were looking at her now like she had a screw loose. She stood up and kept her head down. There was no way she wanted anybody asking if she was alright. Because, the way she was feeling, she would have let them have it both barrels. She was going home, where she felt safe, where she could relax with her family. And, if Gino didn't like it, he could take a running jump. This was her life and she needed to take control. But to do that she needed to clear her head somewhere where he wasn't breathing down her neck, ruling her, making her decisions. She needed her mam. She would help her, tell her what to do.

Leanne turned on to her street and noticed a few of the neighbours out in their gardens. Gossiping they were, whispering, looking over at her. The next door neighbour stopped her before she entered the house. 'Be careful going inside there, love. Your dad has just been dragged out kicking and screaming by some men. I would have helped him, but it was too late, they'd already slung him in the back of the car. What's he been up to then? Because those men seemed pretty pissed off with him? I wouldn't like to be in his shoes. He was shouting and screaming that it wasn't him, whatever he'd done.'

Leanne shoved her key into the door, noticing the wood was all chipped and the paint scuffed. It looked like someone had kicked the thing in. She was determined not to show she was worried, and replied. 'Not got a clue. You know what our house is like: never a dull moment.'

She was inside the house now, door firmly shut behind her, but the damage was even clearer from the inside. The door frame was splintered, plaster hanging off the wall. This was bad, really bad. She cursed herself for letting Gino talk her into leaving her phone dead for so long. But surely someone would have come to find her if Jayden was in real trouble? Who had he pissed off now? And more importantly, where was everyone else?

'Mam, hello, is anyone in?' Slowly, she paced the hallway, aware that somebody could jump out on her at any second. 'Hello, is anybody in?' she shouted again. Still no reply. She couldn't remember the house feeling this cold or quiet. Her hand slowly opened the living room door. Nothing. A couple of pictures were missing and it looked like her mam'd had a good tidy-up but nothing more. She walked further into the living room and started to relax. The neighbours had probably got it wrong again. They were always doing that. Nosey they were, nothing better to do each day except look at other people's lives and judge them.

Leanne ran upstairs and checked each bedroom. 'Alex, are you in?' She opened his bedroom door and scanned around the room. Now this was strange. Her brother was always home, playing on his PlayStation, flopped on the sofa watching television, filling his face. Even odder, his PlayStation wasn't anywhere. She wondered if he and Jayden had had some big falling out. But why would someone be after Jay if it was just a domestic?

She went into her own bedroom and plugged her mobile phone on charge. After a few seconds, all her messages started to come through. There was message alert after message alert. Sitting on the floor near to where her phone was plugged in, she started to read the texts from her mum, from her brother:

> **Please ring me. Need you.**

> **Leanne you need to come home, where the hell r u?**

> **Leanne ring me.**

The messages were all more or less the same. She rang her mother's number and listened to the ringing tone, no answer. Sat thinking for a few seconds. She stood up and walked one way then the other. Was she even safe in the house anymore? What the hell had gone on and who were the men who had taken Jayden away? She needed out of here, and quick.

Leanne stood looking at her nana's front door. It all seemed quiet on the western front. No need to knock, she just walked inside. 'Nana, it's only me.' She walked into the front room and smiled at Grace. At last, a familiar face. 'Have you seen my mam, Nana?'

Grace sat upright in her seat and held her head high. 'Have I bleeding hell. Alex is here all full of cuts and bruises, and he's telling me he fell or some cock-and-bull story. I don't believe him, so I hope you are going to tell me the truth and not insult my intelligence too? Even your mother fed me some line about the bailiffs. So you'd better persuade your brother here to tell all.'

Leanne shot a look over at Alex. 'Wow, what's happened to you?'

He wriggled about on the chair and gave her a look that told her not to delve deeper. 'No big drama like she's making out. I fell, that's all. Came off my bike.'

Leanne sat down next to him and held his chin in her hand. 'Looks sore, did you go to the 'ozzy?'

'Nah, just a few scratches, nothing to worry about now.'

Leanne turned to face her nana, but before she could speak, Alex piped up.

'Why don't you tell nana your news? She's going to find out soon anyway. It's better coming from you than someone else, isn't it?'

Leanne went white. She glared at her brother. What a bleeding stirrer he was.

Grace was alert, arms folded. 'So, come on then, like he said, tell me.'

Leanne gulped. This was not what she needed right now. But Grace wouldn't let up. 'I'm pregnant.'

Grace looked taken aback, not sure if she'd heard her right. 'What did you say?'

'I said I'm pregnant. Not a big thing, Nana. I'm seventeen.' She knew she was going to get an earful.

Grace pointed her crooked finger over at her granddaughter. 'Are you right in the bleeding head, girl? I thought you knew better than that. How many times have we spoke about young girls having babies? And, since when was you having sex, and who with? I didn't even know you had a boyfriend.'

Leanne's voice was low, ashamed that she had let her nana down. Grace was right, in the past they had both sat there and slagged off young girls having babies. She realised now how easy it was to make assumptions about other people's lives. But here she was today in the same boat as them. Her head was going a hundred miles an hour and she could have burst out crying right there and then. 'Nana, please don't go on at me. My head is not in a good place at the moment.'

'Your head hasn't been in the right place since you dropped your knickers, love. What happened to using a condom or being on that pill or something?'

Alex wasn't smiling anymore and knew he had to bail his sister out. 'Nana, chill now. Don't have a go at her, it should be a happy time.'

Grace spoke through clenched teeth. 'I had high hopes for her, I did. You ask Marjorie next door; I always said our Leanne would have a great career one day. Well, that's gone tits up now, hasn't it?'

Leanne was sick to death of people making her feel rotten. She screamed, 'Alright, for crying out loud! I get that you're upset. I don't even know if I'm having the baby yet, so please get off my back. It's still early days.'

Alex looked surprised. He thought this story was cut and dry, what had changed? He patted his sister's arm and tried to make up for letting the cat out of the bag. He knew she needed some brotherly love. 'I'll brew up. Nana, do you want a cup of tea?'

Grace held her head back, looked at the ceiling and rolled her eyes. 'Go on then, put a splash of that brandy from the kitchen side in it. In fact, put two in. I need something to steady my nerves. I'll just nip to the loo.'

Alex watched her leave and spoke to his sister. 'Soz about that. I only said it to stop her giving me the third degree. There's stuff you need to know, but Nan can't hear it. But what's this about not having the baby? I thought you were happy?'

Leanne knew she needed to get this all off her chest. If she'd still been talking to Kerry, she could have counted on her, but she didn't know if she'd even answer her call. She lifted her head and her eyes clouded over. 'I'm not sure anymore. Gino is not who I thought he was. He's like a jailer not a boyfriend.'

Alex's nostrils flared. 'If he's laid one finger on you I'll stab the bastard up.'

'No, he's not touched me. Not–' She stopped herself just in time before it all spilled out. 'It's all this living at his house and that with his mam. I'm not cut out for that house, she's nasty. I need some time on my own to think. But never mind me. Quick, tell me what's gone on with you. I have just been home, and the guy over the road said Jayden had been dragged out of the house by some heavies.'

Alex covered his face with his hands. Leanne pulled them away. 'Tell me now, what the fuck is happening? Quick, before she gets back.'

Alex was trembling. 'My dad has had someone fuck him over. He was on a drop and someone ambushed him, roughed him and nicked the drugs. Then the original buyers came to our house and kicked the fuck out of me. I didn't know who the hell they were at the time though. I thought I was a dead man. They said they had him and that they wanted money from us, otherwise they would do him in. My mam went around to some guy's house who he was dropping for but I've not heard anything else since. She carted me here and said she would sort it out. I didn't even know they'd let him go. So who's taken him this time?'

Leanne stood up, delving her hand in her pocket for her mobile phone. She tried ringing her mam again, still no reply. 'Fuck me,' she mumbled under her breath.

Alex gave her the look and made sure she sat back down. Grace was back in the room, and she could tell they had been talking, she wasn't daft.

'You can say what you want about me, kids, but I say what I see. I've just had a little think and we can't change you being tubbed, can we? I'll just have to live with it.'

Leanne shook her head. 'I'm sorry if I've let you down, Nana. I didn't set out to get pregnant. It was an accident. I was going to go for the pill but I didn't get there in time. I'm a fool and I know it without you rubbing salt in the wounds.'

Grace looked over at Leanne. She wasn't a bad girl, she always had a good head on her shoulders. It was time to make amends. 'I'm sorry, cock. I can't help my mouth sometimes. I think its these bloody blood pressure tablets I'm on. I don't seem to have a filter anymore. If you're happy then so am I. I'll tell Marjorie to let the shoplifters know and I'll start getting some bits for the baby. Is your mam happy too?' She raised her eyebrows, waiting on a reply.

'She was like you, Nana. Upset at first, but once she thought about it, she was coming around to the idea. But the more I think about it, the more I'm not sure what I should do.'

Grace sat back, confused. 'What, you are thinking about getting an abortion?'

Leanne couldn't meet her nana's gaze; it was something going through her mind and even saying it scared the life out of her. But she was a woman with a choice, nothing to be ashamed of. 'Nana, I'm a young girl, and me and Kerry have always said we wanted to travel the world, work away, make great memories, but if I keep the baby, I'll never get the chance to do it again. Not just because I'd have a kid, but because I'd be part of the Gallaghers, and they'd never let me out of their sight. At first, I was all up for it, but now I'm over the shock I'm not so sure. I can only just look after myself and the thought of being responsible for a baby terrifies me.'

Grace sucked on her bottom lip. She knew exactly how her granddaughter felt. She'd been in the same boat when she was younger, had to make a choice. Sadness filled her face as she spoke. 'A woman has the right to choose. Forget what's on the news. A child is a big commitment, I know that more than anyone. If you want my advice, sit down and think about you, no one else, just you, because no matter what your boyfriend is telling you now, you will be the one doing everything, not him. So sit down and think.'

Leanne nodded. Her nana was right. This was her body, her child and her decision. But what about Gino? How would he take the news? Leanne nodded again, slowly. She'd had enough of him and his orders. She was going to take her life back in her own hands.

Chapter Twenty-Seven

Macy sat in the pub with Bobby. He said they needed somewhere quiet to talk without people listening in. Macy was eager to get talking. 'So, tell me again, did Terry say he was going to sort this mess out or what?'

Bobby swigged a mouthful of his lager. 'Yes, like I said, you just need to keep away from your house for a few days in case things kick off. What about getting a hotel, keeping under the radar?'

'I can't Bobby, the kids, what about them? I can't even reach our Leanne – her phone's been dead for days and then finally I got a missed call this morning after endless messages. I wanted to see if you'd heard anything, then I need to call her right back. How do I even start to tell her all this?'

'If she's anything like you, Mace, she's a tough kid. Tell her Jayden's brought shit to your door but you're sorting it. Once they are looked after, we can concentrate on everything else.'

'Right, let me just go and ring her and see where she is.'

Bobby moved his legs so she could get past him. As he watched her leave the bar, he went on his phone and started to look for a hotel room in the area. She would want him to stay with her for sure, someone to protect her. He rubbed his hands together as he imagined himself snuggled up next to her for the night. Finally: he'd waited so long for this.

Outside the pub, Macy pressed the mobile phone to her ear. 'Leanne, bleeding hell, why haven't you been answering your phone? Are you OK? Where are you?' She listened to the reply and walked about the car park. 'Go outside with your phone so Nana can't hear you. I don't want her knowing anything. You know what she's like, she won't settle if she knows troubles brewing.' Macy spoke with her daughter and filled her in on the full story, barely leaving a moment for her daughter to get a word in edgeways. 'I want you and Alex to stay at Nana's tonight. I need to make sure none of you are in any danger. Ring me if anything happens or you hear anything. I'm trying to sort things out at my end and the minute I hear anything I will let you know.'

Leanne finally got chance to speak. 'Mam, I went home before I came here, and Les from over the road said men had come in the house and took Jayden. I don't know if he's lying but that's what he said.'

Macy stood thinking for a few seconds. Les was a right gossipmonger and he was forever making stories up about residents in the area. He was a couple of butties short of a picnic and nobody ever believed a word he said. 'Oh, ignore him, love. Jayden was in bed when I left him. He's probably pissed off to Simon's to get stoned, if I know him.'

The call ended and Macy stood looking at up at the grey clouds hung overhead. At least her children were safe for now. She just needed to make sure Jayden was out of the firing line. Les was probably getting confused and thinking about the other night when the heavies got Alex. Jayden would be fine. She dialled his number and it rang out. Even Jayden couldn't get abducted twice in the same week, surely? Yeah, he was probably out necking a lager to drown his sorrows – that was more his style. He was probably getting high somewhere to numb his bruises.

Macy walked back into the pub and plonked down next to Bobby. 'Fucking hell. Leanne's fine, but someone's told her Jay's not. I think I'm going to have a nervous breakdown.'

He reached over and started to massage her shoulders, his fingers kneading the nape of her neck. 'You need a good massage. I'm good at them, you know?'

She relaxed as his fat fingers dug into her flesh. She felt the tension in her shoulders loosening. 'Bobby, I hope all this turns out right. Jayden is a lot of things, but he doesn't deserve all this. I need him to be alright. He's not answering my calls. Tell me what Terry said quickly, then I've got to go see where Jay is.'

'He will be fine. Let's book a hotel room for now and make sure you are safe.'

Macy seemed to have lost the will to live and simply nodded her head. 'I'll give you that. I need sleep, Bobby, a good night's sleep and I will be fine. If you sort that out, I'll go search for Jayden – see what pub he's ended up in.'

Bobby unlocked his phone and went back to looking for the nearest hotels. Bingo, he found one only three miles from where they were. A nice set up too: a jacuzzi, four-poster bed, the works.

'I'll book it now, Macy. You know Bobby always looks after you.' He stepped away from the table, tapping away on his phone.

Macy let him take the lead. She didn't care where she laid her head tonight as long as she got some sleep. Her mind was doing overtime and every time she closed her eyes she imagined men taking Jay.

Until her phone lit up with a text. It was Jayden. She breathed a sigh of relief as she read the words.

Feeling better. Gone for a few scoops xxx

She figured he must be pissed already if he was texting like that. She couldn't remember the last time he'd put kisses on a message.

Bobby placed his phone on the table. 'Job's a good un, all booked. We can nip to the offy and get a bottle of wine on the way, if you want? A few drinks will help you unwind.'

Macy seemed in a world of her own, away with the fairies. She went along with everything he was saying. Her eyelids kept dropping. She was ready for sleep.

Bobby opened the door and walked inside first. This was a top gaff. Clean, fresh and tidy. Not grubby like some of the dives he'd stayed in when he was younger. 'Take a look at this, Macy, I think you're going to be proud of me for getting this.'

Macy would have slept on a hammock right now. She walked into the room and headed straight for the bed. She flicked her shoes off and lay down, looping her arms over her head.

Bobby was still looking around the room. 'Should I open a bottle of wine?'

'Yes, do me a large one, Bobby, anything to help me relax. I haven't felt like this since we had that shit going on years ago.'

Bobby froze on the spot, his breathing seemed to stop. They never spoke about this, it was a topic they put to bed years ago. Why was she bringing it up now? He never replied in hope she would change the subject, but she didn't.

She rolled on her side and stared at the ceiling. 'Do you ever think about it, Bobby? That night, us? The people we might have been if that day had been different?'

He paced about the room, wanting to change the subject, anything rather than talk about the past. He passed her a large glass of wine and gripped the remote. 'We might get a decent film on at this time. A bit of action or crime is right up my street. What about you?'

'I don't really ever get time to watch the TV, Bobby. So I can't say what I like anymore. In fact, I don't know me anymore, who I am, and what I like. I just follow the crowd, anything for an easy life. Anyway, usually I'm too cream-crackered to watch anything on the box.' Macy picked her glass up and took a large mouthful of her wine. She sat thinking for a few seconds before she continued. 'I loved the Square back then, but I hated me, Bobby. I had no respect for myself, blazing bud like it was nobody's business, fighting, part of a gang, terrorising the residents. It's something I'm not proud of. How do you think it makes me feel when Leanne asks me about her dad, and I have to tell her I barely knew him? I only had his bleeding name; I couldn't even tell her what he looked like because it was just a quick leg-over.'

Bobby sighed. 'Don't be so hard on yourself, Macy. It was just life growing up back then. You weren't the only one at it, you know. Look at me, I was banging anything with a pulse. Any new girl that set foot on the Square, the lads were all over them like a rash. Like I said, it was the norm in those days. We were young, living for the day.'

Macy snivelled and pinched the bridge of her nose. 'Still doesn't stop me thinking about it, does it. If I had my time again, I would have been so different, kept my legs shut. I don't regret Leanne, but I could have waited. I could have had a bit of a leg to stand on when I tell her now that she shouldn't have wasted so much time hanging about on the Square, getting herself up the duff before she's seen the world beyond Manchester. If only I'd told the lads to take a hike rather than taking them down the alley.'

Bobby burst out laughing. 'Then you wouldn't have been the laugh you were, the daring girl who held no fear. All the lads wanted a piece of you, Macy. You were the top girl back then, and hard as fuck, may I add. Nobody messed with you, did they?'

Macy sat up and rested her drink on the top of her knees. 'Yeah, I was a right bitch back then. I took no shit from nobody, never let anybody speak down to me. Bloody hell, what happened to me? How did I end up in hiding?'

Bobby could see she was getting upset. He dug his hand into his pocket and pulled out a bag of weed. He dangled it in front of her eyes. 'Say hello to your old friend. Nice bit of bud for us, help us relax, take the stress away.'

Macy smirked and looked at the weed. 'Jeez, Bobby, what are you trying to do to me? I've not smoked that since I was a kid.'

'I often have it at night, just to chill out, it helps me unwind.' Bobby smiled.

Macy looked at him in more detail. He'd been her friend since being a kid and even when she looked at him now she could still see his face as a teenager. 'We've been through some shit, us, Bobby. And I know we fell out for a time, but we have been through some shit together and I think that holds us together. It's the tough times that bond you as much as the happy ones, innit?'

Bobby's breathing changed and he was looking right at her, ready to say something. He coughed to clear his throat, then reached over and touched the tips of her cold fingers. 'I've always had a thing for you, Macy. Maybe I should have told you this years ago, but I mean more than just fancying you, more than just thinking you're a good laugh. I really like you. I never found the courage to say what was in my heart. If I had a magic wand now, at this very minute, I would take us back to being younger. To the night we were in the alleyway together. Things would be so different then. I would make all that shit disappear.'

Now it was Bobby who was getting upset. His smooth guy act had fallen away and he was baring his true feelings, it seemed, for once. Macy watched him as he continued.

'That night was one of the best nights of my life. Me and you were together and at last you were kissing me, and that twat came and spoilt it. Why didn't he just walk away, leave us to it when he saw we were having an intimate moment? Nothing would have happened then, it would have been sweet. But no, he had to come up to you, touching your face, your hair, trying to take you away from me when I'd waited like forever to get the chance with you. He grabbed me, Macy, remember? Threw me to the floor like a kid, mocked me in front of you, and there was no way I could allow that. I only pointed the gun at him to scare him, to make him go away, but still he carried on touching you, goading me. I was that mad I barely even realised I'd pulled the trigger. I never meant to kill him, Macy, on my life, I only wanted to show him that he was messing with the wrong person. Nathan Barnes. I may have killed the guy – but he's ruined my life sure as I ended his.'

Macy shook her head slowly. 'Bobby, that night has haunted me, and you know I've never told anyone what went on. But I've never told you about how it was for me after. You scarpered, but I was the one who got rid of the gun, I was the one who had to face the police questioning, and I never said a word. How do you think it makes me feel when Jeanette Barnes shouts abuse at me about her brother? Nathan was an alright lad from what I can remember and, because of me, he lost his life. If he didn't think he stood a chance with me, he would never have come down that alley to us.'

'Don't say that, Mace – whoever else is to blame, it's definitely not you.' Bobby had the good grace to look ashamed at what he'd put teenage Macy through. But just like in all the years in between, he never apologised.

They both sat thinking in silence. Bobby rolled the spliff on the bed and lit it before he lay back. 'We have a bond, Macy, a secret, a story nobody knows but us two. I should have done more when the police questioned you, but I knew you would never grass me up. It was weeks before I even left the house, you know; I wasn't sleeping and every night as I closed my eyes I relived that moment in my head.'

'Same. Some nights I never closed my eyes. My mam knew something was wrong and I can't tell you the number of times she pleaded with me to tell her the truth. I changed after that night, Bobby. I promised myself I would change, be a better person, and maybe I would have done it anyway, but a few weeks later I found out I was pregnant. If the memories of the night you shot Nathan weren't enough to keep me off the Square, the thought of a baby was. Especially as I knew I'd be raising it alone. That kid was only ever going to have me to depend on. It made me grow up fast.'

Bobby shot a look over at her. 'I always thought Leanne was my kid, because we'd basically done it, hadn't we? Just because we didn't get to finish doesn't mean the kid isn't mine.'

Macy winced. 'You know how it was – I ended most evenings with a different lad. It made me feel like I could forget everything else for a few minutes. It was always more likely that Leanne's dad was one of the other lads. Like you said, you and me – we were unfinished business. And you know what, a part of me is glad I never found out. Leanne and me are a duo – men have come and gone, but mothers and daughters? Well, that's forever.' Macy reached over and took the spliff from his hand. She could do with some oblivion tonight.

An hour later, both of them were pissed and stoned. Macy had finally stopped sending Jayden messages and seemed relaxed for the first time in days. Maybe it was the weight of finally having said Nathan's name out loud, perhaps it was the release of Bobby telling her not to blame herself, but for the first time in forever, she was letting herself remember her past without fear or guilt.

Finally Bobby looked directly into her eyes. 'Macy, I think you're as beautiful now as you were then. Everything about you rocks my world. No other woman has ever come close to you. I wish me and you could have got together years ago. Our lives would have been so different.'

She never moved a muscle, only stared into his big blue eyes. 'Bobby,' she paused. 'My head is in pieces right now. Jayden is a wanted man. Leanne is trying to make the biggest decision of her life, and Alex is having to lie to his own nan about why he's black and blue. I shouldn't even be here with you. I should be at home trying to sort this shit out.'

But Bobby was fed up of waiting and went in for the kiss.

Macy had already imagined how outraged she'd feel – being hit on when she had so much to sort out. But when it finally happened, she felt herself giving in. He excited her, made her heart beat faster. He wanted her. This was their time; nobody would ever find out. Their secret. Macy was lost in the moment. Soon their bodies were entwined and, piece by piece, he removed her clothing. He nurtured every inch of her flesh, no rushing. As he kissed her stomach, her back arched. She was a woman starved of sex and attention, and her body felt lit up with pleasure. His head disappeared between her legs, and she squeezed the edge of the pillow as warmth filtered her body. Never, ever, had any man made her feel like this. Groaning, scratching his back, pressing herself against him. She'd never let go like this before. She was in heaven for sure as she reached climax. And he'd not finished with her yet. No, he entered her and began to pleasure her more. Her fingernails dug into his shoulders and their eyes met. A stare that told them they'd finally faced the demons they'd both been battling in private since the night Nathan Barnes died.

Macy lay in Bobby's arms and, for the first time in a long time, she felt safe. He made her feel like a woman, like she was something special. She was still reeling from the fact that here was a man who knew her very worst secret and still craved her. She realised that, ever since Nathan, a part of her had felt unworthy of love – paying the price for keeping such a secret. And, for one night, she felt free of it.

He moved his head slightly and kissed the top of her head. 'That was amazing. The best sex ever.'

She dug her head deep into his chest, unable to look at him. 'Stop it, Bobby, you know I'm shy.'

He burst out laughing and rolled her on her side so he could see her face. 'You are far from shy, love. Some of those moves you did to me are illegal in some countries.'

She laughed and lay back on his chest, running a single finger up and down his golden skin. 'Bobby, you say you've felt like this since we were kids. Why have you never told me before?'

'What could I say after Nathan? I was a killer. You deserved better. Then, when I was with Justine, I thought I was over you and I'd moved on. But every night when I closed my eyes it was your face I saw, and I couldn't get you out of my head. All I ever wanted after that was you by my side, in my bed.'

Macy lifted a gentle smile. It all made sense now, the comments he used to make to her, the way he stared at her. 'I can't lie. That's nice to hear, Bobby. Nobody has ever given a flying fuck about me. Alright I met Jayden, but once I got pregnant with Alex he stopped trying. He plodded along and let our relationship die. I tried to mend it so many times, but you can only try for so long and then you give up, don't you?'

'Yeah, Dawn's a good girl, but she's not you. And like I said, I thought I owed you a chance at a better life without what I did haunting you. But then when you got with Jayden, that waste of space, it made me think that maybe I still stood a chance.'

Macy said, 'Maybe you have always been at the back of my mind too.' What was she doing? She couldn't let herself be drawn back to the past. She squeezed her eyes together, aware of what she'd just said, wishing she could take it back.

Bobby held her tighter in his arms and looked straight in her eyes. 'I want us to be together. Always have. We are a good team at work – and we'll be even better outside it.'

Macy pulled away and took a moment to regain her thoughts. 'Bobby, stop this, this is not the right time to be planning a future together. My life is upside down and men have been at my house, hitting my son, threatening to hurt us all. Tonight was good, I'm not going to lie, but that's all it is, all it can be: a night together.'

Bobby huffed and reached over for his fags. This was not part of his plan. 'So, you are selling me out for that wanker, the one who you have said yourself is nothing but a lazy freeloader. Think about it, Macy, think about what I am offering you here. A way out, a new start. We can move if you want to, go to a new area.'

'And what about Dawn? Are you just going to walk in and tell her it's over?'

'If it means I can have you, then yes. You're not getting it, are you, Macy?' He dropped his head in his hands. 'You are the only person who can make me feel better about myself. We share a secret, a past together. I never have to hide anything from you. I can be myself. You're a liar if you say you don't feel that too.'

The truth stung but it also made her realise – Bobby wanted her as a link to the past. She'd wanted Bobby as a way of closing that chapter of her life for good. Laying that ghost to rest. But what had she done? Now he thought there was a chance, he wouldn't let her go, she could feel it. She felt uneasy. Bobby was pissed and stoned, yes, but still saying some stuff that didn't sit right with her. This man claimed he had loved her from afar for years, but he was also still the same boy who'd shot a kid at point blank range. She'd stayed silent partly out of loyalty, the code of the Square, but also, she admitted to herself now, because she knew deep down he was unstable. She'd had to protect herself and her baby – and silence had been the only tool she had. But she was a grown woman now and couldn't be falling into men's traps again. She pulled the duvet over her body and closed her eyes. She needed sleep and a clear head in the morning to do whatever it took to stop everyone who was threatening her family.

Chapter Twenty-Eight

G ino checked his watch: it was ten past ten. No one was ever late to meet him on the Square. Kerry should have been here for ten, he'd told her to meet him. Where the hell was she? The Square was quiet tonight but from the corner of his eye he clocked a black BMW parked up with a few heads sat in it. He walked back to the group and nodded at Jacko and Kyle. 'Yo, check the beamer over there.'

'Want us to go and have a butcher's?' Kyle asked. 'It might be plain clothes.'

Gino sucked hard on his gums. 'Jacko, you go, see what the score is. Make sure you are not carrying anything on you, just in case.'

Kyle stood at Gino's side and they watched with caution as Jacko got on his toes.

Jacko stood at the side of the car and nodded at the driver. 'Yo, what's happening bruv?'

The electric window came down slowly, and Jacko could see the man's face for the first time. He looked like a man not to be messed with for sure. Certainly not the kind to bother with introductions. 'Where's the main man?' the driver asked.

Jacko stood back, aware now that this could be trouble. 'Who's asking?'

The man spoke through gritted teeth. '*I'm* fucking asking, so don't give me fucking attitude otherwise I'll be out of this car and smacking your arse.'

The other men in the car chuckled loudly.

Jacko pressed his shoulders back and his nostrils flared. 'Yo prick, who do you think you are talking to?'

It happened so fast: before Jacko knew it, his face was pressed to the floor and his hand was up his back.

'I said get me the main man, because it sure as fuck isn't you.'

Jacko struggled but was going nowhere fast.

Gino and Kyle had seen from where they were stood what was going on and already they were on their way over, tooled up, ready to rumble. Gino swung a silver machete around in the air as he sprinted over. He was ready to use it too, take every one of them down. Just before he swung it at the man who was dealing with Jacko, he froze. Slowly, he lowered the machete back to the side of his leg.

The man smiled at him and released his grip on Jacko. 'Hello son, I told you I would be back.'

Gino swallowed hard, taking a few seconds to digest what was going on. He helped Jacko up from the ground and stood back with his boys at either side of him. Jacko was ready to steam in, but Gino held him back. 'It's my old man.'

'Oi, less of the old,' his father joked.

Gino was the spit of his father and he could never have denied he was his son, ringers of each other.

'Your dad's a prick then,' Jacko whispered into his ear.

'What are you doing down these ends then? You never said you were coming over.' Gino looked puzzled.

Tyson Gallagher smiled a beaming white smile, walked over to his boy and patted the top of his head. 'Not a nice way to welcome me, is it, son?'

'Like I said, to what do I owe the honour of the visit?'

Tyson looked at his son's mates and gave them the eye. 'You two can fuck off while I have a word with my boy. Daddy's here now and he doesn't need looking after.'

Gino eyeballed Kyle, who slunk off. Jacko followed, his pride hurt more than his grazed face. Both of them kept turning back to see what Tyson's next move was. They were working out that, no matter how big you thought you were in this game, there was always someone bigger than you ready to take you down.

Tyson opened the back door of the car. 'Sit yourself down, son.'

Gino could see another two men in the back of the car and one sat in the front. If he got in the car he'd be trapped and outnumbered but his dad stood waiting until he squeezed into the back. He was spooked but tried his best to hold himself together.

'Who's running the Square, son?'

'Me of course. I have it all boxed off and I don't need any help from anyone, so don't be getting any smart ideas about coming back here trying to fuck my shit up. If you want to supply me, then great, let's talk. But this is still my patch.'

'Oi, cheeky bollocks, watch your mouth, have some respect.' Tyson eyeballed Gino through the rear-view mirror. 'Who do you get your food from?'

Gino was suspicious. 'Some guy I know. Why, what you offering?'

His father licked his front teeth and spoke in a serious tone. 'I need to know – since you'll be stopping buying from them. Because you will be working for me in the future. Me and the boys are moving down these ends and taking over supplying the shit around here. I'll let you keep the Square if you want to save face – but you buy from me, sell for me. I did tell you I used to run this Square, didn't I? And trust me, once this place is in your veins, it never really leaves you.'

Gino gripped the back of the seat in front and dug his fingers deep into the black leather. 'Nah, I'm sorted doing what I'm doing my way, and my plan is to take over more – I want more not less. Like I said, I'll buy your gear, if it's a good price, but I'm not letting you come here and think you can dome me and take what I've worked for. Sack that. Go back to where you come from and work your own area.'

Tyson twisted his body quickly and gripped his son by the scruff of his neck. 'Sort your attitude out little boy. I've told you what is happening, so you can play by my rules or do one. This was my square long before it was yours so don't give me all that *I've worked hard* shit, because me and this place go back years. You was just a twinkle in my eye when I ruled this area.'

'So, if it was yours, why did you leave it if it meant that much to you?'

'I had my reasons, but I'm back now, and you and fucking dumb and dumber over there will be working for me. I'll ask again, who do you get your food from, is it Terry Dolan?'

Gino's eyes were wide. No way he was being a grass, and his dad could tell by the look in his eye that he would rather die than give him a name. If this had have been anyone else, they would have been on the floor now with a chalk mark around them. Tyson gripped the steering wheel and squeezed it. 'Fine. You're not going to tell me? It won't change anything. I'll be back here tomorrow night and we can sit down properly and work out who's doing what. It is what it is.'

Gino was fuming. Who the fuck did this guy think he was coming here and making rules for him and his boys? No way. If he wanted war, then he would fight him to the death for the Square. This was his baby, and he wasn't giving it up without a fight. Gino opened the car door and stood at the driver's window. 'Like I said, this is my manor. I'll fight all the way for it. I don't care if you're blood or not. This is my home and you're not evicting me from it after being here for two fucking minutes, get a grip.'

Tyson nodded his head and started the car's engine up. The tunes were on as he screeched out from the car park.

Gino sprinted back to his boys. 'Right, dad or not, this is war. That weapon thinks he can come here chatting shit to me and take what I've grafted my balls off for years while he's been on the missing list. I want anyone who's anyone here tomorrow night. Get what we need, Jacko. Guns, bats, knives, the full fucking shebang. Shit just got real.'

Gino knew heads were going to roll. This was his turf and nobody was taking it away from him.

———

Later that night Gino walked down the path to his front door. There was somebody sitting at his doorstep.

'Wow, I thought you said you would meet me at yours at ten. I've been sat here like forever.' Kerry looked confused.

Gino shook his head. 'Nah, you muppet, you need to clean your ears out and listen properly. I said meet me on the Square.'

Kerry stood up, bottles clinking together in her blue plastic bag. 'I knocked on a couple of times, but it doesn't seem like anyone's in. I was going to get on my toes, but I thought I would give it ten more minutes.'

Gino screwed his face up and shoved his key in the door. 'I bet my mam has fallen asleep or something, but Leanne should have let you in.'

Kerry nodded. 'That's what I thought, but she might have spotted me and decided she still doesn't want to speak to me.'

The door was open now, and Kerry followed Gino into the hall. He went ahead into the living room and clocked his mam on the sofa, fast asleep, snoring her head off, the television blaring. 'Mam, wow, no need for the box being on that loud.'

His mam stirred, still half asleep. She stood up and wobbled to the door. 'I'm off to bed, son, see you in the morning. I can't keep my eyes open.'

As she left, he shouted after her. 'Where's Leanne, is she in bed? Daft bint didn't even shift her arse to answer the door for her friend.'

Jean yawned. 'She pissed off hours ago. I'm not being funny love, but she's a moody cow that one. I don't know if I'm coming or going with her.'

Gino slammed his hand against the doorframe, aware that it was only having Kerry the other side of the wall that stopped him properly going off on one.

'Oi, come in.' He called out to Kerry. 'Sit down then, I didn't have you down as the shy type,' he chuckled.

'I'm not, just didn't want to stay if I'm not welcome. Where's Leanne, does she know I'm here?'

'Just going to bell her, she must have nipped out.'

Kerry could see he was fuming about something and watched him from the corner of her eye as he went into the kitchen.

Gino rang Leanne's number and listened to it ring out. No reply. His fingers pounded each letter as he sent a text message:

Where r u? I told you not to go out, bitch

He pressed send and held his head back with his eyes closed. She would be back home soon and then she would get told. Who the hell did she think she was taking the piss out of him when he'd told her how the land lay? Gino stomped back into the living room and nodded his head over at the bag Kerry was holding. 'Pass us one then, we may as well start without her. I bet she's at her mam's. She's not answering her phone.'

Kerry reached inside the bag and pulled out the vodka. She had a few bottles of beer too and she passed one over to him. 'I thought she was blanking me for a minute, you know. She can be a right stubborn cow when she's got a bee in her bonnet.'

Gino opened the bottle with his teeth.

Kerry held the vodka up and smiled over at him. 'Have you got a glass, or should I neck it from the bottle?'

'I'll put some tunes on. What about a bit of Aitch? He's only from Moston you know. The lad done good for himself and he's smashing it now. It's good to see a local lad putting us people on the map. It shows you can do whatever you want to do if you have passion and a dream.'

Kerry burst out laughing. 'Fucking hell, what's up with you being all motivational and that.'

He swigged the bottle of beer. 'I like to see people doing well. Not people licking shot like me of course, because I want to be the top dog, but in other areas, yes, I want every-one to do well. We all have to make a crust, don't we?'

The music started and Gino was singing along to the track. He pulled her over to look at his playlist on his phone. She leant over him and he could smell her perfume tickling his nostrils. He turned his head from the screen and looked up to her as she sat on the side of the chair.

Kerry followed his eyes and smirked. 'Wow, pervert, you are.' She yanked her top up and sat back.

Gino sniggered. He wasn't bothered that she'd seen him. 'Nice pair, just saying.'

Kerry blushed and flicked her hair back from her shoulder. She carried on looking at his music.

The drink flowed and soon Kerry was in the middle of the living room showing Gino her moves, twerking, slut-dropping. Gino stood up and cut a few shapes next to her. They were both laughing, and it wasn't long before he had his hands around her waist. He saw his chance and went for it. He put the lips on her and tried his luck.

It cut through the buzz of the alcohol like a knife. Kerry pulled away from him. 'Stop! Fucking hell Gino, why did you kiss me? You're with my best friend. I need to go home. This should not have happened. Where are my shoes?'

Gino moved back in towards her. 'You want it just like I do. I've seen the way you have been looking at me. Why would you even sit here with me if you didn't want a bit of me, eh?'

Kerry scurried about the front room trying to find her other shoe, her back facing him. Gino moved behind her and covered her mouth with his hand. In seconds she was on the floor, and he was on top of her, biting her, kissing her. 'You know you want it, so shut the fuck up and enjoy it.'

Kerry kicked straight into fight-or-flight, squirming about, punching, kicking. She caught him with an upper-cut and startled him. She jumped up from the floor and ran towards the living room door. Hands shaking, she pressed the handle down and ran down the hallway straight out of the front door.

She shouted behind her so everyone could hear. 'Out of fucking order, Gino! How dare you think you can force

yourself on me like that. You're a fucking weirdo.' She staggered down the street, always checking behind her. She got on
her phone and rang a taxi straight away. Her voice was desperate, and she was screaming down the phone. 'Hurry up, please
hurry up.' The call made, she stood in a doorway in the shadows. Her blouse was ripped, and she could feel the stinging on
her neck where he had bit her. 'Bastard, dirty no good bastard,'
she mumbled under her breath. Why did he think he could
have sex with her? She never gave him any signs. There she
was just having a few drinks and a dance and he thought he
then had a right to have sex with her. Should she phone the
police, report him, tell them what he had done to her? Would
they believe her, say she was asking for it, drinking and danc-
ing with him? She held her head back against the cold brick
wall and tears ran down her cheeks. She needed to tell her
friend what had happened – she had to find Leanne before
Gino got to her and told a different story. He'd say she was
gagging for it, that he was the one fighting her off. Kerry
stepped out from the shadows as the taxi pulled up. She
hurried into the back of the car and told the driver to take her
home. As she sat back, she squeezed her fists. 'You'll pay for
this, Gino Gallagher, you'll fucking pay for this.'

Gino sat in the chair still listening to his music. He texted
Leanne again:

Where r u slut? You're a slapper. Think u can
have me over, just u watch bitch, I'll make sure

nobody ever looks at u again when I slice yr
fucking face up.

He pressed the send button. 'Fuck women, who needs them
anyway.'

Chapter Twenty-Nine

Jayden sat in the chair facing Terry, two men either side of him. He was in a bad way, breathing like a horse that had just run the Grand National, and was bleeding from his nose, thick clotted blood.

'I'll ask you again, who the fuck took the drugs? I trusted you to drop off the weed and now I've got some pricks at my door because of you. You better start speaking, you daft twat, because I'll finish you, mate. On my life, I'll fuck you up good and proper and you will be in a wheelchair if you are lucky.'

One of the men dragged at Jayden's hair and lifted his head up. Jayden was coughing and spluttering, his lungs flooding.

His voice was low: 'I only done what you told me to do. When I was parked up, I was ambushed. I didn't see their faces, only a tattoo on his arms. They fucked me over and minutes later the other lot come and dragged me away saying I had set it all up. Terry, I would never double-cross you. You must believe me.' Jayden coughed again, breathing raggedly. 'I admit I told them your name. I had no choice, they'd been to my house, my family were in danger.' He sobbed and his words could hardly be made out.

Terry stood with his shoulders back, planning his next move. 'We need to find out who the fuck these men are. Word on the street is the King Pin is called Tyson, used to live in the area. He was buying a big drop to grow his patch, or so my boys say that set up the deal with his deputies. I'm waiting on an update where the prick is and I will pay him a visit. This should have been a cut-and-dry job. This is what happens when you let pricks like you do your drops. I should have stuck to my team instead of letting this fuck-up near me.' Terry booted the chair and nearly knocked it over. He turned to his heavies. 'These lads will be back, and I need to be ready when they do. At the end of the day, someone owes for four boxes of food, and I'll tell you now I won't be paying for it. Get the word out to everyone who is anyone and see who is selling cheap. Somebody knows something and I won't rest till I find out who had me over. I'll cut their bollocks off and make a necklace out of them. Get on the blowers, phone everyone. I want names before the day is out.' Terry shot a look over at Jayden and spat at him. 'Get rid of this clown, throw him in the river or something. Find me this Tyson, the fucking main man.'

Terry marched from the room.

Jayden was heaved from the chair and dragged outside. As the glow from the streetlights hit his eyes, he winced. Then it went dark again as he was shoved into another car boot. He heard the sound of a car engine starting, darkness and rumbling. He struggled to bring his hand up and slowly he made the sign of the cross across his body. Nobody could help him now except the big man in the sky.

Terry sat in his car facing the Square. A few new faces had been seen there over the last few days: older men, or so his source had told him. He sat smoking, watching the goings-on with eager eyes. He watched Gino serving someone up and sat up straight in his seat. 'What do we know about that muppet? I know he buys our stuff but low level. He's been on here a while though, has he got boys, elders?'

The large man at the side of him rested his chunky fingers on the dashboard and eyed up the Square. 'Deals a bit of weed. His old man used to run the Square years ago, a bit of a head back in the day, did a bunk when he became a dad though. You know the sort.'

Terry studied Gino. Something didn't sit right with him. 'It's not fucking rocket science, is it? Jayden comes from these ends, and he must have told somebody what he was doing. The rest is history. Some shady fucker has set him up. I want a stakeout here every night. A few of us need to watch this Square with clear eyes, see who comes who goes, any more new faces and all that.'

The men agreed. Terry was right, Jayden must have been mouthing off telling the world and his wife his business. All it took was someone to follow him and they would be quids in. Easy peasy when you think about it. Could it have been this kid Gino? Did he have the stones to pull off a stunt like this? Jayden was an easy mark, and doing him over would have looked like easy money to someone. Money was power and there was no honour amongst thieves, was there?

Gino didn't notice Terry's car parked up. He was paranoid but only had eyes peeled for his dad's motor. His old man had told him he would be back, and it was only a matter of time before he tried to take the power from Gino and reclaim the Square as his own. He'd asked nicely, but he wasn't the kind of man to take no for an answer. It was his kingdom; he reigned there for years before Gino was born. But, he'd had his time and now it was Gino's time to shine, the heir to the throne.

Jacko and Kyle stood by Gino. All of them were edgy tonight and there was an eerie silence in the Square. Gino looked at his phone again: no messages, no missed calls. Not a word from Leanne. Not a word from his dad.

'Get the rest of the firm down here. I have a feeling about tonight; something doesn't feel right. Get the straps on, get tooled up, get ready to fight for what is ours. Dad or no dad, he doesn't rule me. I'll fight him for it. We'll fight them all.'

Jacko still held a grudge against Gino's dad, wanted to cut him deep for humiliating him. Tyson had put him on his arse, embarrassed him in front of his crew. Nobody fucked with Jacko, fucking nobody.

Kyle zipped his coat up fully as a cold northerly wind rushed through the Square. It was like the ghosts of this place were all sprinting past them, warning them that trouble was brewing, to be ready for what was coming.

Gino patted his jacket pocket. Ready for war, ready to do whatever he had to do to keep his name, his area. There was no room for fear anymore, this was about pride, name sake, and he was willing to die to save what was his. Gino had been just fifteen when he took over the Square. And he'd only got there through blood. He'd messed up the young guy who'd ran the patch before him, stabbed him fifteen times in his legs and chest. The bloke was in hospital for months, and there was a time when Gino thought he was going to get slammed for it. But, nobody said a word to the dibble. They knew to keep silent, never breathe a word of what they'd heard, seen, or witnessed. Gino was the man after that on Tavistock Square and, apart from the odd few pricks who got a bit gobby, he had never really had a challenge. He kept his circle tight, looked after his boys, made sure their pockets were lined when the count was in. These were his brothers, his warriors, the men he took with him to any beef. They'd all die for each other and to protect the Square. Gino had come from nothing back then. His mother was living from hand to mouth most of the time and poverty was a word he knew well. No food in the cupboards, knocking on neighbours' doors for a few slices of bread, a bit of milk, a tenner to lend his mother until pay-day. Yes, he knew what it was like to be poor, and he told himself once he started earning that he would never see empty cupboards again. Gino had always bunged his mother a few quid from day one. With the first bit of money he earned he bought them both steak pudding, chips, peas and gravy from the chippy with a buttered muffin each. He'd always seen the puddings in the chippy, the steam coming from the pan when the woman opened the lid to take one out, and his mouth had watered wondering what it would be like. He'd set his sights on bigger things than a chippy tea these days, but sometimes he reckoned no success would ever taste as sweet as that meal.

Gino was dressed like a main man these days, not over the top bling, but clean smart clothes, box-fresh trainers. His mam used to go to Wyndsor's for his shoes back in the day and if he closed his eyes he could still hear the kids laughing at his unbranded trainers, pointing at him. *Adidas four stripes* they called his trainers, snides, poor kids' footwear. Kids could be so cruel sometimes and he never forgot the way he felt back then.

Gino listened to Jacko and Kyle getting the team ready at the side of him. This was game on, and he was ready to play. Winner takes all.

Leanne looked at her phone and felt sick at each message she read. It was like a cloud had been lifted from her head and she could see clearly now, see Gino for the cocky bully he really was. She'd typed a reply out four or five times and deleted it before she sent it. She was raging inside, angry with herself that she'd let a man treat her like that. She'd not slept properly, and her head was still filled with questions, decisions she had to make. Should she keep the baby, could she be a single parent? Where the hell was her mother when she needed her most? She had tried so many times to ring her and still she was blanking her. Leanne shot a look at the clock and decided if she had not heard from her in the next hour she was going home. Sack sitting here at her nana's house any longer. If men came through her door, then so what? The mood she was in she would have wiped the floor with the lot of them. But, she decided, before she went home she was going to Gino's and getting any of her belongings left there. After today, she hoped she'd never darken that door again. She'd been so afraid of standing up to Gino, afraid of what he'd do. But her family were in deep enough shit with everything Jayden had done – it was time she faced her fear.

Leanne stood knocking at Gino's door, ready to give him a mouthful. How dare he call her a slag and a slapper on his text messages? She had been a good girlfriend and one he should have been proud of. Abuse it and lose it, she supposed. But it was Jean who opened the front door and looked Leanne up and down. Trouble was brewing and she could see in her eye she was ready to have a pop.

'And where do you think you have been? My boy has been worried sick, ringing you, walking the floors all night he has.'

Leanne eyeballed her, never flinching. And who was she anyway to be asking her questions? She wasn't her mother. 'I've come to get my stuff. And as for your blue-eyed boy, do you mean the one who has been sending me abusive texts all night long calling me every name under the sun?'

Jean huffed. 'I don't blame him. He was worried. It would have been good manners to let him know when you were staying out. Girls these days have no bleeding morals.'

And there it was, just what Leanne needed to tell this old trout exactly what she thought about her. She inhaled and bent forward slightly. 'Listen up, Mrs Know-It-All. Your son is a control freak, and looking at you I know where he gets it from. I would rather die a painful death than live under your roof. You expect me to get up each morning and clean your house while you and Gino kick back and do nothing? You have watched too much Cinderella. So please, let me get my things and I'm gone from here. I can assure you I will never cross your door again. And as for me giving you a grandchild, think again. None of you deserve a child in your life, because, if they lived with you, they would end up like you two, sick and twisted in the head.'

Jean stood back from the door, hands gripping the door-frame. 'You tried trapping my boy, saw he was on a good thing and couldn't wait to get your greedy little claws into him. I told him straight that I didn't like the look of you.'

This was war now. 'He's a bully and he'll never change. In fact, love, keep my belongings. I need nothing from either of you anymore. I might have lost some clothes but I've found me, yes me, the girl I used to be, so kiss my arse. Goodbye.' Leanne was smiling from cheek to cheek as she walked down the garden path. She turned back and rammed two fingers in the air at Jean. 'One each for you and your son,' she shouted.

Leanne marched down the street like a Suffragette. She was ready to burn her bra, swing it in the air and show these men that women do have a voice and are not to be treated like second-class citizens. Skivvy, punchbag, floozy – she wasn't any of those things for anyone anymore. Fuck men, and fuck the control they thought they had over her. She felt an inner strength now, courage rising from her feet to her head. She was a lioness, a warrior, a contender.

Leanne knocked on Kerry's front door and stood back looking up at the top window. Maureen, her mam, moved the blinds back and smiled down at her. 'Come in, the door is open,' she mouthed.

Moe was daft as a brush but had a heart of gold and always had time for Leanne. They'd chatted for hours when she was growing up and she had told Leanne all about her failed relationships and the hardships she'd suffered in her life.

Moe was at the top of the stairs, looking down. 'Bleeding hell, I thought you had died. Where have you been? I've not seen you for ages.'

Leanne kept her voice low, not sure what Kerry had told her mother about the beef they had. 'Oh, I'm here now. Just been mad busy with stuff. Is Kez in?'

'Yes, come up love, she's still in bed. I don't know what time she rolled in last night but, judging by all the banging in her room, she must have had an argument with someone.'

Leanne was already on her way up the stairs. She opened the bedroom door. It was dark in the room and the curtains were shut. She inhaled and could smell stale booze and fags.

Kerry stirred; aware someone was in her bedroom. 'Get out of my room. How many times do I have to tell you that when my door is closed it means I'm asleep? Mam, get out, will you?'

Leanne was not sure how her friend would take her being here. 'It's not your mam, it's Leanne.'

Slowly, Kerry rubbed her knuckles into her eyes and tried to focus. She looked rough, smeared make-up, puffy swollen eyes. She sat up and pulled the duvet under her chin. She was anxious, Leanne could see: no eye contact, playing with her hair.

Leanne sat on the end of the bed and stared at the wall for a few seconds. 'So, do you want to sort this out or what? We are supposed to be best friends and well, to tell you the truth, I missed you.'

Kerry's bottom lip trembled, and she started to blubber. 'I've missed you too. My life has been so miserable without you. When me and Leon were over all I wanted was you to talk too.'

Leanne's eyes widened. 'God! When did you break up with Leon?'

'A while ago. The guy was full of shit and not the man I thought he was.'

Leanne rubbed her hands together. 'So, we are both single ladies then?'

Kerry was puzzled and Leanne knew she had to spell it out to her. 'I've finished with Gino. He's horrible Kerry, you don't know the half of it. I've been a right dickhead and I pretended everything was rosy in the garden when it was far from it.'

Kerry went white, scratching at her skin as if thousands of ants were running about on her. 'I went to Gino's house last night to see you but you weren't there. Gino was ringing you all night. He said you had gone out.'

Leanne was listening now; this was news to her. 'And you were there, sat with Gino without me? What did he say? What did you two talk about? I thought you both hated each other.'

'Please just listen. If you hadn't come here today, I would have come to your house to see you. I don't know how to say this so I may as well come right out with it: Gino tried kissing me, more than that, he tried having sex with me. Leanne, on my life I was scared for my life, I pushed him off me. I bit him, punched him, he wasn't stopping. I was scared out of my life.'

Leanne held the bottom of her stomach. She was heaving, all the colour drained from her face. Any second now she was going to spew up. She ran to the bathroom. She locked the door behind her and ran to the toilet bowl as the vomit sprayed from her mouth. It was a reminder that she had another problem far bigger than the one she had just left behind her. She sat on the floor at the side of the toilet and pulled her knees to her chest. If this was morning sickness, then God help her. She couldn't handle this. She needed her mother to rub her back, hold her hair back, tell her everything was going to be OK.

There was a knocking at the bathroom door. Kerry's voice, soft. 'Open the door, Leels, are you OK?'

Was she OK?, she asked herself. How the hell had she got to this? Her life in tatters, her best friend being attacked by her baby-daddy, and her family being threatened by gangsters. No, she wouldn't wallow. She remembered the feeling she had walking away from Gino's house. She stood up and rinsed her mouth. She looked at herself in the mirror and nodded her head. A look that told her she was going to be more than OK. She was going to prove it to everyone.

Kerry was sheepish when Leanne finally opened the bathroom door. 'Can I please tell you exactly what happened? I swear down on my life I would never ever touch your man, I would rather die. Girl code and all that. It was all him, Leanne, he's a wrong un. Look at my neck, my arms. These bruises are real, and last night I was in two minds whether to walk right into the police station and tell them that he attempted to rape me. Because that's what it was, it was rape.' Kerry burst out crying, waiting for comforting arms around her from her best friend.

But Leanne was frozen. She knew what kind of man Gino was. She had never told anyone he had forced her to have sex the night she lost her virginity. She prepared in her mind what she was going to say next. She was ready. 'Kerry, I believe you. I'm just glad you got away. I should have done the same thing. But you telling me this has made me realise what I think I knew all along. I need you to come with me to the clinic. I don't want a baby – not yet, and certainly not with Gino. He doesn't deserve to be a father. And I'm too young, I need to live my life, travel, go and do all the things we spoke about. Please tell me I am doing the right thing?'

Kerry wrapped her arms around Leanne and squeezed her tight. 'Of course you are. You know your own body and mind best of all. It's still early days – you can't be far gone. Gino is a dangerous man. He tried to get in your head and isolate you so you had nobody. I've missed you so much and I am never, ever, ever, falling out with you again. Men will never come between us again. Sisters before misters and all that.'

The two of them hugged each other and there were genuine tears shed between them. Life had taught them both some serious lessons, and they were still standing tall.

'What about Gino, have you told him yet?' Kerry asked.

Leanne spoke through gritted teeth. Just the mention of his name made her blood boil. She hated him with a vengeance, wanted to hurt him, make him pay for being a rapist. 'No, I owe him nothing. I wouldn't piss on him if he was on fire. The guy gives me the ick. I'm done there, trust me, that door has well and truly closed and I will never open it again. Help me get booked into the clinic and help me sort my life out.'

Kerry looked her friend in the eyes, serious. 'Leanne, I'm scared for you. Gino is a nutter, he has a screw loose. He won't let you go without a fight – especially knowing you're pregnant. You know that more than anyone.'

'Then fight I will, Kerry. Fool me once then shame on you, fool me twice then shame on me.'

Chapter Thirty

M acy sat curtain-twitching. Up and down she was, like cheap knickers. Every time a car pulled onto the street she was at the window. Bobby had told her it was all going to be alright but still she had a feeling in her gut that told her something wasn't right. Alongside the guilt at having spent last night with Bobby was a growing sense of dread that something awful had happened to Jay. Him going walkabout was normal – but not with all this shit going on. All day she'd been sat here, waiting, hoping that Jayden would come through the front door and tell her everything was going to be alright. He'd messed up loads of times before and, somehow, he always fixed it. He would always come up smelling of roses no matter what had happened.

Darkness fell and Macy could see a few kids sat on their bikes outside her house. Just teenagers they were, kids who were not old enough yet to be on the Square, kids who were still wet behind the ears. A shadow was walking down the path and, with her heart in her mouth, she stood up and scanned around the front room looking for the baseball bat. If this was trouble, then she was ready. Quickly, she scurried into the hallway, prepared for action. Anyone coming through that door uninvited would be whacked on the head. She had a great swing on her and hopefully it would put them out cold.

Her heart was pounding, not sure if the person outside was going to knock or just kick the thing down again. But instead, she heard a key in the lock.

The front door opened, and she dropped the bat. She flicked the hallway light on, and relief flooded her. 'Bleeding hell, Leanne, I nearly whacked this over your head. Why didn't you ring me and tell me you were coming back? I thought it was trouble.'

'Wow, since when was you ready to total someone, Mam? I didn't have you down as some lunatic.'

Macy trudged back into the front room as Leanne and Kerry followed her.

Kerry whispered behind her hand. 'What the fuck is going on? Is your mam alright, or what?'

'Yeah, we've just had some shit going on with Jayden, that's all. Some guys have given him a beating and came through our door slapping our kid about. Alex is alright now but it put the fear of God in him.'

They were all in the living room now and Macy sparked up a fag. Sitting down, she kept her eyes on the front window, watching for any movement. 'Jayden's gone again, Leanne. I'm worried about him, scared he is in serious trouble.'

Leanne rolled her eyes and shot a look over at her mother. 'Mam, he's always in trouble. He always turns up.

Look at that time he had beef with the Smiths, and they told him he was going in a body bag,' she chuckled. 'He ended up best of mates with them, on a bender for two days if you remember properly. He's probably in the boozer as we speak. He won't be arsed about putting your mind at rest, he just cares about himself. And let me tell you now, the way that man spoke to me I'll be glad if they have battered him good and proper. Mam, I don't get on with him, I never have.'

Macy sucked hard on her cigarette. 'Not what I need to hear right now is it, Leanne? Let's make sure he is alright first, then we can sort out what he's said to you. He sent me a text saying he was out on the lash but it's been silent ever since.'

Leanne looked uneasy. 'I hate to say it, but we'll have to ring the dibble if he's not home soon. Tell them you heard he had some trouble with some gangsters and he's not been in touch since. You don't have to give them names, only report him missing.'

Macy sat chewing on her fingernails. She'd thought about this, but the police at her house, the neighbours whispering behind her back? No, there was no way she could get the rozzers involved.

Leanne licked her dry cracked lips. 'Mam, I know you have your own troubles at the moment, but I've decided I don't want to have this baby. I've not let on, but Gino is not a good guy.' She knew if she told her mam the full story right now she'd be over there, and she'd be inside on GBH charges before you knew it. The truth would have to wait. 'Do you know he even tried it on with Kerry?'

Macy stubbed her fag out and sat back looking at Kerry and then Leanne. 'Well, that is no good, is it? You're only a few weeks gone and already he is cheating on you. I'll stand by you no matter what you decide. I've still not met the guy yet but, after hearing that, make sure you keep the wanker away from me. I'll cut his balls off if he even tries to step over this door. Bleeding hell Leanne, you don't half pick them, don't you? Who wants a lad who is out in the mix, dealing drugs, fighting all the time and, as you have just found out, cheating too? I was that girl once and thought I knew it all about guys. I went for Mr Popular, Mr Drug-Dealer, and Mr Hard Man, and all of them were nothing but trouble.'

Leanne went bright red. 'So you know what it's like, but I guess we have to find out ourselves, just like you did.'

Macy shook away the memories rising up again. Nathan. Bobby. That night. 'I was an idiot and I'm trying to stop you making the same mistakes as I did. I'm not proud of who I was back then, and I cringe when I think about it. You're set for better things, Lee, baby or no baby. I want you to know your worth.'

Leanne blushed and checked her mobile phone: just as she thought, more abuse from Gino. She wondered if his mam had told him she was canning him. There was no going back as she typed out her next text:

> Do one, you lying, cheating, prick. Kerry told me all about what you did to her. I can't believe I ever thought me and you could be a thing. I'm booking in for an abortion - you're

not fit to be a dad and I'm not ready to be a
mum. Enjoy your life, loser.

She read the message once and then pressed the send button
with force.

———————

It was three o'clock in the morning when the police arrived
at Macy's house. She could hear the banging on the door
and jumped up out of bed thinking it was trouble. 'Fuck,
fuck,' she mumbled. She quickly grabbed her light blue
housecoat and shoved it on. If they asked if she knew
anything about any trouble, then the answer was no. Her
lips were sealed, she was no snitch. She turned the landing
light on and ran down the stairs. She opened the front door
and stood with her poker face on.

'I'm PC Charles, we've met before, if you recall. I'm here
about Jayden Foster,' the copper said.

She knew this officer. He'd been to her house a few times
in the past when her other half had been caught robbing.
'He's not here, if that's what you mean.'

The officer and his colleague looked awkward. He said
softly 'Macy, can we come in please?'

She eyeballed him and thought about if she had anything
in the house that she shouldn't have. 'Do you have to? I
don't want the neighbours talking. You know as well as me,
it doesn't take a lot to get these lot gossiping, does it?'

The officer kept a straight face. 'I think you will need to
sit down.'

Macy swallowed hard, a rush of adrenaline kicking in. 'Hurry up then, I swear, five minutes you've got and that's it.'

Leanne appeared at the top of the stairs and shouted down. 'Mam, who is it, are you alright?'

Macy turned and walked into the house. 'I'm fine, just the dibble here to speak to me. Go back to bed, love. I'll be up in five.'

PC Charles waited until Macy had sat down. He looked over at his colleague before he began. 'A body had been found in the River Irk in Collyhurst. We believe it is Jayden. He had a letter from the benefit agency in his back pocket.'

Macy felt like they were speaking a foreign language, barely taking it in. 'No, what on earth would he be doing down near the river?'

'His body was badly beaten, and we are now treating this as a murder case. The investigating officers will be here soon, and they will be asking you questions about Jayden's final hours.'

Macy went white, her airways closing as the meaning of the words hit home. She stood up and started pacing the front room, trying to take it in.

'It's not him, not Jayden. You must have got it wrong.' She looked at the officers in hope they could change what they had just said.

'Would you like me to get you a drink of tea or something, Macy? Please come and sit down, I know this must be a big shock for you.'

Leanne came barging into the front room now. 'I thought you lot would have been gone by now. Mam, why are they still here?'

Macy was in shock, staring into space as she spoke. 'They have found a body in the river. They think it's Jayden.'

Leanne froze, aware all eyes were on her. Then she ran to her mother's side and hugged her. 'Oh Mam, what the fuck? You said he was on a bender – has he fallen in pissed or something?'

Macy shook her head. She could feel it in the marrow of her bones: the police were right. This was no accident, and if there was to be any justice, it was time for something very rare indeed round this place – the truth.

The two officers sat with them and started to take a short statement about the last time Jayden was home. Macy didn't care anymore, and she was singing like a budgie. After all, her man was dead, and someone was going to pay for it. The drugs, the kidnapping, Alex getting beaten – she left none of it out. And through it all, she stayed dry-eyed and steady-voiced. There would be time enough for tears later.

The officers left after a few hours, telling Macy to expect the investigating officers to be there soon. Macy just wanted the family to have a bit of time together before the next round of questions started.

Leanne walked them to the door and came back speechless. There were no words to say, nothing could bring her step-father back. Leanne sat and watched Macy sob her heart out.

'He can't be gone; they must have got it wrong. You watch, he'll come through the door soon and tell us it was all a big mix-up. He's an idiot, I know, but he wouldn't get himself killed, wouldn't go and leave us...'

Leanne had to tell her mother straight, tell her Jayden was dead, he wasn't coming back. 'Mam, they identified him. It's him.'

Macy smashed her clenched fist into the arm of the chair, dust flying up. 'No, no, no.' Death was so final. No words or pills or potions could bring a loved one back. Macy would never hear his voice again, never lie next to him in bed again. Even the arguing, the fights, she'd miss it all.

Morning light cracked in through the blinds. Leanne was asleep next to her mother. But Macy was wide awake. All she'd done all night was chain smoke. She chewed on her cheek and got up from her seat. She wanted answers, she wanted to know who was responsible for ending Jayden's life. But worst of all, first thing, she had to go round to her mum's and tell Alex that his dad was dead, tell him that he would never see him again. Life could be so cruel sometimes, but death was crueller. Macy lifted her head slowly and stared at the ceiling. Then she dragged herself upstairs and started to get ready. Somebody somewhere knew who had done her other half in and as God was her witness she was going to find out.

Macy walked slowly into Queen's Park. She'd always played in here growing up and as a teenager she'd had sex here a few times. The graveyard, bizarrely, had always felt like a safe place, a location she always ended up when she was steaming drunk. With caution she opened the graveyard gates now, always checking behind her, always making sure she was alone. Slowly she started to read the names on the headstones, studying them, looking for a familiar name. Her feet stopped suddenly when she came to the resting place of a man called John Duram. Rubbing at her arms, she zipped her coat up as the cold wind started to pick up. From her pocket she pulled out a small silver trowel. The one she used to plant her flowers in the summer. Dropping to her knees she moved an old flowerpot with *brother* written on it in gold writing. She squirmed as she spotted a big fat worm wriggling about in the dark brown soil underneath, black beetles running about. It all reminded her a bit too closely of what was going on under the soil. Shuddering, she pulled her hood up and checked she was still alone. Digging, digging, sweating, grunting and groaning, Macy carried on until she stared down at a blue plastic bag and dragged it with force from the hole. With haste she filled the hole back up and placed the black flowerpot back where it was originally. She sat down on her bum to rest briefly and spoke to the headstone. 'Thanks, John, for keeping this safe. It's been our secret for years and I thank you for that. Rest in peace, mate.'

Macy made the sign of the cross across her body and shoved the blue bag inside her thick padded coat. She jumped to her feet and, with her head dipped low, made her way back through the park. There was nobody about yet except the birds.

Macy hit the main road and tried her best to keep a low profile. She headed back home, to her manor, to where she would sit down and plan her revenge on those who had taken her son's father from her. But first, it was time to go and see Alex. The sun was up and she couldn't put it off any longer.

Nearly back on home turf, Macy realised which way the route was taking her. She stood facing the Square and stopped dead in her tracks. It was like the place was drawing her back in, willing her to step back to where her story first began. With small steps she walked onto Tavistock Square. She stood with her back against the cold brick wall and dug her hand in her pocket for a cigarette. Slowly she flicked the lighter underneath it. Closing her eyes, she was back to that night when she was a young girl, the screams, the shouting, the blue police sirens. She tossed her cigarette butt away with a quick flick – it was time to lay some ghosts to rest.

She walked through the place and looked at it afresh. It still looked the same. Landmarks were still there, graffiti of the old crews' names on the walls. But finally, she felt she was going to be free of the hold it had over her – and her family.

Macy went to her mother's house wishing she was there with other news. But Alex was sat waiting for her – she had to face it. She had rang her mother earlier and told her the awful news, but there was no way she was telling her son over the phone – or making Grace tell her own grandson that his father had passed away – no way in this world. This was a mother's job. That was it, she figured: being a mum meant you got the very best bits of life – and the very worst.

Macy stood at the front door as Marjorie opened it with a look of despair in her eyes. The old lady was blubbering already, her voice low. 'I'm so sorry love, I have no words to take away the pain you must be feeling in your heart. Me and your mam are sat in the kitchen. Alex is in the living room waiting for you. Shout if you need anything. Your mam is in bits, and I've just poured her a glass of brandy to help calm her nerves.'

Macy raised a gentle smile. 'Thanks Marj, I don't know how I am still standing. I've not slept a wink and my head is spinning. Do me a favour, please do me a large glass of brandy too. I need something to take the edge off the way I am feeling.'

Macy stepped inside the house and gripped the living room door handle. She inhaled deeply before she entered.

Alex was alert – but with no clue how serious the news was. 'What's up? Nana has been acting really weird, she's being overly nice to me. I think she's losing the plot or something. Honest, she can't do enough for me. I could get used to this. I might end up living here.'

Macy sat down next to her son, reached over and touched his fingers.

He pulled his hand away: sack all that soppy shit.

'Alex, the police came to the house last night. They found a body in the river.' Her words stuck in her throat and tears started to flood from her eyes as she continued. 'It was your dad.'

Alex stared at his mother, suddenly looking like a little boy. 'What?'

'Your dad is dead, son. I'm so sorry.' Macy broke down crying. She reached over to hold her son in her arms, and he howled out like an injured animal. Macy could do nothing to take away the pain he was feeling in his heart.

Marjorie and Grace come into the front room now and it was obvious that Alex knew his father was gone.

Macy spoke in a gentle tone. 'Son, we will get through this together, we will, honest.'

Alex finally lifted his head. 'How Mam? Nothing will bring him back. What did the police say? Did you tell them about the men who come to our house? Was it them?'

Alex knew he'd said something he shouldn't have, and his eyes widened, looking at Grace.

'I bleeding knew it. Didn't I say to you Marj that something more was to this story. You better tell me the full story now because, if you don't, I'll report this my bleeding self. I was never buying that bailiffs story and him falling off his bike.'

Macy sighed. The cat was out of the bag and her mother wouldn't rest until she knew the full story. 'Jayden was trying to earn some extra money. You know what he's like.'

Grace seconded that with a nod of the head.

'He was dropping some weed off in Blackpool. Anyway, to cut a long story short, he was had over, someone got to him before he dropped the drugs off to the people it was intended for. So, some men come to our house looking for the missing drugs and couldn't find anything. Alex was there and they gave him a beating, threatening to come back if the drugs didn't turn up. Jayden was kidnapped by them, but they let him go as some kind of warning. They messed him up bad and flung him out of the car on our street.'

Grace was horrified as the story unfolded.

'So, he was home safe then,' Marjorie said. 'Why would they take him again?'

'I don't get it either,' said Macy. 'The last I heard he was going for a few beers but they must have come back and took him again. Leanne said the neighbours saw him being dragged out of the house. There was a lot of drugs involved and I should have known it wouldn't have been left. Who in their right mind would lose forty or fifty grand? I guess it was easier to blame the guy who lost it than go looking for whoever was bold enough to nick it in the first place.'

Alex snarled at them all. 'We should have been at home with him, stuck by him, been there when they come for him.'

Macy shook her head. 'Don't you think I know that now? Cudda, wudda, shudda won't bring him back will it?' Macy broke down crying again and her body was shaking from head to toe. 'What will I do without him, Mam? What will we all do?'

Alex moved onto the sofa and rested his head on her shoulder. She stroked his head. 'It's all going to be fine son. We will find these pricks and make sure they pay for this. They'll all pay, trust me, as long as I've got a breath left in my body, they'll all go to hell for this.'

Chapter Thirty-One

Leanne had been at her nana's all day with her family. It was a sad time and a lot of the neighbours had been calling in to offer their condolences. Grace had Marjorie running around brewing up, making sandwiches, answering the phone; she was like her personal assistant. Kerry had kept to her word and phoned the clinic for a consultation for the following day, but Leanne couldn't think about anything except the moment. Voices of people speaking in the room, clouds of smoke filling the air, phone constantly ringing. Leanne checked her own mobile phone and went into the toilet to read the latest message Gino had sent her. With shaking hands, she started to read what he had written:

> Meet me tonight at nine bells on the Square.
> If u don't come yr house will be torched, I'll
> make yr life a misery, trust me, turn up or
> I will come looking for u.

Her heart was racing, and she shoved the phone into her pocket. She clenched her teeth and went back to join the others.

Macy answered her phone and went into the kitchen for a bit of privacy. 'Hiya Bobby, on my life I can't believe it. Jayden was a lot of things, but he didn't deserve to die.' She listened to Bobby on the other end of the phone and walked about the kitchen. 'I'll be there as soon as I can. My family need me at the moment and I can't get away. I'll ring you soon, is that alright?' The phone call ended just as Leanne walked into the kitchen.

'Who was that, Mam?'

'Just Bobby checking in on me. He's been my pillar of strength through all of this. I don't know what I would have done without him, to tell you the truth.'

Leanne looked puzzled. 'All I seem to hear these days is Bobby this and Bobby that.'

'We go back a lot of years, love. We've been through a lot together. We fell out for a few years, but he's always been in my life, like a guardian angel, I suppose.'

Leanne sat down at the kitchen table and stroked her finger around the rim of a cup that was left there. 'Gino wants to see me tonight. I'm going to tell him to his face that it's over: us, the pregnancy, the whole lot. He hurt me, Mam. How the hell can you tell somebody that you love them while you're hurting them? Tell them you want to live together one day, then hit on your mate the next day?'

Macy plonked down next to her daughter and sighed. 'That's life, love. Some men are alright but most of them will shag anything with a pulse. Jayden thinks I didn't know about the slapper he'd been bedding for the last year on the Two Hundred estate, but I did. I chose to look the other way. Like I said, it's life.'

Leanne was outraged. She banged her flat palm on the table causing it to shake. 'Mam, why did you not call him out on it? Fancy knowing your man was playing away from home and turning a blind eye to it! Why, why, would you even do that?'

Macy was getting used to speaking the truth now. 'Because, if you really want to know, I had no interest in him like that anymore. We'd stopped being close like that ages ago. He knocked me sick when his hands even touched me. When I heard that he was sleeping with somebody else I switched off from him, it was the last straw. I know I should have confronted him but the thought of being alone outweighed what he was up to. His mate was sleeping with brasses, and I bet Jayden was too.' Macy sighed. 'It's water under the bridge now, love. It was only the other week I seen all the scratches on his back, and I was ready to tell him what I knew, but something inside stopped me. I couldn't be arsed with all the drama.'

Leanne reached over and hugged her mother. How on earth had she kept that to herself? It must have been destroying her inside. 'I'm not having the baby. I've seen the light where men are concerned, and I'll never let anyone treat me that way again.'

Macy agreed, nodding her head. She could tell her daughter had more to say.

'He hit me, Mam, not just once, a few times. He said he was sorry, and I thought he was, but it happened time and time again. His mam was horrible to me too. I could never have lived at their house with them two. I would have been a prisoner, a servant for them both. I should have listened to you, listened to your advice when we had our chats.'

Macy was aware that their chats had not happened for a long time due to her workload and already she was feeling guilty. Her poor daughter was suffering domestic violence and she never spotted the signs. 'I'm so sorry, Leanne. Where the hell has my head been at these last few months? I've been that set on work and earning a quid that I've let you and Alex down. I've been a shit mother, haven't I?'

'Shit happens, Mam. And I've let you down too. Jayden was having an affair and sleeping with brasses, and you kept all that to yourself. Maybe, if I wasn't that infatuated with Gino, I would have sensed something was wrong. So we are both to blame. Anyway, we have to put it behind us now and look forward. The only time I want to look back is to see how far I have come. I'm so sorry about Jayden, and my heart breaks for our Alex, but knowing what I know now, I won't be shedding a tear for him.'

Macy's eyes flooded with tears, remembering she would never see Jayden again. 'But, still, he was there for us all. He was a good dad sometimes to Alex and he did try his best. I know he messed up a lot, but he's gone now and none of that seems to matter.'

Leanne stood up and touched her mam's shoulder. 'I'm going home now. Are you and Alex coming too? I love Nana and all that, but I just want a bit of normality for us all. Life is going to be hard for these next few months and the sooner we all go back home, the sooner we can start moving on with our lives.'

Macy lifted her eyes and smiled at Leanne. 'You're probably right. Do you need me to come tonight while you meet Gino? If he's heavy with his hands, I think I should be there as back-up. I'll take my bat and if he lays one finger on you I'll crack his skull right open. I won't forget what he has done to you. How dare he think he can slap you about? Jayden had his faults, but if he'd got wind of this he would have gone around to his house and smashed his head in.'

———

Bobby sat in the car outside Macy's house waiting for her to come outside. He was going to take her out for a drive, get her away from all the stress for a while, take her for a few beers. He rolled a spliff and placed it on the dashboard. Macy opened the passenger door and jumped inside.

She kept looking at her house. 'I've left Leanne to sit in with Alex – he's coping better than I thought. The rozzers have not long gone. Question after question they asked me. My head is going to pop with all the stress.'

Bobby started the engine up, and took the spliff from the dashboard. He passed it to Macy. 'Here, spark that up and chill out.'

Macy held the joint in her hand and shot a look over at Bobby. 'So, fill me in. What do you know? Was it Terry and his boys who finished Jayden off? Don't lie to me because I know that you know something. At first I thought it might have been that first beating catching up with him, or that he'd staggered into the river, pissed. But I've seen the police report now. Some fucker picked on him while he was weak and finished him off. And I'm going to find that murderous bastard. I'm sure it wasn't the same gang that took him the first time – they'd let him go as a warning, they'd had their chance to do him in.'

Bobby kept his eyes on the road and joined the main traffic, he turned the music up slightly. 'Look. Word on the street was that Jayden was a grass. We all know what happens to snitches around here, don't we, so I'm not going to fight his corner and say that he didn't deserve it, because he did. And, let's face it, he probably had something to do with the drugs going missing too. I've heard whispers that he had a buyer set up for it.'

Macy spoke through gritted teeth. 'Did he fuck. Jayden wouldn't know who to sell that amount of weed to. He was small-time and without help he has no contacts.'

Bobby started to hum along to the radio and only when the song changed did he reply. 'Only telling you what I heard. Don't shoot the messenger.'

Macy sat thinking; something didn't sit right with her. She looked at the joint for a few seconds and passed it back to Bobby. 'I don't need this shit. Been down that road years ago and I swore to myself I would never go there again. I had it the other night for old times' sake but I'm not a kid anymore. You should sack it too; it messes with your head.'

Bobby chuckled. 'Please yourself. Anyway, I know it's early days, but we need to get back out there grafting.

Money doesn't grow on trees. Life goes on, love. And you're a single mum now – you've got to bring home the bacon.'

Macy sat playing with her fingers, aware that he was right, but it felt like the wrong time for him to be pushing her back to work. Sure, she no longer had Jayden's money, but that was fuck all anyway.

'Give me a bit of time, Bobby, it's early days and I need to make sure the kids are alright before I go back out grafting. All I need is getting nicked and going to jail. Who would look after the kids then, eh?'

Bobby carried on driving and every now and then looked over at her, a shifty look. 'Fancy a few beers?'

Macy's nerves were in bits. 'Only if you've got news on which of Terry's goons did for Jayden. I can't be long. I need to get back home to the kids. Leanne has got something she needs to sort. The lad she's been seeing has been slapping her about, the prick. She has only just told me, fuming I am. Gino, from the Square, do you know him?'

Bobby nearly choked, coughing. 'Nah, never heard of him.'

'Well, when I get my hands on him, he will be a dead man walking. '

Bobby pulled into the pub car park. He'd gone quiet. He reached over for the lighter and lit the joint up. He put his seat back and opened the window. Macy sat watching him, remembering him back in the day when he never had a spliff out of his mouth.

'Fancy a few puffs?' He held the spliff out to her with a big smile on his face.

'No thanks. Come on, put that out and let's get in the pub. I've told you before that I don't have long.'

Bobby pressed the button to close the window and opened the car door. 'Ready when you are.'

Macy sat in the pub, nursing her drink. Every time she took a swig, she felt sick to the stomach. Not even the warm buzz of the alcohol could mask the constant thought that Jayden was gone. The story was going around and around in her head.

'Bobby, I've been thinking, and things just don't make sense in my head.'

He moved in closer to her and looked deep into her eyes. 'What do you mean?'

'Right, so only a few people knew Jayden was doing drops, so who the fuck set him up? He was going to Blackpool, so it's not like a chance thing, is it? Simon, Terry, it's a short fucking list. '

'Chancers, grafters, must have spotted him somewhere and thought he looked suss. They probably thought they would have a look at him, and they come up trumps. It happens all the time, Macy.'

'Since when? Nah, something doesn't sit right with me with this.'

Bobby rolled his eyes, no interest whatsoever. He wouldn't lose any sleep over Jayden, he owed him nothing. 'Macy, I know I shouldn't be saying this, but I can't stop thinking about you. I'm going to put my heart on the line here again and tell you something.'

Macy necked another mouthful of her beer. He was stoned and doing her head in. All she wanted to do was go back home to her children.

'Macy, it's always been you. I've loved you like forever. I told you as much the other night. And now that Jayden's gone, you're going to need someone to look after you…'

Macy squirmed, straightening her clothing. 'Bobby, what I need are some answers. What I need is justice for Jayden. What I need is my daughter to be safe from some handsy little prick who thinks he's the big man. I need to go home. My partner has just been found dead and I don't need to be hearing things like this. Drink up and take me home.'

He leered over at her as his hand squeezed her thigh under the table. 'Forget all that for an hour, Macy. Let's get a room and fuck the living daylights out of each other. You have nobody to answer to anymore. We can be together.'

Macy gripped his hand and moved it from her leg. 'Bobby, fuck off saying stuff like that. Take me home, otherwise I'll walk or get a taxi. There is no me and you, and there will never be again.'

He sat back with his arms folded, staring at her. 'We'll see. You know more than me that we will be together one day. We have a bond nobody can break, secrets we share, are you forgetting that?'

Macy stood up and made sure nobody could hear her. 'It's your secret, Bobby, not mine. Don't forget that. I'm gone.'

Macy walked into the car park and pulled her mobile phone out from her pocket. She tried ringing Leanne's number but there was no answer. Quickly she rang a taxi. She wanted away from this place as quickly as she could.

She stood waiting for her taxi when she spotted Bobby swaying out of the pub's double doors. She hid out of sight and watched him wobble towards the car. There was no way he should have been driving in this state, but she had bigger fish to fry, no time to stop him getting behind the wheel. He was big and daft enough to look after himself. She watched as he sped out from the car park. She let out a sigh of relief and went and stood outside the pub. Her taxi was on its way. She wanted to be at home with her family. She should have never left them. The last thing she needed was another man causing trouble in her life. She patted her handbag to check the blue carrier bag was still inside. Sometimes you had to stop waiting for other people to come up with the answers.

Chapter Thirty-Two

Leanne stood looking over at Tavistock Square. It was noisy and the gang was out in force. But tonight there seemed to be a few new faces scattered about the Square, older guys. Leanne craned her neck as she saw Gino running to a car that had pulled up. He passed the driver something and then ran back to where he'd been standing. She wasn't used to seeing him doing any of the running. Something had changed.

One of the older men was now at Gino's side, whispering in his ear, nudging him. Whatever he was saying to him, you could see he wasn't happy. Jacko and Kyle were up to something and from nowhere a gang of lads come and stood on the other side of the Square. Gino sprinted over to them and they all huddled together. Leanne stood back out of sight. Her heart was racing. She could see the glint of a machete being pulled out and voices were getting louder.

Gino shouted over to the older man. 'No one runs this place except me. Five minutes you have to fuck off, then you'll find out what I am about.'

Leanne backed away, further into the shadows.

Gino's dad Tyson stepped out into the pool of light from a streetlamp and stood in front of his boys. He eyeballed Gino and licked his lips slowly. This was war: street style. It was the elders versus the youngers.

The shopkeeper must have seen what was about to happen and with trembling hands he ran to the shop door and locked up, lights off: he wanted no part of this.

The quiet was punctured by a slow beat, getting louder, faster. Soon there was noise everywhere: shouting, threatening and beneath it all the pulse of hammers banging against steel bins. It was ready to kick off.

Gino and around twenty others started to edge forward, goading their opponents. Tyson stepped forward and nodded his head over at his son.

'If this is how you want to roll then so be it. This Square is mine and it's always been mine. You've just been keeping it warm for me. You and your fucking muppets can do one before you all end up in body bags.'

Gino was chomping on the bit, ready for action, his wingmen at either side of him. From out of his jacket he pulled an iron bar and gripped it tightly. Jacko was the first man to attack, and the rest followed. This was a war zone now, a blood bath. Mr Patel from the shop stood in the window with his phone in his hand and it was obvious he was calling the police. Silver blades swung high in the air, fists curled into tight balls. Kicking, screaming, shouting.

Gino was having a one-on-one with his old man. Each of them going for gold. Everything was to fight for: both of them wanted to rule the Square. Gino took a dig to his ribs that brought him to his knees. He was no match for his old man. Yet. His dad stood over him ready to give him the killer blow, but hesitated. Gino's eyes were wide open, and you could see his fear. Jacko saved his bacon just in time as he struck Tyson over the head with a claw hammer. He dragged Gino to his feet and carried on fighting. Gino was pouring blood, from his mouth, from his nose. He had to get away, get to safety. The fight went on for around ten minutes but it looked and felt like some epic battle. Bodies lying all over the place, some still moving and some not.

From the alley, Leanne watched Gino leaving the battle-field and never flinched. Blue lights and police sirens rang out. The dibble were here and team-handed, but it was too late. The damage had been done. The gangs ran off in different directions. The only ones who stayed were the ones unable to move.

Gino was out of sight in some nearby bushes. He was injured badly. Wiping his hand across his face, he looked down at the bright red blood. Every bone in his body was on fire. He was struggling to breathe and a pain in his chest was getting worse by the second. He needed urgent medical help. His eyes closed for a few seconds, until he heard a rustle and sensed someone standing over him.

Leanne stood looking down at Gino. She was powerful now; he was the underdog. 'I saw everything that happened, and you deserve all that was coming to you. I should have left you here to keel over and die on your own for the way you have treated me.'

Gino looked up at her and she could see he was holding his side. He'd been stabbed.

'Defenceless, aren't you? Just like I was when you terrorised me. Go on, tell me how it feels when you can't do a thing to protect yourself. When someone else is calling all the shots.' She swung her foot back but, before she could boot him in his ribs, he fell on his side. She bent down and pulled his head up by his hair, looking straight into his eyes. 'You'll never, ever treat another women like you treated me, you prick. Look at you, you're nothing, pathetic.'

Gino struggled to get his words out, no fight left in him. 'Just like your brother was when I kicked the fuck out of him.' He let out a small menacing laugh.

Leanne froze, slowly taking in what he meant. 'Say it again?'

Gino was on his final breaths for sure. Blood was pumping out of his side. 'It was me who took the weed from your old man, the stuff my dad was buying. I never told my old man that I was skimming both sides. Then me and my dad's boys from Blackpool went to your gaff and went through your door. Why pay Terry's prices for weed – or my dad's – when I could nick it off Jayden and get him framed for it. Clever, aren't I?'

Leanne stood listening as he continued.

'You're a fucking nothing, Leanne, fuck all without me. Ring me an ambulance. You can't let the father of your child die. Go on, ring a fucking ambulance.'

She checked around her. The police had swarmed the Square and now it was a crime scene. The helicopter was out in the night sky and all the neighbourhood was stood at their doors watching the arrests and men being put into ambulances. She looked at Gino again and smirked. 'Die here for all I care. The Square will be a better place without you. How could you do this to my mam and my family? Jayden is dead now because of you. Who killed him? Go on, you've told me everything else, you may as well clear your chest before you meet your maker.'

Gino was coughing up thick clotted blood. It bubbled from his mouth. He reached his hand up to Leanne, eyes wide. 'Help, please, help me.'

She stood over him. 'Tell me who killed Jayden, and I will.'

Gino was in pain and on his last legs. If he didn't get help soon he was a goner. 'Terry and his boys. Your mam thinks her friend has got her back, but he's in it deep too. He's had her over. We all want money and power, all of us.' Gino's body melted into the floor and his eyes stared up into the night sky.

Leanne stood looking down at him, her chest rising frantically. A wave of rage ran through her body and her nostrils flared as she watched his body shudder a few times. Then he was no longer moving; his body was still. She reached down, patted his pockets and pulled out a wad of cash with a phone number written on a sticky label with blue biro. It was a big fat wad; more money than she had ever seen in her life.

She snarled down at her ex, 'You won't be needing this now, will you.'

She turned and walked out from the bushes, zipped her coat up tightly and headed onto the main road with haste. She wanted away from here as fast as she could.

As she walked along the main road, she met Kerry who was with another girl. 'Oh my God, Leanne. The pigs are everywhere. It's kicked off on the Square with Gino and his boys and some other gang who thought they were taking over things. The news reporters are there and everything. Everyone is saying it was Gino's dad and his boys who started it, but nobody knows for sure. Some of them are dead and some are in a bad way. I don't know what happened to Gino but I'm sure we'll find out soon enough. Bloody hell, did you even get chance to speak to him?'

Leanne was cool as a cucumber. She never flinched. 'No, I decided there was no need. My mind is made up and it's nothing to do with him. He is an arsehole and he will get what's coming to him. I'm at the clinic tomorrow, and after that hopefully I can put all this nightmare behind me.'

Kerry hugged her. 'You're right in not going to see him. If you'd been on the Square you would have been in the middle of all that shit. Someone must have been looking after you for sure. Thank your lucky stars you weren't there.'

Leanne hugged her friend and squeezed her tightly. 'I think you're right – I've got a feeling my luck is about to change.'

Chapter Thirty-Three

Macy lay awake in bed. She got up and walked out of her bedroom. There was a light still on in her son's bedroom and she made her way towards it. Slowly she opened the door and dipped her head inside. 'Alex, are you still awake too?'

His head appeared from under his duvet, and she could see he had been crying, his eyes red raw. She rushed to him and sat on the edge of the bed. She hugged him and rocked him to and fro. 'Come on son, get it out. I've not stopped crying either.'

Alex blubbered, 'Mam, I miss him so much. I know what he was, but he was still my dad. What am I going to do without him? We play *Call of Duty* together, hours we play the game, just me and him.'

Macy had no words to heal her son's broken heart. If he had just lost a toy or something, she could have replaced it, but his heart was broken and, as far as she knew, there was no remedy for a broken heart except time. She moved him over in his bed and lay next to him, stroking his face. 'We've got a long road ahead of us, son. It's going to be hard, but we will get through it together. We will never forget him, and I'll always tell you the mad stories about him. He was a lovable rogue, you know. He had his faults, but he had a big heart.'

Alex snivelled, 'And will Bobby be here in his place? Because that's what he told me. He said one day he would be here with us, and he'd look after me.'

Macy was suddenly alert. 'When did he tell you that?'

'When he was here when I got beaten up. He called it a man-to-man chat. To tell you the truth, I wasn't listening proper, but he seems to think somewhere along the line you and him will be together.'

'Not a bleeding earthly, son. And when I see him, I'll be having words saying things like that to you. Who the bleeding hell does he think he is?'

Alex snuggled into his mother's bosom and closed his eyes. 'Will you stay here with me until I go asleep, Mam? I know I'm like a big baby, but I need you near me tonight. I feel safe when you're here.'

'Ssshh, I'm going nowhere, son. You go to sleep. I'll be right here with you.'

After she'd watched Alex finally drift off, Macy heard the front door close, and she could hear Leanne and Kerry coming up the stairs. Slowly, she slipped out of bed and made her way onto the landing.

'I thought you would have been asleep, Mam?'

'I wish. Alex was upset so I stayed in bed with him until he drifted off. The poor thing is heartbroken.'

Kerry was eager to fill Macy in on the night's events. 'Macy, come in here with us while I tell you about all the trouble on the Square. Loads of police swarmed it tonight, ambulances all over…'

Macy followed them both into Leanne's bedroom and flicked on the lamp. Kerry ran to the bathroom for a quick wee. As soon as Macy came into the bedroom, Leanne made her swear down she would not repeat what she told her to anyone else, not even mention it when Kerry come back into the bedroom. Macy agreed, eager to hear what she had to say.

'Mam, it was Gino who set up the lads to come here. It was him who battered our Alex. I found out tonight. He knew who had Jayden over too. I'm not sure who told him that Jayden was carrying the drugs, but he said something about *your friend*. Terry Dolan and his boys were the ones who are responsible for killing Jayden, but it's not like anyone would call Terry *your friend*, is it? There was something about his dad's Blackpool gang too. I don't get it – Gino nicked the gear that his dad was meant to be buying? Madness. It's all hearsay at the moment, but there is no smoke without fire, is there?'

Macy looked puzzled and started chewing on her fingernails. Kerry was back in the bedroom now, and the talk changed to what Leanne was facing.

'What time are you at the clinic tomorrow, love? I'll come with you.'

'Mam, you've got enough going on. Kerry will come with me. I'll be fine, stop worrying about me. I'm a big girl now.'

Macy smiled. 'You'll always be my little girl no matter how old you are. I'm too tired to talk tonight but we'll sort it out in the morning.'

Macy climbed back into her bed, staring out at the night sky. It was a full moon tonight and she couldn't help but study it. As a child she would often talk to the moon and, even as a teenager, she continued to talk to the sky. It knew all her secrets. It knew what she covered up, it knew the tears she'd cried, and it knew about the nights she had spent with Bobby. Holding the edge of the duvet, she started to drift off to sleep. Her brain was overtired, and she still had a million and one questions running around her mind. Things were just not adding up. So Gino nicked Jayden's drop but his dad beat him up? She replayed every day with Jayden running up to his death. Everything he had told her. The arguments they'd had when she told him she was going back grafting with Bobby. Macy was still looking at the moon for answers, but she was none the wiser. The police would be back again in the morning no doubt and hope-fully they could shine some light on Jayden's murder. But what her daughter had just told her was lying heavy on her mind. Was Gino's dad the centre of it all? She'd have to ask Bobby – if he was still speaking to her after she turned him down. It felt like there was no one left in her corner.

Chapter Thirty-Four

Bobby sat with Macy in the car after the police had attended again the next day. She'd thought telling them everything she knew about Jayden would solve things – but it was the same old shit, them asking questions she didn't know the answer to. She switched off from them in the end and told them straight that her family were grieving and they wanted to be left alone. And it seemed like the police were moving on too – Jayden's death was already old news. Now the coppers had him as a foot soldier, they weren't bothered. Their focus was on the Square and last night's carnage.

Two deaths up to now and five men in critical conditions in the hospital, the police told Macy. Gino's body had been found by a dog walker in the early hours of the morning and, when they told Macy and asked if she knew Gino, she decided this time she was going to play dumb. She didn't want any coppers coming near Leanne and linking her to him, so she found a way to tell the truth – but far from the whole truth.

'Gino Gallagher? Never met the kid,' she swore.

The less said the better, in her eyes. After the dibble left and she had to tell her daughter about Gino, Macy thought Leanne took the news of his death well. She never shed a tear. Then she turned on her heel and told her she meant it when she wanted Kerry, not her, at the clinic later that day.

So Macy had called Bobby and, like a bad penny, he was there again. Just as a shoulder to cry on today, he said. No come-ons, no graft, just him being here supporting his friend, he said.

But Macy's mind was still whirring and she wasn't in the mood to take any shit. The moment she got the chance she challenged Bobby. 'Our Alex said something strange last night and it's not sitting right with me. Did you tell him you would be looking after us and all that?'

Bobby shifted in the driver's seat and tried to make light of the matter. 'Yeah, it was when he was in a bad way. I only told him that I had his back and all that, and if he wanted me, just to give me a ring.'

'Did you say anything about me and you being together?'

Bobby fidgeted more, no eye contact. 'Erm, no, why?'

Macy held her head to one side, thinking. 'Oh my God, it was you, wasn't it? It was you.'

Bobby never flinched, still looking out of the car window.

She poked a single finger deep into his chest. 'Bobby, I've worked it all out. You knew Jayden was doing drops and I don't know how but you are involved with Gino from the Square. Probably buying your weed from him. Fuck me, this can't be true.' She was near hysterical, breathing doubled. She was at him again, eyes bulging from the sockets. 'Go on, tell me I'm not right.'

Bobby twisted to face her. There was a pause that told Macy all she needed to know. She barely listened to his feeble attempt to deny it.

'Nah, you're pissing in the wind, Macy. I'm gutted you could even think that of me. You're not thinking straight.'

Silence, neither of them speaking. He let her calm down before he spoke again. 'Macy, I'm sorry I put pressure on you the other night. It was too soon, I get it. Yeah, I'm not going to lie, I'm glad to see the back of Jayden. He was never no good for you in my eyes. It should have been me, always me who was with you. But I can wait. I've waited all these years already.'

She was livid. How dare he bring it back up when she had just lost her partner? 'How many times do I have to tell you that we are not a thing! I don't know what is going on in that head of yours, but it's all a crock of shit. You need to wake up. We've been stuck in the past, stuck together by that night you killed Nathan. But I've realised now, I let your secret chain me up. I let my fear hold me back – and where has it got me? Nowhere. I'm as tied to the Square as I was when I was drinking there every night. But those days are done. It's ruined my life, but over my dead body will it mess up Leanne's. I'm done with the past, and I'm done with you.'

Bobby snarled over at her, 'You don't mean that, you're just upset and trying to hurt me. You always hurt the ones you love, and I'll take it on the chin because I know you are grieving. Wait a few months, and you'll see what I have seen for years.'

She slammed her flat palm on the dashboard. 'Are you not listening to a word I have said? You will never be by my side.'

Bobby lost the plot, and this was a side of him she'd not seen for a long time. His ears pinned back, and his nostrils flared as he reached over and gripped her by the neck. 'You're mine now. It's my fucking turn. You kept my secret all these years – that shows you loved me. I've always wanted you, but had to stand back and watch you make mistake after mistake with all those losers you bedded. I had a shot at you that night when we were kids and what happened in that alleyway still fucking haunts me. If that hadn't happened you would have seen then how much of a catch I was. But no, it was all fucked up by Nathan Barnes. I could have saved you from everything, your life with that prick, the pregnancy to a random lad you didn't even fucking know. We could have had it all, but you would never give me a decent shot. Well, now it's my time. I'm the only who can keep you safe while you've got Terry Dolan on one side and Tyson Gallagher on the other. You need me, Macy.'

She wriggled and pushed her hand into his face. Who the hell did he think he was manhandling her like this? 'Bobby, this is a life you have made up in your head. You are away with the fairies. Yes, we slept together but it stops there. Any chance we ever had of being a thing died along with Nathan in that alleyway. I know we've had a drunken thing here and there – but that was weakness, Bobby – we're no good for each other.'

Bobby was raging now, his dreams broken, the life he had planned in his head falling apart. There was no happy ending, no running away into the sunset together. He released his grip on her and popped a cigarette from the packet next to him. He lit it and sucked on it with all his might. Turning his head slowly, he eyeballed her and smirked. 'So, that's it then. No me and you?'

She turned and looked out of the window and never replied. He carried on talking and all she could do was listen as the truth unfolded.

'You may as well hear it from me then. It was me who set Jayden up. The guy is a wanker and he makes my blood boil. I tipped off Gino about his drop – I knew he was a right head-the-ball who'd lose no opportunity of free weed. I just didn't know his own dad was the buyer he was fucking over. Then Jayden shafted us when he blabbed Terry's name. It was his own fault, what did he expect? Terry was always going to catch up with him – I only led him to Jay a bit faster. He never went for that beer the night you were with me, Mace. I told them he was home alone. Even told them to take his phone and text you some story. I needed time to show you I was your future.'

Macy felt sick. That last text from Jayden. The kisses he never usually sent. She'd been with Bobby while Terry's men were taking revenge on Jayden.

Bobby carried on. 'I've been texting Gino for days trying to get my cut from the drugs. The night he died he should have been handing it over to me. Twenty bags the kid owed me. So, it was all for fuck-all really. I never got the money, and I never got you. That money was for us to set up somewhere new, me and you and the kids.'

Macy opened the window and sucked in mouthfuls of cold air. She was in shock. 'How did you ever think you would get away with it? I hate you, Bobby; hate you like I've never hated anyone in my whole fucking life. You remind me of every moment in my life I'm ashamed of. And I won't let you drag me back there.'

Macy rushed out of the car and Bobby watched her go into the house.

Stood behind the door, her heart was beating faster than ever. Mouth dry, body trembling, she walked one way then the other. She punched and kicked the wardrobe door, smashing at it, trying her best to destroy it. She fell to her knees and slammed her fist into the floor. What a bloody mess her life was. Now she had a choice to make: should she go straight into the police station and tell them what she knew, or hold another secret for Bobby until her dying breath? Footsteps stopped outside her bedroom. She quickly dried her eyes and pulled the wet strands of hair from her cheek. The door opened slowly, and Leanne was stood there.

'Mam, I'm bleeding. Every time I go to the toilet, there's more blood. I have really bad stomach ache too. I think I'm having a miscarriage.'

Macy had to put her own troubles to the back of her mind and deal with what was right in front of her. 'We need to get you to the hospital. Sit down here on the bed while I phone a taxi. No point in waiting for an ambulance: it could take forever.'

Leanne held the bottom of her stomach as a pain surged down her back, pains like hot pokers were being stabbed into her belly.

Leanne lay on the hospital bed and bit down hard on her bottom lip. Her fears had been right: she was having a miscarriage. She looked over at her mother, sadly. 'It was for the best, Mam, and it has stopped me having to go to the clinic this afternoon. I was dreading making that decision. You don't hate me for what I was going to do, do you, Mam?'

Macy was at her side holding her hand tightly. 'Do I 'eck, love. I'll always stand by anything you do. God moves in mysterious ways, and it was him who decided you didn't have to make any choices. He made them for you.'

Leanne looked pale but there was a peace about her that Macy hadn't seen in a long time. 'It's all going to be alright, Mam. I know you might not think so now, but it will be. I'm going to travel and do all the things I said I would, and I'll make sure you don't have to go out shoplifting again – and don't say you don't know what I'm talking about, because I know that's what you have been doing. You're better than that, and I don't want to ever risk losing you if you go to prison. I want to tell you something, something that I think will change everything.'

Macy swallowed hard, eyes wide, nervous. 'What do you need to tell me, Leanne? Please, don't let it be bad news. I don't think my heart could take it.'

Leanne smiled and stroked her mother's face. 'You're right. We've all had enough to deal with today. Let's wait til I get out of here. But just so you know: no, it's definitely not more bad news.'

Chapter Thirty-Five

Macy placed the blue bag on the doorstep of Jeanette Barnes' house and hid away in the shadows of the night. She watched as the hallway light flicked on and watched as Jeanette picked the bag up.

Her job was done now and her conscience was clean. For years she had tossed and turned carrying the truth about the death of Nathan Barnes. She'd always thought she was protecting Bobby by staying silent, and keeping to the code of the Square by not going to the police. But she saw now that Bobby wasn't the one she should have been protecting. And while she was still mourning Jayden, she realised that knowing the truth was the first step towards healing. And that was one thing she could give Jeanette. It might be eighteen years too late, but she saw now she hadn't needed to go to the cops. Just giving the family what they needed was enough. Now she knew the family would find out the truth about the night Nathan died.

Bobby's fingerprints were all over the gun and he would be arrested if Jeanette took the evidence to the police. There was a letter in the bag too, telling Jeanette that her brother was an innocent victim. Macy never named herself, only told the family that she had hidden the gun away for years to protect a man she thought was her friend. She told them how sorry she was and hoped that they could find forgiveness in their hearts.

Macy headed back home and stood on the Square, looking around. There was an eerie silence, no youths shouting or screaming, no drugs being dealt. An emptiness, a ghost town. Just one black car parked to the side of the Square. The wind picked up and howled past her ears. It was time to move away from Harpurhey, time to leave the Square behind forever. She whispered her peace to Tavistock Square and slowly walked away from it, never looking back once.

Epilogue

ONE MONTH LATER

Jayden's funeral had been a nice quiet service and, despite everything, Macy and her family had given him a good send-off. Macy had worried that the day would be ruined by Terry's heavies or Tyson's squad lurking and watching, but it remained peaceful.

Bobby had been arrested for the murder of Nathan Barnes. He was going to get slammed for a lot of years. For a long time, Macy thought she deserved the same – until she realised she'd been serving her time ever since that night, carrying the guilt. And finally she was free.

Leanne seemed like her old self. She was always by her mother's side and Alex was never far from them both. He was the man of the house now and he pledged that, not only would nobody ever hurt his family again, he was going to make something of his life and not end up in the dead-end that his dad had been trapped in. And, by the look in his eyes, he meant it.

Leanne didn't attend Gino's funeral and she never spoke about the night he died to anyone. Just like her mother, the Square had given her a secret to keep. But there was one part she had to share. The night of the funeral, while half the estate was at the wake, Leanne was having a quiet night in with her family.

'Mam,' Leanne called from the kitchen.

'What now, Leanne? I've just sat down, what do you want?' she yelled back.

'Come in here a minute, will you? I need you to see something.'

Macy struggled to stand up from her seat. These last few weeks had taken it out of her and she was getting pains in places she had never felt before. Maybe it was age, maybe it was stress. She plodded into the kitchen, and you could tell all she wanted to do was rest.

Leanne stood in front of the kitchen table and slowly moved away.

Macy covered her mouth with two hands and looked at her daughter. 'Where has all this money come from? Leanne – is it blood money? Do you know something…?'

'Ask no questions and I'll tell no lies. All I will say is that no one's going to miss it. I told you I would look after us all, and I will.'

Macy lifted her eyes up to the ceiling and her mouth moved but no words came out.

'Mam, we have over twenty grand here. It's our chance to get away from here, start again. We can leave Harpurhey, leave all those memories behind us. Alex and I can start over somewhere new. You and Nana can live somewhere

where you're not always dreading the next knock on the door. We can be happy. We've said all the goodbyes we need to. I wanted the funerals over with before I told you. Sometimes you don't believe a problem is gone until it's dead and buried.'

Macy started to ask a question then realised some things were better not said. She walked over to the money and picked up a bundle to convince herself it was real. 'I think you have hit the nail on the head, love. The sooner the better for me. Goodbye history, goodbye misery.'

Leanne held her mother in her arms and swung her around the kitchen. She looked into her eyes and filled up as Macy spoke.

'Promise me one thing, Leanne. Forget what hurt you, but never forget what it taught you.'

Acknowledgements

Thank you to James for his support.

My children: Ashley, Blake, Declan, Darcy and all my grandchildren.

Thanks to Gen, Megan, and Alice as well as all the crew at HarperNorth.

Finally, thank you to all my readers and followers.

Harper
North

Book Credits

HarperNorth would like to thank the following staff
and contributors for their involvement in making
this book a reality:

Hannah Avery
Fionnuala Barrett
Claire Boal
Sarah Burke
Alan Cracknell
Jonathan de Peyer
Anna Derkacz
Tom Dunstan
Kate Elton
Laura Gerrard
Simon Gerratt
Monica Green
CJ Harter

Megan Jones
Jean-Marie Kelly
Sammy Luton
Oliver Malcolm
Alice Murphy-Pyle
Adam Murray
Genevieve Pegg
Agnes Rigou
Florence Shepherd
Emma Sullivan
Katrina Troy
Sarah Whittaker

For more unmissable reads,
sign up to the HarperNorth newsletter at
www.harpernorth.co.uk

or find us on Twitter at
@HarperNorthUK

Harper
North